PERFECT MURDER

By

Don Higgins

W & B Publishers
USA

W & B Publishers

For information:
W & B Publishers
Post Office Box 193
Colfax, NC 27235
www.a-argusbooks.com

ISBN: 978-0-6922742-2-4
ISBN: 06922742-2-7

Book Cover designed by Dubya
Cover art by Don Higgins

Printed in the United States of America

CHAPTER ONE

HAL REINER SAT at his desk in the silent squad room except for the hum of the air-conditioner. Outside, the overcast sky represented the prevailing mood within the Beaverton, Oregon police department. An increase in felony crimes, mostly drug abuse violations, hampered the overworked guardians of service and protection. The two-story brick building housed insufficient personnel to satisfy a population of 60,000 residents. One secretary and two forensic investigators along with seven homicide detectives occupied the upper floor of the city hall. Scattered desks encircled the central office of Lieutenant Abrams, except for two desks off by themselves in one corner of the large room—like outcasts. At one of the desks, Detective Hal Reiner stared at paper work, mulling over upsetting words spoken in the latest argument with his wife.

"Are you afraid I'll make you feel something?" Evelyn said, knowing it was a sore spot in his persona. "After seven years of marriage," she continued her diatribe, "I'm convinced you won't change your ways. If there was any love for you, it can't possibly compete with your blasé attitude. I'm thinking seriously about a divorce."

Through the open door of his office, Lt. Josh Abrams waved his arm trying to get Hal's attention but finally resorted to the intercom. Hal looked up, motioned with his hand, then got up slowly, anticipating he might be in for a reprimand. He walked at a modest pace toward the lieutenant's office. As he approached, he saw a woman sitting in front of Abram's desk. Her profile suggested someone in her early thirties. As he walked into the office, she turned with a pleasant smile. The blond hair looked natural, cut short, and she had on a pants suit which revealed a trim body.

"Have a seat," Abrams said, motioning to a chair beside the woman. "Hal, this is Karen Holmes, your new partner."

After a moment of silence while he digested the news, Hal said, "A new partner already?" He frowned and turned to Karen. "I just got rid of one." With a quick smile that didn't seem genuine, he held out his hand. "Hi."

"Hal Reiner," Abrams said to Karen. "He's been with the department seven years and still hasn't learned anything." A just-noticeable grin surfaced on Abrams face.

Karen shook hands with Hal and asked, "Did you want to get rid of your partner?"

Hal pulled on an earlobe, then glanced at Abrams. "Let's just say I wasn't overly downcast at hearing about him leaving."

"His partner retired," Abrams clarified.

"I suppose we had our good moments," Hal said to Abrams.

"And bad moments as well." Abrams' grin suddenly disappeared. He leaned forward in his chair, turning his attention to Hal. "Karen was a vice officer in Castletown and recently got promoted into homicide. I believe she'll have a lot to offer, but she's new to the area, so she'll need your experience and support."

Hal nodded. "I think I can handle that." He glanced her way. "Welcome aboard."

"Thank you, Detective. I think I've always wanted to be in homicide. I've always loved a good mystery. One of my hobbies is solving sudoku puzzles." She laughed. "But seriously, I'm all for putting away the bad guys, especially the ones who think they've committed the perfect murder."

Hal gazed at her. "You think the perfect murder is a no-go?"

"I do. Killing another person is not spring house cleaning, if you know what I mean. There's almost always some forensic evidence left at the scene; there's testimony from witnesses, even the perpetrator's confession. It comes out sooner or later."

Hal glanced at Abrams then back to Karen. "What about the thousands of unsolved cold cases?"

"They'll be solved eventually. Fortunately, there's no time constraints on murder. Am I right?"

Abrams nodded.

She cocked her head with an expression of resolve. "Today with DNA, chemical analyses, expert medical at our disposal, perps getting away with murder—highly improbable, detective."

"Improbable, but possible, right?" Hal didn't wait for an answer; he got up and motioned toward the door. "I'll show you to your desk. We're off by ourselves over there in the corner of the room," he said pointing."

"It's his preference to be off by himself," Abrams said to Karen.

Karen glanced at Abrams with a curious look.

"Hal is the department hermit. Most of the squad agrees he likes to be left alone. He's a thinker, doesn't say much, but when he does, it's important." Abrams' expression suggested praise. "Hal is a top-notch investigator. You will do well to take note of his experience." He held up a hand in a gesture of earnest. "If being off by yourself is a problem, let me know. Other arrangements can be made."

"No, I'd rather be close to my partner," she replied. Thank you." Karen followed Hal across the room at his slow pace. A few detectives looked up, but Hal didn't stop to introduce her. "I assume Lt. Abrams gave you a tour, and introduced you to the personnel. We'll get you set up at your desk."

"I don't mind the corner of the room. It does seem a little strange with everyone else some distance away, but I'm game as long as there's no problem with the others."

"Me."

She gave him a puzzled look.

"It seems I'm the outcast of the department."

"Why?"

"Don't know."

She smiled. "I hope whatever it is doesn't rub off on me."

He pointed. "That's your desk, across from mine, the one with the copier on it."

"A copier? Am I the custodian of the departmental copier?"

"When my old partner vacated the desk, the copier found its way there, but we'll find a new location for it."

"I'm glad to hear that," she replied, approaching the desk. "I should start unpacking my box of personal things. I'll have to go get them. They're in my car."

"No need to explain everything."

"I meant I won't need any help."

"Good."

She let his comment pass. "I'll get them now." She turned to leave then said, "I'm really looking forward to working in the department. Eager to get started on a case. She remained standing until Hal sat down at his desk. When Hal didn't reply, she pranced across the room toward the elevator.

Hal glanced around the department to see if anyone was gawking. With a hand supporting his head, he stared at the opposite wall wondering if he would be able to weather his new chatty partner, especially her in-your-face temperament. He'd need to wait and see if the problem was unworkable. Suddenly, he sensed someone staring at him.

Pushing the copier to one side, Karen sat her box on the desk. "Back already," she said in a bouncy tone. "I have a question."

"Speak."

"Can we get someone to move the copier?"

"I can only do one thing at a time," he replied, then nodded his agreement and grabbed the phone on his desk.

Looking around the room, she inquired, "There seems to be a lot of empty desks. Are ten people the full complement of the department?"

"We're short-handed. That's all I know. Ask Abrams."

She shrugged. "I was just making conversation." She opened the desk drawer. "Ohh, the drawer is full." She stared at him until he finally looked up.

"You chatter all the time?"

"Oh, sorry." After a momentary pause, she said, "I am a talkative person. Verbalizing my feelings helps me better understand..."

"It doesn't help me."

Her eyes ran appraisingly over the muscular 5' 10" frame, but he had stooped shoulders. A square face, not unpleasant to look at, but his expression showed no emotion.

Hal finally got the secretary. "Doris, get someone to remove the copier and junk in Manchester's desk."

"Thank you." Karen opened her box and removed a few personal objects. She noticed Hal watching. "I have a question. Do you have a problem with me as your partner?"

He shook his head. "Not yet."

"I don't want to be a burden, but I'm eager to learn all I can, and be a contributor. Detective Reiner, I know I'm new and I don't have much experience, but I'm willing to learn. I'll need your input, please, no matter how insignificant." She held out a hand. "Can we agree on that?"

He shook her hand weakly. "When I have something significant to say, you'll be the first one to hear it, okay?" He glanced at her packing box. "Okay, I think we understand each other. After you get settled in, for starters, we'll go over the Christianson case, a double murder."

"A double murder?" she repeated, waiting for clarification.

"We'll talk about it when you get settled in, okay?" With a sudden move, he opened the bottom desk drawer, suggestion the end of the conversation.

As she put items away in her desk, he glanced at her a few times, wondering whether her sudden presence had some profound meaning or merely the roll of the dice. Now that his marriage seemed to be unraveling, he had another female to worry about. Karen was about his age, he guessed, and noted that she didn't wear a wedding ring. The thought of woman in a romantic way at this time in his life appalled him. Karen's constant babbling quickly squashed any thoughts of romance in addition to her aggressive attitude. And he had his hands full with Evelyn.

"I'm almost done," Karen said brightly. "It's almost noon. Maybe we could get a bite to eat soon unless you have other plans."

He nodded, then said, "There's a café down the street if you don't mind fast food."

She laughed. "When I'm hungry, I'll eat most anything."

Karen's open-mindedness is the one thing he did admire. Not like his wife, Evelyn, who saw everything in terms of black or white. Her narrow-minded attitude had become a stumbling block in any attempt to restore a healthy relationship. She hadn't mentioned divorce before, but from recent conversations he felt certain it was on her agenda. With her vindictive attitude, he knew she would try to get all she could in a divorce settlement. The second car, the house, a meager savings account and his retirement benefits. He had earned his pension and at retirement he wouldn't share it with anyone. His pension was non-negotiable. Fortunately, they had no children, except for their godchild, Rodney, his brother's eight-year-old son. They didn't see Rodney that often anyway. Evelyn was infertile because of her diabetes. Early in the marriage they had talked about adopting. He was glad nothing came of it. Nothing to hamper their separation appeared significant, with the exception of his pension.

During lunch, Hal allowed Karen to tell him non-stop about her time and experiences with the Castletown police department. He only heard bits and pieces, enough to nod occasionally.

"But I dropped out of college in my senior year," Karen said, cutting a piece of meat with her fork. "You probably think I was foolish… Hal?"

"Sometimes we have to do what we have to do. What did your folks say?"

"I thought my dad would disown me. Mother couldn't understand why I wanted to be a policewoman. I told her I wanted to make our streets safer from violence. My younger sister understood and came to my aid."

***

Michael had graduated college with a business degree, employed as a comptroller, a prestigious position with a large company. Many times his father had denounced his job as a policeman. The old man looked upon his entry into homicide as a shortcoming, even lower on the success ladder than a street sweeper. He would never forget the scolding words.

"It's going to be your ruin. Looking at dead bodies all the time has to affect your mind. It's not a step up; it's lower than a ditch digger at a cemetery."

***

Suddenly, Karen's voice brought him to the present. "You'll have to tell me about some of your experiences here in Beaverton," She wiped her mouth with a napkin.

Hal didn't answer, but slid out from the booth. "Let's get back to work. He grabbed the check. "I'll buy."

**

They returned to their desks in the squad room, and hearing the familiar ring, Hal picked up the phone. "My brother? Yes, send him back."

Karen inspected the man approaching Hal's desk. She took note of his muscular build, blue eyes, and short, blond hair, nearly identical to Hal.

"Michael, this is Karen Holmes, my new partner. Michael's my brother."

"Are you twins?" she asked, her eyes big with wonder.

"No," Michael replied with a friendly smile. "But I'm one year and three minutes older than Hal. All through our childhood I kept reminding him that he must look up to me as the wiser one."

Karen laughed. "I know what you mean. I have a sister a year younger and I remind her of that ancient wisdom whenever she tries to outfox me. As kids, we were the same size, and she had the gall to borrow my clothes, if you know what I mean."

Michael shook his head. "I don't remember stealing his clothes." He glanced at Hal. "I do remember one time in high school, Hal made a date with a girlfriend, and then decided he didn't want to go out with her, and asked me to take his place. I thought she was pretty so I agreed. I think that was the only time we took advantage of our resemblance."

Karen wrinkled her nose. "You guys pulled the old switcheroo on that poor girl! Did she ever find out?"

Michael glanced at Hal. "I never told."

Hal didn't reply.

"I went out with her two more times," Michael said, grinning.

Hal gazed at his brother. "What do you want?"

"Nothing. Just stopped by to return your Dremel set." Michael said, pulling a plastic case from a handbag. "I spoke with Evelyn, invited you both to a family get-together if you want to come. Rodney asked about you."

"I've been busy with a heavy case load."

"Father will be there."

Hal rubbed his neck. "It's doubtful if I'll be able to come."

He handed Hal the Dremel set. "I was in the neighborhood, and thought I'd better give it to you. Had it long enough." He extended a hand to Karen. "Glad to have met you." He turned to Hal. "Don't be a recluse. Stop by the house one in a while." Michael waited for a moment, then left.

"Your brother seems nice."

Suddenly aware of Karen standing next to him, he replied curtly, "Grab a chair and we'll go over the Christianson case file."

***

On the outskirts of Beaverton, a simple poker game was in progress with deadly consequences. Within the middle-class neighborhood of landscaped yards and mature trees along the street easement nestled the Blydair residence. Vigil Blydair slid the deck of cards along the surface of the table with a flamboyant movement focusing intense green eyes on his wife, Betty.

"Cut?"

The petite woman with bangs and innocent looking brown eyes cut the deck in half and patted it as a
signal of completion. Glancing at her husband with a
slight grin, she said, "I trust you, Virg, but feel obliged
to maintain your honesty for the sake of our guests." He
nodded, knowing she was trying to be funny, then
glanced around the poker table at the other players.

Directly to his left sat Tanya Costello, a heavy-set
woman in her thirties with a round face, and large gray
eyes that seemed to be on the move observing everything at once. Red hair done up high in a bun made her
neck appear elongated.

Her husband, Mark Costello, sat next to Tanya in
what appeared to be an uncomfortable position. Thick
eyebrows and sagging jowls went well with his skepti-
cism. And on occasion, before speaking, he would lift
his chin as a signal of some profound utterance in the
making.

Pedro Gonzales of Mexican descent came next
around the periphery of the table. Slight in build, he
looked like a teen-ager even though he was approaching
30. His thick black hair gave a painted-on appearance.
Worried eyes and a dimpled cheek on his boyish face
suggested a tame disposition.

Jerry Cosgrove loomed even larger than his
heavy-set frame. Bushy eyebrows and a big grin added
to his jovial attitude, but his small beady eyes exempli-
fied a cruel temperament behind the comic mask. He
grunted often from no obvious cause. His favorite pas-
time was belittling others, but always with a wry grin.

Lori Evans sat next to Jerry; an attractive young
woman of 29 years. Large blue eyes appeared even larg-

er on the small face. Slim-figured with large breasts, although she didn't promote her sexiness, but any sexist remark directed at her would be met with a strong reprimand.

Next to Lori, Betty Blydair assumed a position of caretaker, her body always at attention waiting for an emergency to happen. She had a comely expression and presumed everyone innocent of any suspicions of wrongdoing. Brown neck-length hair with bangs, pleasing brown eyes promoted her benevolent nature.

Virgil Blydair completed the circle. Tall with long arms, he appeared lanky in his chair. Small green eyes, blond curly hair, and a comely smile seemed to advertise his witty behavior. He, like Jerry Cosgrove, enjoyed the give and take of controversy. Virgil leaned forward ready to deal the cards, stuck in stop-motion, deliberately waiting for someone to question his pause.

"You stuck in a rut?" Jerry chastised Virgil. "Come on, I'm ready to win the first hand."

"A little suspense before we start," Virgil replied, then leaned forward. "Okay, let's begin the games with five-card draw, jacks or better to open." He tossed four quarters in the center of the table, then gave a nod of his head. "One dollar ante, everyone. I've got the coin box by my feet if anyone needs change."

Mark's brow deepened. "Hell yes, we need change. How about bringing that coin box up here on the table."

"He hides it by his feet so no one will steal from it," Jerry remarked.

"Let's just say I'm keeping everyone honest," Virgil said, placing the coin box in the middle of the table. Everyone took nickels, dimes and quarters and tossed in five dollar bills in exchange.

After returning the coin box to the floor, Virgil dealt out the cards and the participants scanned their hands for any discards. After dealing replacement cards, Mark opened and betting continued at a rapid pace until Virgil peeled off a straight flush winning the pot.

Jerry looked at Tanya with a teasing expression. "This wetback next to me is giving me bad luck. He should be out in the fields picking berries. Why don't you trade places with him? Better yet," he added with a just-noticeable grin, "sit on my lap."

"I don't appreciate your rude humor," Mark said. "You and your wisecracks will get you in trouble."

"It may be worth it," Jerry replied, his crooked grin still in place, then turned and glanced at Lori. "I haven't once made a move on you, right?"

She didn't answer him.

"Not yet, anyway." He laughed in bursts.

Pedro didn't look at Jerry, but with lips pressed tightly together, his expression showed discomfort.

Mark dealt out the first card face up to each player. "This is five card stud. Nothing wild, high card wins. Tanya, you can start the bet."

She tossed out two quarters. After the second card was dealt face up, Lori and Pedro folded. Betting continued until the last card was dealt face down. After two raises, Virgil showed his hand. "Looks like ace, king is high. I win again."

"I think he's hiding extra cards up his sleeve," Jerry said. "He's got tricky fingers."

Virgil scoffed. "If you'd watch your cards instead of the ladies present, you'd have a better chance at winning, old man."

When Lori noticed Pedro looking at her with a solemn expression, she gave him a reassuring smile, got up, walked to his side and gave him a kiss on the cheek. Without a word, she returned to her seat.

Jerry did a double-take, glancing at Pedro, then at Lori. "Hey, sweetie, if it's romance you want, I'm closer." He puckered his lips. "I'll give you a real kiss."

"You'd get a slap in the face," she said calmly.

Betty looked at Jerry and said, "Be nice."

Pedro dealt two cards face down to everyone.

"What're we playing—seven card stud?" Mark inquired.

Pedro nodded.

"No speaka da Anglish," Jerry quipped. "Everyone be on alert, this hand is mine. Yep, a full house, aces over is gonna win this hand, folks." He jabbed a finger into his chest. "I raise the ante. Everyone put in two bucks."

After putting in her ante, Tanya caught Betty's eye. "Have you been following the new Dallas TV show?" She paused briefly, then added, "But of course, you have. I'm surprised, but glad Larry Hagman is one of the returning stars. I can hardly wait to see if J. R will get the ranch back from Bobby."

Jerry laughed in bursts. "That'll take the rest of the year to resolve!"

Tanya shook her head, scoffing.

The deal passed to Jerry. "Five card stud. Nothing wild." Jerry began dealing the cards, two face down, then one card face up. A heaping pile of coins lay in the center of the table as jerry dealt the last face card up. Jerry called and raised Mark. "This is my time to win," Jerry said, raising his chin.

Mark turned over his hidden cards which revealed a club flush beating Jerry's three queens.

"Damn! Lost again." Jerry wrinkled his nose. He took a swallow of his beer.

Virgil glanced at Jerry's cache of coins. "Looks like you could use more change."

"I'll bring it to you," Virgil said, getting up. "How's that for service."

As Virgil moved around the table, Jerry commented, "He doesn't trust me taking coins out of the box? Talk about calling the kettle black. Virgil is the one that has slippery fingers in the till." When Virgil got to his side, Jerry scratched his chin, looking up with a sinister expression. "You better remember what I told you last week on the phone."

Virgil put the coin box on the table in front of Jerry. While Jerry checked his billfold, Virgil took a pill from his pants pocket and popped it in his mouth. And tipped his can of beer to his lips. "For my thyroid condition," he said. "Gives me energy to hold a deck of cards with one hand!"

No one laughed. "We're waiting, impatiently, old man," Virgil said to Jerry, pointing at the coin box. Silence and an atmosphere of apprehension embraced the occupants as Jerry picked out various denominations of coins, and then tossed a ten dollar bill in the box.

"My mother, my father, my wife thank you," Virgil said, nodding to Jerry. "But yours truly withholds thanks, except to say, keep losing." Virgil returned to his seat, held up his can of beer and announced, "Toast! To a great evening of poker!"

Everyone drank from their beer cans. Lori passed the deal to Betty. Betty began dealing another hand of seven card stud. As Betty dealt out cards to the players, Jerry quipped, "A man was complaining to a friend— 'I had it all—money, a gorgeous house, a big car, the love of a beautiful woman, then POW! It was all gone.' 'What happened? asked the friend.' 'My wife found out about her.'"

"Not that funny," Virgil said. "This one is better. "Two blondes were walking down the road and the first blonde said, 'Look at that dog with one eye!' The other blonde covers one eye and asks, Where?'"

Jerry shrugged, then took a big swallow of beer.

Play continued with sporadic conversation relating to the poker hands.

Lori's smile raised a dimple in her cheek. "I won!" she exclaimed, and scooped the pot toward her.

Tanya watched Jerry rubbing his arms. "What are you doing?"

"I got this tingling all over my arms. Feels like a thousand bugs attacking me." He licked his lips, then put a hand on his beer belly, grunting. "Stomach cramps, too."

"Would you like an anti-acid tablet?" Betty asked.

"Nah." He took another large swallow of beer. "Come on, slow poke, let's play. I got a feeling I'm the winner this time."

"Keep that thought, Jerry, your optimism is hilarious." Virgil leaned forward ready to deal the cards. "Okay, this hand will be five-card draw, jacks or better to open." He tossed in four quarters, then gave a nod of his head. "One dollar in the pot everyone."

Lori excused herself to go to the bathroom. As she passed Pedro's chair, she stooped down and kissed him, then continued on. Everyone knew it was a sign to Jerry to let him know Pedro was her boy friend.

"Shall we wait for Lori?" Virgil asked.

"Hell no!" Mark exclaimed. "Let's play."

Everyone put in their ante except Jerry.

"We're one dollar shy," Mark said, then glared at Jerry. "I didn't see you ante up. Are you playing?"

The other players glanced at Jerry's limp position in the chair; his chin resting on his chest with no discernible movement.

"We're waiting," Tanya said with a degree of agitation in her voice.

Mark reached over and nudged Jerry's arm. "Good god! I believe the man's fallen asleep."

Virgil knocked on the table with his knuckles. "Hey, Jerry! Wake up! Are you playing or sleeping?"

With no response, Betty got up and went to Jerry's side. She patted him on the face and then after a moment, she felt of his pulse. "I'm not feeling anything. Virgil, you better call emergency."

Virgil grabbed his cell phone and dialed 9-1-1.

***

"Hello!

9-1-1 operator. "What is your emergency?"

"We can't get any response from our friend. I don't know—maybe he's had a heart attack."

9-1-1 operator: Is he breathing?

"I don't think so. We can't feel a pulse. We need a paramedic."

9-1-1 operator: Where is the person now?

"Still sitting in his chair at the table... at my house—1244 Benedict Way."

9-1-1 operator: And you are...?

"Virgil Blydair."

9-1-1 operator: Stay on the line, Mr. Blydair. The paramedics are on their way."

CHAPTER TWO

THREE DAYS LATER at the precinct station, Lieutenant Abrams handed Hal a folder. "New case. A middle-
aged man died of heart failure while playing a game of
poker at a friend's house with six other players. The victim name's is Jerry Cosgrove. The case is a little late
coming. Everyone including the medics thought the
cause of the heart attack was arteriosclerosis, including
the medics. An autopsy was done. I just received a call
from the medical examiner. He's confirmed the man
died of heart failure." The lieutenant's eyes rolled up.
"But he said toxicology has proven there was poison in
his system. Aconite, a perennial plant grown wild locally, is used to treat a variety of diseases, but deadly if any
part of the raw root is ingested. The pathologist said the
poison attacks the heart directly. The poison was found
in Cosgrove's beer. See if you can muster out a confession." As Hal got to the door, Abrams asked, "How's
your new partner working out?"

"Too early to tell."

"Well, you're the senior detective, so start thinking positive about your working relationship, okay."

Hal headed back to his desk, stopping at the side
of Karen's desk. "You got a minute?"

"Sixty seconds?" She grinned. "I would say 99%
of the time that's a given."

"New case." He pulled a chair next to her desk

and sat down. He gave her the file and both read in silence she flipped the pages at a reading pace.

"Doesn't sound complicated," Karen said. "Since we know the victim was killed at the scene, someone at the poker party had to be the perpetrator, right?"

He frowned. "It appears that way. But the situation is strange. A man is poisoned from drinking the same beer as the rest of the poker players." He raised his eyebrows. "None of the other players had any trace of the poison in their beer." Hal rubbed the back of his neck, thinking. "One of them has to be the perpetrator."

"Unless they're all in collusion with one another."

He looked at her, somewhat startled. "Highly unlikely."

She grinned. "You mean six people holding onto a secret is like the saying, two people can keep a secret if one of them is dead?" She waited for a reply, but with silence, she continued, "Detective Reiner…"

"Skip the redundant label," he interrupted. "Call me Hal. I'll call you Karen."

She blinked her eyes. "Okay. You know, even if there is only one perpetrator, couldn't he or she be in collusion with an accomplice? The file points out two married couples and perhaps Gonzales and Evans are an item."

"We'll sound that out during the interrogation."

"If we interview each of the players separately to weed out any concealment by an accomplice, not only for what is said, but what each one might reveal with their demeanor seems to be our best approach. Don't you think so, Hal?"

He nodded, but didn't reply.

She lifted an eyebrow. "I'm pretty good at reading

body language."

"Are you a psychic?" He rolled his eyes.

She laughed. No, but I've taken a couple of courses on Kinesics, which is the study of body language, bodily gestures and facial expressions. Experts in the field agree that nearly 80 % of all human communication is non-verbal." Hal folded his arms across his chest. "How we position our bodies," she continued, smiling, "often reveals our feelings like the way you have your arms cross tight against your chest suggests you are skeptical."

"Okay, okay, I've heard enough. You've convinced me you're not a psychic. I'll let you be in charge of the non-verbal communications. In the meantime, I'll arrange for the interviews of the Cosgrove poisoning, but one of the first things to do is research aconite."

She gave him the file. "I'm excited. I'm looking forward to working with you on this challenging case."

He sat down at his desk, swiveling his chair away from her on-going gaze of attention. Confusion engulfed him suddenly. A new partner who gabbed too much, an additional case that had all the makings of endless interviews, and his marriage was falling apart. He opened the lower desk drawer and looked inside absently.

***

The following day at the precinct, Betty Blydair sat erect in her chair as Hal and Karen entered the interrogation room.

"I'm Detective Hal Reiner and this is Detective Karen Holmes," he said abruptly.

The threesome exchanged handshakes.

"We're interviewing those of you at the poker

game for information about the death of Jerry Cosgrove."

"I've been in a state of shock ever since last Friday. Jerry was only forty years old. I don't think he had any heart trouble." She put a hand to her cheek. "He *was* overweight. Oh dear, one never knows when it's time to meet one's maker."

Karen nodded. "Mr. Cosgrove died of heart failure, but the cause was poison in his system."

"What?" Her brown eyes widened. "Poison? Whatever do you mean?"

"Aconite, an alkaloid toxin. Very potent. The poison in his beer prompted his heart attack."

Betty put a hand to her mouth. "Are you saying he was poisoned that evening at my home?"

"Yes, that's what we're saying," Hal remarked, watching her demeanor.

"Really? But...I don't see how that's possible. We were all playing poker together. Poor Jerry. How could someone have done it?"

"That's what we're trying to find out," Hal said. He put his notepad on the table and sat down.

Karen sat down across from Betty, and opened her notepad, then looked at the petite woman in a gesture of friendship. "Mrs. Blydair, we know you and your husband came here voluntarily, and we appreciate your cooperation in this homicide case. We'll need to know exactly what transpired that evening from the time your friends arrived at your house until your husband called emergency services. Please relate the smallest of details as you remember them."

Betty wiped her brow with downcast eyes. "Where do I start?"

"At the beginning," Hal replied.

"Would you like something to drink?" Karen asked.

Betty nodded. "A glass of water would be nice."

Karen left the office and returned with a glass of water, giving it to Betty with a napkin.

After taking a sip of water, Betty spoke with a noticeable calm about her. "We've been meeting the last Friday of each month since March of this year. Jerry Cosgrove, Mark and Tanya Costello, Lori Evans, Pedro Gonzales and of course, my husband, Virgil, and myself. It's the only time we spend time together at our poker parties." She paused. "Except we knew the Costello's from the Elks Club. And we did know Jerry before. We were in business with him until we had a falling out of sorts. Jerry accused my husband of stealing from the company funds—an untruth it was—and Jerry threatened to sue, but he stopped the lawsuit when we bought him out with a very generous offer. That was nearly three years ago."

"That ended the dispute?" Hal inquired. "You didn't try to get even in some way?"

"No, sir. The matter sort of went in hibernation," she said, smiling. "The only thing is—Jerry does have an inconsiderate habit of reminding Virgil of 'slippery fingers in the till'—Jerry's words. But he usually says it with a smile. Jerry's peculiar humor is one of his amiable traits. There's never a dull moment when he's around. I suppose that's why we've kept him as a friend, inviting him to the poker parties." She gazed at Karen. "I might be naive, but I like to treat everyone with kindness no matter what they've said or done. After our tea and muffins in the kitchen, we all went to the living room and played poker."

"Was everyone in the kitchen while you were having tea and muffins?" Hal asked, writing in his notepad. "Or did guests wander in?"

"Everyone arrived around seven o'clock, and all of us sat at our kitchen table until we moved into the living room for the poker games at exactly seven-thirty."

"How can you be so certain of the time?"

Betty's gaze roamed around the room. "I confess I have this thing about planned events. I strive...well, the truth is, I mandated that our meetings take place in a scheduled manner." She brushed at her bangs with a wave of a hand. "I admit to my fanaticism keeping a tight schedule. It's one of my personality quirks, if you will, but one that I hold in esteem. With one eye on my watch, it was my custom to announce, 'Time for poker,' whether or not everyone had finished their appetizers. I loathe events that play out in a random fashion." She looked at Hal. "But to answer your question properly, Detective Reiner, it was exactly 7:30 when we all left the kitchen together."

Karen wrote in her notepad, glanced at Hal, and then asked Betty, "Did all of your friends arrive at your home at the same time?"

"Pretty much, yes. Mark and Tanya arrived at seven. I was in the process of making corn muffins. Tea and muffins was our customary staple each time we met..." She paused then added, "And beer during our poker games." She glanced up at the ceiling as though it helped her memory. "Within minutes, Lori Evans and Pedro Gonzales arrived."

"They came together?"

"Oh, sorry. No, Pedro came about two minutes after Lori."

Karen wrote in her notepad. "And where was your husband at this time?"

"Helping me in the kitchen."

"And when did Mr. Cosgrove arrive?"

"He came perhaps a minute or two before the Costello's. We all gathered at the kitchen table and talked of mundane things munching on muffins and sipping tea."

Hal leaned forward, firmness in his voice. "Anything significant happen while everyone was in the kitchen?"

Betty looked surprised. "Oh yes, it did. Well, I'm not sure how significant, but Jerry and Pedro had a slight confrontation. Jerry remarked about Pedro being late. He said, 'Hey, Wetback, late again. Were you held up at the border?' were his words if I remember correctly. I don't think Pedro said anything in return, but I could tell he didn't like the criticism."

"How could you tell?"

"His mannerism and expression, tightly pressed lips and a stiff upper body."

Karen glanced at Hal momentarily, then asked Betty, "And you took that to mean…what?"

"That Pedro was irate at Jerry's words."

"Was there any physical contact between the two?" Karen asked.

"No. Pedro is a small person. Jerry is heavier set and taller, although I don't believe Jerry would strike anyone; he likes to talk tough, but he's a pansy if you know what I mean." With raised eyebrows, she added, "Actually, they both live in the same apartment complex, Jerry and Pedro, and I would think Jerry would get his fill of teasing Pedro."

"Was there any other disagreements or altercations?" Hal inquired.

"No." Betty shook her head for added confirmation. "Then we all went into the living room..."

"All at the same time?" Karen asked.

"I came in a few minutes later. I got beer from the fridge, put the cans on a tray, including a bowl of nuts, and then took the tray into the living room."

"The beer was unopened?"

"Oh yes. I don't like to open those tabs on top. Too often it results in a broken nail."

"Who opened your can?" Hal asked for clarification.

"My husband. He's always considerate enough to do that for me. Is that important?"

Hal put down his pen and flexed his fingers. "Everything is important in a homicide investigation."

Karen tapped her pen on the table. "All of the guests were at the table when you walked in with the tray?"

"Yes, everyone was in the room the entire time," she said, then paused for a moment. "I think Lori went into the bathroom once, but was only gone for a few minutes. But no one else left the table while we played poker and munched on peanuts." She sighed. "I'm not much of a beer drinker, but I sipped a few..."

"Mrs. Blydair," Hal intervened, leaning forward. "You mentioned Ms. Evans going to the bathroom. Did she take her beer with her?"

"I don't think so. She did stop by Pedro's side and gave him a kiss."

"Tell me, did everyone drink from their beer cans if you can recall?"

"I'm not certain about everyone, sorry. I did see my husband and Jerry open their cans right away and take a drink."

Karen jotted in her notebook. "You played poker with money or chips?"

"Coins. Before we started playing, Virgil pushed a coin box filled with nickels, dimes and quarters in the middle of the table so everyone could get change." She hesitated, then said, "I believe it was after the first few hands when Jerry asked for more change because he was losing. He always does. Virgil got up, took the box to his side and held the box in front of Jerry." She paused, thinking. "I remember now Jerry's exact words. 'Put the box down. I don't steal money like some people I know.' I looked at Virgil, but he didn't respond to Jerry's dig."

Hal's eyes narrowed. "Your husband didn't react at all?"

"Only a wry grin, which *is* his custom. He sees humor in everything."

Karen nodded. "So, the poker games continued without interruption until you discovered Mr. Cosgrove unresponsive?"

"Yes."

"Tell us about that."

"I believe it was Tanya who noticed Jerry's limp position in the chair—his chin resting on his chest and no movement discernible. Mark reached over and nudged Jerry's arm. He said, 'Good God! I believe the man's fallen asleep.' I got up and went to Jerry's side. I slapped his cheek, and then after a moment, I felt for his pulse. Nothing. I told Virgil to call 9-1-1."

After Hal finished writing in his notepad, he got

up. "Mrs. Blydair, you're free to go unless you prefer to stay here until we've interviewed you husband."

"Or you can be seated in the main office," Karen added.

"I'll wait here for my husband."

Karen stood up, pressing down her skirt. "These chairs aren't very comfortable. Would you like a pillow?"

"No thank you, I'm fine."

***

After closing the door behind them, Hal said, "A pillow! Are you pampering the suspect?"

"I was trying to be considerate, to put her mind at ease with a few caring words," she said defensively.

Hal snorted. "My father used to tell me, 'If you keep your mouth shut, flies won't get in.'"

"What's that supposed to mean?"

"You're a smart lady, you figure it out."

"I thought a suspect was considered innocent until proven guilty."

Hal grinned. "Did her body language tell you that?"

Karen gave him a blank look. "My opinion, for whatever it's worth, I thought she was straight-forward with her responses. I hope all of our suspects are as open. Do you really believe she put the poison in the beer?"

"She admitted being alone in the kitchen with the beer. Maybe she added the poison then."

"But, she said the cans were unopened. If she was lying, wouldn't she know her testimony would be double checked?"

"Maybe so. We'll have forensics check out the cans for any sign of holes." He stepped forward motioning with his arm toward the adjacent interrogation room. "Let's talk with the husband. Maybe we can put some of these thorny questions to rest."

***

Entering the room, Hal and Karen sat across from Virgil Blydair. The introductions were short. Karen explained they were investigating the death of Cosgrove. After what seemed to be a prolonged pause, Virgil spoke with a hearty grin. "It seems implausible that someone at the poker games could have poisoned him. I mean we were all drinking from our cans of Budweiser in plain sight of everyone." Virgil lifted his hands to the air. "Surely someone would have noticed if the poison was dumped in Jerry's can, eh?"

"The fact remains Mr. Cosgrove's beer had poison in it," Hal remarked.

"In the beer!" Virgil rubbed the back of his neck. "What about the tea and muffins we had in the kitchen?"

"The toxin wasn't present in the tea or muffins, only the beer," Karen replied. "Toxicology tests were run on the tea cups and muffins as well as the beer cans. Only the can that Mr. Cosgrove was drinking from had a large amount of aconite, a very potent poison."

Hal looked directly in Virgil's eyes. "Mr. Blydair, you don't seem overly concerned about Mr. Cosgrove's death."

Virgil laughed. "It's been a week, my dear fellow. At first, yes, I felt a degree of sadness, but now after the fact, my feelings for him are neutral, especially now that I'm probably considered a suspect, eh?"

"At this time you are considered a person of interest as well as the other five people at the poker game." Karen advised. She glanced at Hal, then continued, "I understand that you were in business with Mr. Cosgrove, but had a disagreement. Would you care to comment?"

Virgil nodded. "That's correct. We were in business together until he accused me of stealing from the company funds."

"Embezzlement?" Hal asked without looking at Virgil.

"In a manner of speaking, yes. But untrue. The dispute happened about two and a half years ago. We kept large amounts of cash in our office. We had a check-cashing business. Jerry discovered our cash drawer empty, and accused me of taking the money. At the time he threatened to sue, but after I bought him out, the unpleasantness went by the wayside. The only thing is—he continues to remind me of the empty cash box."

Karen winced. "Doesn't that make you angry?"

"No, as long as he says it with a smile. I don't get mad, I get even."

Hal and Karen glanced at each other.

Virgil's grin erupted. "Just kidding. I wouldn't do anything to keep him from *not* coming to the poker games. He's a lousy player and loses his money every time we play. I suppose you could say I tolerate him. He's witty. I admit I don't care for his attitude—racist and sexist—but my wife, Betty, she felt we should remain friends with him. I agreed."

Hal wrote in his notepad, then inquired, "Everyone had a beer at the poker table?"

"Yes. Bud Light, 12 oz. cans."

"I suppose everyone grabbed a can from the fridge on the way to the living room," Karen said suggesting a difference in testimony.

"No. Betty brought in the beer on a tray after the rest of us sat down at the poker table."

Hal raised his head. "Opened?"

"No. The cans were unopened. She hates busting those tabs open; breaks her nails."

"You're certain of that?"

Smiling, Virgil asked, "Of breaking her nails?"

Hal frowned. "That the cans were unopened."

With a devilish grin, Virgil brushed at the table with the palm of his hand. "Sorry, Detective Reiner, you can't trick me into denying that which I saw with my own eyes. Regarding the opening of beer cans—yes, I saw everyone at the poker table opening up their beer, except I opened Betty's can for her..." He paused with his smile receding, "to save her from breaking a finger-nail."

Hearing Blydair's words, Hal recalled the time when Evelyn broke a finger nail trying to adjust a knob on their Jacuzzi. She spends great deal of time in their Jacuzzi. The thought occurred to him that she could fall, hitting her head on the tile and drown in the tub

Karen noticed Hal's bent-over frame. "Tell me, Mr. Blydair, was the seating arrangement at the poker table always the same?"

"Oh yes. Betty wouldn't have it any other way. She has a passion for order. I sat facing the kitchen. To my left, Tanya Costello. Next to her, Mark Costello, then Pedro Gonzales and Jerry Cosgrove sat across from me. Then Lori Evans and Betty next to me. For the last eight months, it's been a standard routine meeting the last Friday of each month."

Hal rubbed his forehead. The interview with the husband was becoming unfruitful. How the poison got into Cosgrove's beer can remained the big question with little to go on. He addressed Virgil. "During the games, do you recall anyone being close to Mr. Cosgrove?"

"Close? You mean close enough to put poison in his beer can?"

"That's exactly what I mean."

Virgil shook his head." My dear fellow, with six people in close proximity to Jerry, someone spooning poison into his beer can would have been too obvious." His grin widened. "But to answer your question specifically, I saw Lori, Tanya and Pedro near Jerry at one time or another...before he became a statistic, that is."

"What were the circumstances of those encounters?" Karen inquired.

"When Jerry made a sexist remark directed to Tanya, she got up, went to his side and hit him on the head lightly. Jerry laughed it off. A little later, on her way to the bathroom, Lori stopped by Jerry's side and told him she didn't like his racist comment to Pedro."

"How close was she to Mr. Cosgrove?"

Virgil held up a thumb and forefinger close together. "That close. I noticed she rested her hand on the table nearly touching his beer can. After Lori returned from the bathroom, Pedro gave her a kiss on the cheek, I assume, to let Jerry know that she was his girl."

There was a moment of silence while Hal and Karen wrote in their notebooks.

"Hey, did you hear the latest blonde joke? A blonde suspects her boyfriend of cheating on her. She buys a gun. When she arrives at his apartment, sure enough, she finds him in the arms of a redhead. Over-come with grief, she points the gun at her own head. The boyfriend yells, 'No, honey, don't do it?' 'Shut up!' she yells. 'You're next.'"

Karen laughed. Hal remained sober-faced.

"Were you close to Mr. Cosgrove at any time?" Hal asked, focusing on Virgil's demeanor.

"Only that one occasion when I took the coin box to him so he could get change, then I returned to my chair.

Karen closed her notebook. "Mr. Blydair, did you have anything to do with Mr. Cosgrove's death?"

"No."

"That will conclude this interview for now," Hal said, getting up. "You and your wife are free to leave."

Leaving the room, Hal said, "Both are strong sus-pects. My gut feeling tells me the Blydairs are involved. Threatened to be sued is a good motive for murder."

"Which was two and half years ago, a long time lapse to get even."

"Hate never forgets," Hal said, looking at the far wall. He shoved his notepad in his shirt pocket. "Let's write up another report with no leads."

"We still have the others to interview," Karen said in an upbeat tone. "We're likely to get a change of story from one of them."

***

On his way to his office, Lt. Abrams stopped by Hal' and Karen's desk. "What's the latest with the inter-views?"

Karen waited for Hal to respond. "Still thinking,"

he said.

"Man of few words," Abrams said to Karen. "Are you getting acclimated to this case yet?"

"I think so," she said. "We just finished interviewing Virgil Blydair. He corroborated his wife's testimony, appeared aboveboard, without any sign of stress, and confirmed that his wife brought in the beer cans on a tray, unopened. He said he saw everyone open their own beer. No confession yet."

"Do you think the Blydairs are involved?"

Karen glanced at Hal. "My partner is suspicious. He thinks the Betty could have added the poison in the beer when she was by herself in the kitchen."

Abrams frowned. "But the cans were unopened, right?"

"Yes, according to her and confirmed by her husband. We'll definitely check that out with the other players. And have forensics check the cans for any holes."

"Adding poison with a needle?" Abrams asked, frowning. "Does aconite come in liquid form?"

"We'll check it out," Hal replied, shrugging. We need to think anything's possible."

"Good thinking. Have forensics inspect the beer cans for any perforations no matter how small. Maybe we can close this case before more complications muddle the task ahead—how the poison got in Cosgrove's beer can."

Hal nodded, and bid Abrams good-bye, then opened the bottom drawer of his desk, looking in. He thought of his wife again. The dread in his gut matched that of his eyes.

CHAPTER THREE

A FEW DAYS later, Hal and Karen interviewed Tanya Costello at the precinct. As soon as they entered, Tanya reeled back in her chair with an open mouth. Her green eyes stared at the opposite wall, then the redhead slapped both hands on the table. "I don't know if I'm more shocked that his death was due to poisoning or if he was poisoned by one of us at the table."

Hal noted her aggressive nature in his notepad. It reminded him of his wife constantly nagging him about his submissive personality. She was right, he knew full well of his laid back temperament, but he wasn't completely at fault with the negative trait. He didn't come by it on his own accord.

Hal and Karen sat down at the table across from her.

"Were you acquainted with Mr. Cosgrove outside of the poker parties?" Karen inquired.

"Me? God, no! Mark and I had met Jerry eight months ago when the Blydairs invited us for poker for the first time; the only time we saw him were at the poker parties. We knew the Blydairs from the Elks Lodge. I don't think Jerry was liked by anyone, except maybe Virgil and Betty. He had a foul mouth. He made sexist remarks to me, and my husband didn't like it one bit. Nor did I."

"Like what would he say?"

"You would be good in the sack. He said that more than once in front of everyone."

"Sounds like motive to want him dead," Hal said, noting the confrontational sound of her voice.

She shook her head. "No, but angry enough to slap his face." She paused. "I did hit him on the head when he made that sexist remark to me."

"When did this happen?"

"Early on. I think it was during the second or third hand of poker. He stared at my chest, then said it, grinning."

"Said what?"

"That I would be good in the sack. I knew what he meant. He always had a stupid grin on his fat face, so most of the time one couldn't tell if he was serious or not, but this time I believed he meant it. He's such an ass."

"But you took it serious enough to get up, walk over, and hit him on the head?" Karen questioned.

"I wasn't about to let him get away with that stupid remark. But there was no force behind my punch. I doubled up my fist and hit him on top of the head lightly; kind of a reminder for him to watch his foul mouth."

"How long were you at his side?" Hal asked.

"I don't know—a minute maybe."

"Did you come in contact with his beer can?"

"What on earth for?" Her eyes showed a sudden awareness. "Oh, you mean to put poison in his beer? No, sir, I did not. I imagine everyone was looking. If I had had the time to touch his beer or the inclination, surely someone would have noticed."

"Maybe, Maybe not," Hal replied. "I think most eyes would have been focused on your fist hitting his head."

"Which he deserved." With puckered lips, she sat a little more rigid in her chair. "Well, I didn't put anything in his drink." She turned to Karen. "Both Lori and Pedro were close enough to put something in his beer can. They sat on each side of him. I'm not saying they did, but I wasn't the only one near Jerry."

Karen nodded. "Mrs. Costello, did you notice any strange behavior from Jerry before you found him dead?"

"I didn't find him dead."

Smiling, Karen remarked, "I meant the six of you at the table."

"Betty was the one who took his pulse. But to answer your question, no I didn't notice any strange behavior. The less I had to look at him, the better. Although I did hear grunting sounds which may have come from him just prior to his collapse."

Hal leaned forward. "He collapsed?" When conducting investigations, he knew that suspect's words were often as important as the context in which they were said.

"Well, I mean when we noticed his head down, arms to his side as though he *had* collapsed. When he didn't answer Virgil's request to ante up in a new game, I glanced at him then noticed his head resting on his chest as though asleep."

"Then you did notice strange behavior."

Tanya looked into Hal's eyes, frowning. "Sir, I meant up to that point I didn't see any strange behavior."

He wasn't sure where he was going with his next question; he was more concerned with her answer. "Did you see Mr. Cosgrove drinking his beer?"

"That I did. When Betty brought in the beer and nuts, she went around the table, and each person took a can. Cosgrove opened his beer and took a swig right away."

"Did you notice if Mrs. Blydair touched any of the cans on the tray?"

"Twelve ounce beer cans on a tray is heavy. Betty is a small woman. I'm sure she used both hands to carry the tray."

"Well, did you notice if she turned the tray to position the beer in front of the next person in line as she went around the table?"

"Especially when she got to Mr. Cosgrove's side," Karen added.

Tanya thought for a moment. "Didn't I just answer that question? Heavens! I wasn't watching her every instant. Why are you asking these asinine questions?"

"The devil is in the details," Hal answered.

Karen addressed Tanya in an appeasing manner. "Mrs. Cosgrove, you came to the interview voluntarily and we appreciate your willingness to testify, but I remind you that anything you say can be used against you."

"Yes, yes, I know. I have nothing to hide. I will answer your questions."

"Any small detail is important in a murder investigation. If you can recall, please, did anything unusual happen when Mr. Cosgrove drank from his beer can?"

"He nearly gagged. This was after he'd taken a few sips. At the time I thought it odd that he would have a delayed reaction. After coughing, groaning, and holding his stomach, he said, 'Beer will be the death of me yet.'" With a smirk, Tanya added, "Rather prophetic, don't you think?"

After a moment, Hal glanced at Karen, motioning to her with a tilt of his head. "I have no more questions."

"Mrs. Costello, thank you for your testimony and your cooperation" Karen said. "You're free to leave now."

She got up immediately and headed for the door. "She turned and said, "I will be more than pleased when this investigation is over."

With a tilt of her head, Karen asked, "Why is that?"

"To know who killed him. In the meantime, I have to wonder who did it."

"You're excused," Hal said to Tanya. "We may want to talk to again."

"No problem," Tanya said and left the room.

***

Hal and Karen returned to their desks in the squad room.

"She seems open, not obviously hiding anything."

Hal shrugged. "She's still a person of interest."

"Of course. I just meant …"

He waved a hand through the air. "No need for an explanation. Let's stick with the facts."

"Okay." She glanced at her notepad. "Are you aware Forensics found a small hole in Cosgrove's can near the top."

"No. When did you find out?"

"This morning."

Hal looked at her with quizzical eyes. "You didn't tell me."

She raised her eyebrows with a slight grin. "You

didn't ask."

"Okay." He nodded. "That throws a new light on how the poison got in Cosgrove's beer. But only even if aconite comes in liquid form."

The phone rang on Hal's desk. He paused for a long moment before answering.

"Your phone is ringing," she said, pointing.

Hal grabbed the phone and pasted it against his ear. "Reiner here," he remarked brusquely.

The caller was his wife. He felt emotionally drained after unrewarding interviews with three suspects and wasn't in the mood for discussing marital differences in front of Karen. "I can't talk about it now." Pause. "Hey, it's my job. What do you expect of me, miracles?" Pause. "We'll discuss it when I get home, if I get home." Long pause. "Yes, I'm angry. I'm working." Pause. "I said I'd talk to you about it at home. Goodbye." He slammed the receiver onto its cradle. "A little disagreement with my wife," he said to Karen. "Are you married?"

"No."

"Then you wouldn't understand."

"Try me," she said in a defensive posture.

He shook his head, then turned in his chair, abruptly, busying himself digging through files on the top of his desk.

***

A few days later, Lori Evans was escorted into an interrogation room. Karen sat on one of the end chairs and readied her pen to take notes. Hal sat across the table from Lori. He looked her over. A young lady in her late twenties, he guessed. She wore a mini-skirt with a matching white, long-sleeved blouse which revealed a slender well-proportioned body. Her demeanor suggested someone who wouldn't hesitate to defend her principles. And yet, she had a calmness about her that intrigued him. Her round face exhibited friendliness; soft, blue eyes suggested integrity. Lori Evans would be the one most likely to give forthright testimony.

"We appreciate you coming in today, Ms. Evans. We know you've given testimony about Mr. Cosgrove's death to the patrol officers at the scene, and we appreciate your cooperation," Karen said. "But new information has come to light that requires further interviews." She paused waiting for a reply, but Lori remained closed-mouthed. "Mr. Cosgrove did die of heart failure, but the cause was due to poison, which means someone at the poker party put a lethal dose of aconite, deadly poison, in his beer."

Lori pressed her hands together. "He was murdered," she said calmly with no outward show of emotion. "I'm not particularly sorry that's he's dead," she added. "He had a foul mouth, and I called him on it more than once."

"You were sitting next to him at the poker table?" Karen asked.

"Yes."

Hal leaned forward. "Then you were within arm's reach of his beer. Is that a fair assumption?"

"Well actually the beer can was on his right side, next to Pedro."

Karen gazed into Lori's eyes. "Ms. Evans, did you put poison in his beer?"

"No."

"But you have motive to kill him, wouldn't you

agree?" Hal inquired.

"His sexist remarks were nauseating to me," she said, placing one hand on top of the other, "and his racism toward Pedro made me furious, but neither was serious enough to kill him."

"What did he say about Pedro?"

"He said, 'This wetback is giving me bad luck,' then he added in a nasty tone, 'The Mexican should be out in the fields picking berries.'"

"What did Pedro say?"

"Pedro said nothing. He's non-confrontational, tries always to shy away from racial remarks, but I knew he was offended. I told Cosgrove to shut his racist mouth."

Karen wrote in her notebook, then asked, "Then Pedro was close enough to reach over and put poison in Cosgrove's beer. Is that what happened?"

Lori shook her head. "He wouldn't do that?"

"You and Pedro were romantically involved?" Karen asked.

"Yes."

"You mentioned sexist remarks. Tell us about that."

"At one point during the games, he told me I would make a good lay in bed, and that I needed a *real* man, that Pedro was a ....I think the term he used was 'shrimp,' and he said he was going to steal me away from Pedro."

Hal got up, walked around the table, stopping behind Lori and inquired, "Did any of the other players say anything during Cosgrove's remarks?"

"I think Tanya said something, but I don't recall what it was."

Hal returned to his seat. He glanced at Karen with raised eyebrows, then asked Lori pointedly, "You don't recall or you wish not to recall?"

"If I remembered I would tell you. At the time I was angry. I got up and stormed over beside Mr. Cosgrove and told him he was an ass."

"How close were you to Mr. Cosgrove?"

"Close, but not touching him. I was between him and Pedro. I put a consoling hand to Pedro's arm."

"Then you were near Mr. Cosgrove beer can," Hal remarked, studying her reaction. "You mentioned before his beer was on his right side, close enough to put poison in the can, would you agree with that?"

Lori shrugged, then replied, "I suppose I was close enough."

"Did you touch his can while you were at his side?"

"Did I touch his can of beer?" A long moment passed before she answered. "No. If I understand what you're implying, Detective Reiner, I didn't put poison in his beer." Her eyelids fluttered. "I couldn't have put poison in his can without being seen. I mean I'm sure everyone was watching me. I don't know who put poison in his beer, but it wasn't me."

"You and Pedro were the last ones to arrive at the Blydair residence before the poker game started, is that correct?" Karen inquired.

Lori ran a hand through her hair. "I arrived a few minutes after seven, then Pedro arrived a few minutes later. We drove there with our own cars. We were in the kitchen with the others. That's when Mr. Cosgrove made his first racist remark to Pedro. He said, 'Hey, Wetback, late again. Were you held up at the border?' I told Mr. Cosgrove to shut his bigoted mouth."

"What did he say?"

"He laughed in my face."

Did anyone else say anything?"

"I don't know. I stepped out of the kitchen for a minute. I needed a little space to cool off."

Hal leaned forward. "Where did you go?"

"On the other side of the doorway to the kitchen, but in plain sight of everyone. It couldn't have been more than a minute or two before I stepped back into the kitchen."

Karen waited while Lori took a sip from her soda. "While playing poker did you notice anything unusual about Mr. Cosgrove's behavior during the games?"

"I don't know how long it was, but after a few games, Mr. Cosgrove rubbed his stomach a few times like he was in pain. He wiggled around in his chair as though he had ants in his pants. I thought I heard him groaning. His behavior didn't seem out of the ordinary. He was always acting out, you know, wanting attention."

"That's all I have for now," Hal said, getting up.

Karen nodded. "You're free to go."

With a pleasant smile, Lori bid them both farewell and left.

***

Outside the room, Karen commented first, "I don't think I would want to be on the receiving end of her anger about Cosgrove's remarks. Although inflammatory remarks aren't usually much of a motive for murder, do you think?"

"Maybe no, maybe yes," Hal replied staring at the

opposite wall. "For some, words can be just as hurtful as physical force. I know about that."

"From personal experience?"

He nodded, then quickly changed the subject. "This case is beginning to look like a confession is needed. Six suspects at the crime scene and they all have degrees of motive."

Hal rubbed the back of his neck. "They're all watching each other, but don't see who put the poison in Cosgrove's can. This case is giving me cramps. Are we into a perfect murder here?"

Karen grinned. "I don't think so."

"Well, let's report our meager results to the boss man."

***

Inside Lt. Abrams office, he motioned for the detectives to be seated. "I can tell from your bleak expressions that no one yet has confessed," the lieutenant said, as Hal and Karen sat down across from his desk.

"Not even close," Hal replied.

"You have two more yet to interview?"

Karen nodded. "Mark Costello and Pedro Gonzales. Costello is scheduled tomorrow morning and Gonzales in the afternoon. When we're done here, Hal and I will visit the law offices of Blankenship and Hoffman in Castletown to see if there's any litigation in process against Virgil Blydair. He and his wife both mentioned Cosgrove threatened them with a lawsuit."

"Alright, jump on it," Abrams said, waving them out. "A long drive to Castletown. You'll be gone most of the day. Good luck!"

Hal and Karen left the department. "I'll drive," Karen said, glancing at Hal. "If you don't mind. I know the area well having lived only a few miles away from their office."

"Okay, okay, you don't have to explain yourself."

"But I feel like I should. Sharing my thoughts helps me to understand if what I'm saying is reasonable. I would think sharing your ideas would serve you as well."

He didn't reply. The thirty minute drive seemed a lot longer as he stared out of the window, watching mostly farmland pass by. Ever since he could remember, sharing his feelings had been a catastrophe of one degree or another. In that respect, his brother was like Karen—wanting to talk at length about every little detail. He wondered why he had such an aversion to speaking out, then instantly, he acknowledged the reason to himself. *Afraid of getting whipped again.*

***

"We're here!" Karen said, in a bubbly tone "Safe and sound." She pulled into a parking lot and stopped the SUV in front of the office building that had a large sign depicting the logo Blankenship and Hoffman. Attorneys at Law.

Inside, Karen showed her badge and explained their reason for wanting information. The secretary spoke to Mr. Hoffman on the phone, then directed Karen and Hal through double doors into a large office.

"We're investigating the homicide of Jerry Cosgrove," Karen said. "I understand he was your client. Is that correct?"

The name sounds familiar," the bald man with a round face replied, then turned to a cluster of file cabinets. He returned to his desk with a file packet. After gleaming through the file, he said, "Yes...well, he was a short term client. We took his deposition regarding a lawsuit against a Mr. Blydair, but he never pursued it. That was nearly three years ago."

"No contact with him as recently as two or three weeks ago?" Karen inquired.

"No."

Karen thanked him for his time and she and Hal left the building. As she paced rapidly toward the SUV, she noticed Hal continuing down the sidewalk. "Where are you going?"

He stopped short of a crumpled paper bag, then reached down and picked it up.

Karen laughed. "Is that evidence?"

"Garbage. I'll put it where it belongs." He walked to a trash container at the end of the building, and tossed it inside.

"You have some redeeming qualities, after all," she said, waiting for a reply.

When he met up with her, he replied, "I didn't want someone tripping over it or stepping on it. It occurred to me someone could trip, fall and break a hip." He shrugged. "Trying to save some one pain."

Her eyes brightened. "Excellent! You're sharing your feelings."

"I don't know about that. Let's get back to the precinct. It'll be evening before we get back." He knew he should be more receptive to his partner. "What does body language tell you about the case? Any gestures suggesting involvement by any of the suspects so far?"

"Thanks for asking. So far, no one in particular stands out."

As she stopped at a signal light, Hal slapped his

forehead. "I don't believe it," he exclaimed, a slight grin showing.

"What?"

"Would you believe our next suspect, Mark Costello is going to confess?"

She looked into his eyes. "What brought that on?"

"Thinking positive. Maybe I'm learning something from you."

"Good thinking."

"As you've said, maybe if I expect a break in the case something good will happen."

With a big smile, she nodded. "Let's shake on that, partner."

"Okay, after we park," he replied, grinning. "You're the one driving."

***

In the department, Karen made out a report, then she and Hal met with Lieutenant Abrams. Karen explained their trip to the law office, another dead end, telling him there was no litigation presently against of the Blydairs.

"But we have high hopes with our interview with Mark Costello," Hal said in a positive tone.

"Your positive attitude is good news," Abrams said.

Nodding her agreement, she punched Hal in the arm.

The detectives went to their desks, filled out paperwork, and bid each other a good evening.

***

Hal left the department satisfied that he had accomplished a few things this day. As soon as he walked in the door, Evelyn stood in the alcove with hands on her hips. "I knew you'd be late. You'll have to prepare your own dinner."

He nodded.

"Try the doorbell," She said pointing.

"He reached around the door casing and pressed the button." He looked at her.

"That's right, it doesn't work."

He closed the door. "I'll call a repairman."

"Can you look at it? You're something of an investigator. Maybe it's something you can fix."

"After I have a bite to eat, I'll take a look."

He fixed himself a sandwich and fried potatoes. While eating and sipping on a beer he watched the news report on TV. Finished eating, he gathered tools and a trouble light and checked the wiring. Luckily, one of the wires had come loose from the switch, a repair he could fix, but it would take the better part of an hour. He took his time, making certain both wires were stripped and secured properly. After installing the connector box he pressed the bell button and the familiar chime filled the house. Approaching the kitchen, he said to Evelyn, "I fixed it."

She remarked with a twist to her mouth, frowning. "What do you want—a medal?"

He didn't answer, but went directly to the den, sat down and stared at the floor. A sudden recollection of the trauma he experienced as a child pervaded his mind. It was in the kitchen that his father beat him with a belt.

"You're to be seen, not heard," he remembered his father saying.

The whipping was especially hurtful because he

was only trying to emulate his brother who had been commended many times for speaking his mind. "Dear old Dad," he said aloud. Suddenly, he sensed someone in the room with him. He looked at Evelyn surprised by her sudden appearance.

"You're having conversations with your father again," she said shaking her head. "You blame him for your shortcomings. Whatever it was happened 30 years ago. Don't you think it's time to put it to rest? And your jealousy of Michael should be addressed." With hands on her waist, she said, "You need to see a professional."

" I'm seeing someone," he lied.

"Who?"

"I'd like to have some privacy if you don't mind."

"You have plenty of that."

Wanting to lessen the chance of her talking about their marital problems to others, he knew he would have to be suspicion free in the event of her death. It was the first time a separation from his wife meant killing her. But it would have to be without fault. The perfect murder fascinated him because it took patience, knowledge of police procedure and unwavering dedication, which he had, despite what others thought.

Wiping his forehead with a handkerchief, Hal got up, left the den and strolled into the living room. "I'm tired. Going to bed," he said to Evelyn.

Following him, she replied, "So early? About the only time we have any conversation is on the weekends."

Without replying, he wandered into the spare bedroom feeling a little lost.

CHAPTER FOUR

WITH A FURROWED brow, Mark Costello held the door open for Karen at the interrogation room. He also waved in Hal. Seating himself at the table near the back wall, Mark placed his palms on the table and remarked grimly, "I think this is a waste of my time, but I'll answer any and all questions to impress upon you that I am cooperating."

"You act like a man who needs to be in charge," Hal said.

"Yes. As manager of a warehouse I have to direct many workers to get things done." He glanced at his watch. "I'd like to get out of here as soon as possible."

"Yes, sir, we understand," Karen said. "We only have a few questions to ask you concerning the death of Jerry Cosgrove. He died from poison in his system which occurred when you were all together drinking from your cans of beer and ..."

"Yes, I know all that," Mark said, nodding. "Listen, the poison would have had to be only in Cosgrove's beer, otherwise all of us would've been dead. After we sat down to play poker, I distinctly remember Betty bringing in cans of Bud Light. Each of us took a can from the tray. They were unopened, and shortly thereafter, each of us flipped open the tab."

Hal angled his head in a motion of concern. "You saw all of them opened?"

"Maybe not everyone, but I heard the pop sound. You can't mistake it."

"It seems odd you would've been listening."

"Well, I wasn't listening deliberately, but like I say, you can't mistake the sound." He raised his hands. "I see no way the poison could have gotten into his can. I would have noticed. His can was always on the table in plain sight."

After a moment of watching Karen observe Cosgrove, Hal inquired, "What was your relationship with Mr. Cosgrove?"

"Zilch! The only time I'd saw him was at the poker games and that was too often."

"You didn't like him?" Karen asked, noting what appeared to be an anxious expression.

"You got that right! The bastard openly wanted to screw my wife. I'd have decked him, had I not been good friends with the Blydairs." He guffawed. "And I didn't want to interrupt our poker games."

"If you disliked him so much, why go to the poker parties?" Hal inquired.

"Playing poker is the only enjoyment I have during the month. I will say one thing for Cosgrove—he was a funny asshole..." He glanced at Karen. "Pardon my French. He did have a good joke to tell, I'll say that much for him. Besides, he always lost, dropping one-hundred bucks or so each time we played. I learned to put up with his sexist remarks."

Hal raised his head. "To you?"

"No. My wife."

"What did he say?" Karen asked.

Mark paused, folded his arms across his chest and remarked, "You'd be good in the sack."

"Did you do anything in response?"

"I held up my fist and told him he'd better watch his mouth or he'd be missing some teeth."

Hal eyeballed Cosgrove. "So you did threaten him."

"In a manner of speaking. I wanted him to know I wouldn't tolerate him disrespecting Tanya."

"Sounds like you were pretty angry."

"I can control my anger. Out of respect for the Blydairs, I wouldn't have hit him. Cosgrove always had a grin on his mug, suggesting his comments were not to be taken serious. But yes, I was mad as hell. After I told him, he began laughing and the incident sort of went by the wayside."

Karen wrote in her notepad. "After the beer was given to you and the others, did you start drinking right away?"

"I did. I took a swig, set my can down, and waited while the first deal was handed out. I sipped on my beer as we played poker. I remember seeing Virgil, and Pedro drinking during the beginning hands. Mark leaned from side to side in his chair, grimacing. "I need to get up and stretch, okay? This hard-back chair is breaking my shoulder blades."

Karen motioned with her hand. "Go ahead."

Mark grunted, then got up slowly turned around and arched his back. "How long is this witch hunt going to take?"

"Sir, it's not a witch hunt, it's a homicide investigation," Karen replied. "You must understand Mr. Cosgrove died from being poisoned at the Blysdair home. These interviews are needed, sir, to narrow the focus on the perpetrator."

Mark sat down, scowling. "I think you got it all wrong about one of us poisoning Cosgrove. Maybe the poison was already in his can of beer from the store where they were purchased. You probably heard about Tylenol capsules laced with cyanide that killed people in Chicago. What about that?"

Hal almost smiled at hearing Cosgrove's suggestion. A good question, one that could provide reasonable doubt to jurors in a court of law. He spoke to Mark. "We know the beer used at the poker party was purchased all at one time, meaning it to be highly unlikely that Cosgrove's beer was the only one with poison. Aconite is a fast-acting very toxic poison," Hal continued. "Cosgrove had enough in his system to kill him within minutes after ingestion."

"Well if one of us killed Cosgrove, he or she must have been a sleight-of-hand artist." Mark paused, stroking his chin. "I think everyone was near Cosgrove at one time or another; except me. Pedro and Lori sat on each side of him. They were closer than anyone else. I would've seen anyone who tried to tamper with Cosgrove's beer can, not that I was looking for that to happen, but someone grabbing it would be like waving a white flag, don't you think?"

"Not necessarily," Hal remarked, leaning forward in a challenging pose.

Before Hal said anymore, Karen asked Mark, "Are you sure you didn't get up from your chair and perhaps walk past Mr. Cosgrove?"

He grunted. "As sure as I'm sitting here now."

Karen flipped a page o her notepad. "What if we were to tell you that you were seen touching Mr. Cosgrove's arm while playing poker?"

Costello's bushy eyebrows lowered. "Hell, that was just before we found him dead. I didn't get out of my chair; I just leaned over and nudged him with my hand thinking he was asleep." He added, smugly, "Hey, there's no way I could've put poison in Cosgrove's beer without five other people seeing me do it."

Hal observed the man across from him. A few facial features reminded him of his father; green eyes, thick eyebrows, scowling most of the time, highly aggressive, opinionated and confrontational. But he knew he shouldn't transfer feelings of his father to this suspect. The traumatic experience happened so long ago. For a brief moment he thought about it, then got up, rubbed his forehead, faking a headache. "I need to get some air," he whispered to Karen.

"Are you okay?"

"Yeah, just need something for my head. I'll step outside for a minute."

She nodded. "I'll take notes."

Once outside of the interrogation room, he walked through the main hall passing some of his colleagues.

"What're doing out here," Gillan said. "Aren't you supposed to be interviewing a witness?"

"I am," Hal said, frowning, a hand to his forehead.

"Well, what are you doing out here?" another detective questioned.

"He's thinking what to ask?" Gillan said, scoffing.

The two detectives laughed.

Hal didn't answer, but he felt his gut churn with irritation. It wasn't altogether clear if they were joking or serious, but past experience, especially with Gillan, suggested contempt. He didn't receive much respect from his colleagues in the squad room, their behavior almost as bad as his wife's. He stopped at his desk and sat down, thinking of Evelyn's remarks before he left for work and recalled her words clearly. Opening the garage door, he heard her voice yell out from the kitchen.

"Wait! I need to show you the mess in the garage." She pushed past him at the door and stepped down into the garage. "I've told you enough times, but it must go in one ear and out the other." She pointed at a collection of cardboard boxes laying on top of one another in a haphazard way. "Will you please cut them up for the trash bin? Remember, they're to be put in the recycle container."

"I know that, but I can't do it now."

"Why not?"

"I'm on my way to work. I don't want to be late."

"They're picking up trash this morning," she said, hands planted on her waist.

"It would take too long. I'll do it the first thing when I get home."

Her last words hurt.

"Never mind. I'll do it! Always your job comes first." She turned abruptly to go inside, and over her shoulder, she said, bitterly, "You're about as helpful as an old dog."

He took a couple of aspirin, returned to the interview room, and seated himself at the table. After Mark finished answering Karen's question, Hal spoke out while glaring at the table top absently, "Just once I'd like to get some respect!"

Karen and Mark stared at him for a moment. He lifted his head with a wry smile and said to Mark, "What I mean is every detail is important. As we said before, this interview is based on your willingness to talk to us.

No one yet is charged with murder, but it's apparent that someone at the poker table poisoned Mr. Cosgrove. We need to have straightforward answers, but having said that it's not a requirement for you to answer any of our questions, and it's your right to have a lawyer present." Hal glanced at Karen briefly.

Mark looked directly at Hal. "I've been as truthful as I can, answered all of your questions. No, I don't need a lawyer," he glanced at his watch, "but I'd like to go. I have things to do."

Karen closed her notepad, then got up. "I have nothing further." She glanced at Hal. With no indication from Hal, she said, "Okay, Mr. Costello, you're free to go."

***

When they got back to their desks, Karen questioned him. "What was that all about?"

"What?"

"When you came back in the room and said something about not getting any respect."

His pen slipped from his hand and dropped on the table making a rattling sound. His hand froze for an instant, and he could almost her hear demanding a reply to her question. He didn't look at her and said, "Nothing important, just thinking out loud." He waved a hand through the air and said quickly, "I don't think Costello is telling us all he knows, but of all the suspects, he's the least likely to have poisoned Cosgrove."

"I agree, but he could very well be an accomplice."

"With his wife?" Hal said, frowning.

She nodded.

He turned away, feeling the desire to argue the

point, but after a moment, he acknowledged her response with a nod, a sign of peace. Letting his emotions run amok wasn't a good idea. He needed to be on the good side of his partner, a commitment he guessed to be favorable for him in the long run, not yet sure what that meant.

Karen motioned toward Lt. Abrams' office. "Are we ready to see the boss?"

"Not really, but he's expecting us." Hal wanted to be alone, feeling disinclined about the case.

In the lieutenant's office, Abrams directed Hal and Karen to be seated. "So, do we have a viable suspect?"

"No, and no confessions," Karen said.

"No contradictions or accusations at all?"

"Not yet. Only a few suppositions," Karen replied, angling her head to one side. "Mark Costello said Evans and Gonzales were closest to the victim, but he didn't accuse them. All the suspects have denied seeing Cosgrove's beer can handled by anyone other than himself."

"What about collusion of two or more?"

"That was our thought, too," Hal replied. "All have an inkling of motive, but it seems to be a one man job," Hal paused, grinning, "or a one woman job. The exception might be the Blydairs."

"And yet, they all seem to give each other a clean bill of health," Karen said.

Abrams frowned. "Are you saying all of them have complicity?" Abrams remarked, scowling.

"I know it's a stretch, but it would explain why they're not dumping on each other."

"And what about litigation by Cosgrove against the Blydairs?"

Hal's shoulder slumped. "Another dead end. Cosgrove did talk to the lawyers about suing Virgil, but didn't pursue it"

Karen explained further, "Hoffman, one of the lawyers, said they took his deposition nearly three years ago which seems to validate Mr. Blydair's claim that the embezzlement charge was vacated."

"Have you finished interrogating all the players?"

"We have Pedro Gonzales left."

Abrams closed a file folder. "Okay, finish interviewing Gonzales, and let me know if anything develops." He shook his head. "This simple case of the victim being poisoned in front of six others is turning out to be a real who-done-it, with only circumstantial evidence at best. We don't even know if one or all six are the perps. We have work to do to keep this case out of the dead files. Our case load is staggering, can't put anyone else on it, so keep at it. Interrogation seems to be our only viable prospect."

***

Escorting Pedro Gonzales into the interrogation room, Hal noticed the slight of build, small man in his late twenties appeared cautious in his mannerisms. Either that or Pedro was putting on an act. Pedro remained non expressive, but managed an affirmative nod when asked of his dislike for Cosgrove.

"Cosgrove called me a wetback," he said, agitation in his voice.

"That made you mad," Karen inquired. "Mad enough to kill him?"

"No. I wouldn't kill anyone." Pedro brushed the top of his butch haircut and said, dryly, "I don't know anything about the poison that killed him or where to get it."

With a wave of her pen at Pedro, Karen said, "What if I told you we have evidence that you purchased poison last week from a store?"

Pedro glanced at Karen then back to Hal. "I got rats in my apartment. I bought rat poison at the hardware store."

"We'll need to verify that," Karen said, flipping a page of her notepad. "What store was it?"

Pedro stared at his shoes, thinking, then gave her the store name and location.

Hal wrote aconite in large letters on his notepad and showed the page to Pedro. "Have you heard of a toxin called aconite?"

"No."

That's what killed Mr. Cosgrove." With intense eyes, Hal watched Pedro's mannerism as he asked another question probing deeper about the rat poison. "What was the name of the rat poison you say you bought?"

Pedro's blank expression revealed his ignorance. "I don't remember."

Hal glanced at Karen. Karen smiled at Pedro. "Relax. You're not a suspect, only a person of interest at this time. You're not obligated to answer any of our questions, do you understand?"

"Yes, miss, but I will answer."

"When you started playing poker the night of Mr. Cosgrove's death," Karen carefully phrased the question, "did you get your beer from the refrigerator?"

"No. Mrs. Blydair brought the beer into the room."

"The cans were already opened?"

"No."

Hal got up, walked around the table and stood in back of Pedro. "How do you know they weren't opened?"

"I could hear the *pop* when the others opened their cans."

Hal looked at Karen, grinning. "Okay, Mr. Gonzales, you sat next to Mr. Cosgrove, is that correct?"

Pedro nodded. "Yes."

"At any time, did you handle or touch Mr. Cosgrove's beer can?"

"No, sir." Pedro flexed his left hand.

"I see you favor your left hand. You're left-handed?"

"Yes."

"So your beer can would have been on your left side, correct?" Hal didn't know where he was going with the question; his goal was to confuse Pedro.

"Yes."

"And we know that Mr. Cosgrove was right-handed, so his beer can was on his right side. Therefore, the beer cans were close together, right?" Not waiting for a reply, Hal added, "Close enough for you to put poison into Cosgrove's beer."

Pedro shook his head. "I never touch his beer."

Hal turned away from Pedro. Glancing at Karen, he said, "Isn't it true Mr. Cosgrove insulted you and your girlfriend, Lori?"

"While we were playing poker?"

"Well, when else would that have transpired?"

"Cosgrove lives in the same apartment complex as me, Pedro replied, softly. "But we never saw him at the apartments when Lori was with me."

"Okay, Mr. Gonzales, focus your attention on the poker party," Karen advised. "Did Mr. Cosgrove make sexist remarks to Lori?"

"Yes."

"Maybe you and Ms. Evans plotted together to kill Mr. Cosgrove," Hal said, returning to his chair.

"No. Lori won't hurt anyone."

Hal leaned forward. "And what about you?"

Pedro folded his arms across his chest. "Yes, angry with him, but I don't hurt him."

"Well, who else had a reason to kill Mr. Cosgrove?" Hal demanded, glaring at Pedro.

Pedro sighed. "Mr. Cosgrove told me Virgil stole money from him."

"When did he tell you?"

"Many months ago."

"Where did he tell you this?"

"At the apartment where I live."

"Yes, we've heard about Cosgrove's lawsuit against Virgil Blydair," Karen acknowledged. "What was said if you remember?"

Pedro shrugged. "Mr. Blydair was a cheat, something like that."

"Is that all he said?"

"All I remember," Pedro said, shrugging. "Long time ago."

"Was anyone else there to hear the conversation?"

"No."

"What about Mr. and Mrs. Costello? Did they have any serious disagreement with Mr. Cosgrove?"

Pedro shrugged. "He said nasty things to Mrs. Costello. Mr. Costello don't like it. Mrs. Costello hit Mr. Cosgrove on the head."

"What did Cosgrove do?"

"Only laugh."

Hal rubbed the back of his neck. "That's all there was to it? No physical contact by Mr. Cosgrove?"

Pedro shook his head. "He only laugh."

Do you have anything else to say about Mr. Cosgrove?"

Pedro looked around the room." Maybe Mr. Cosgrove put poison in his beer."

"Why do you say that?" Hal asked, scowling. "Are you saying he killed himself intentionally?"

Pedro looked away. "Maybe."

Karen leaned closer. "Why do you think Mr. Cosgrove killed himself?"

"He not happy. Lost his job."

Hal rolled his eyes at Pedro. "How do you know that?"

Pedro shrugged. "I hear it from someone."

"Who?"

Pausing momentarily, he rubbed his nose. "I don't remember," he said with an apologetic expression."

Hal glared at Pedro. "You don't remember or you choose not to remember?"

"Pedro looked down at the table, not answering."

Hal shook his head, scowling. "You're not being truthful with us, Mr. Gonzales. There was no suicide note, and Mr. and Mrs. Blydair said Mr. Cosgrove was usually in good spirits, joking around, certainly not depressed." Hal clasped his hands together on the table. "In other words, you're speculating, and you don't have any evidence that Mr. Cosgrove wanted to end his life?"

Not expecting answer, Hal closed his notepad and glanced at Karen. "Do you have any more questions?"

"No." She reached over and patted Pedro's hand. "Mr. Gonzales, we thank you for your cooperation. You're free to go."

Hal stood up. "Don't leave Beaverton without letting us know. We may want to talk to you again."

Hal and Karen escorted Pedro out of the precinct and returned to their desks.

"He's definitely a person of interest," Hal said. "What's your take on him?"

"His answers were straightforward, although at times he appeared confused. He admitted to buying rat poison if it was indeed rat poison. It's easy enough to check out his story. All in all, I don't see him as a viable suspect based on his statements and behavior."

"On his gestures," Hal said without criticism.

He knew witnesses weren't entirely truthful when presenting testimony. It wasn't as if he dealt with people of pristine character. He felt forced to double check other witness statements for reliability. He tried to never let his ego enter any decision regarding guilt or innocence, but the Cosgrove poisoning was getting to him with the growing awareness it could turn into a cold case bound for the basement archives. The perfect murder? The thought fascinated him and at the same time offended his ego if the testy case couldn't be solved.

He said to Karen, "Now we have to see if there's any merit to the suggestion that Cosgrove's committed suicide. But even if Cosgrove didn't put the poison in his beer can, we still have the problem of how someone else did, assuming all of them aren't in collusion."

Karen glanced at her notepad. "I'm grateful we don't have more suspects. Did you see the report from the lab?"

"I haven't looked in my basket."

"Forensics determined it would be impossible to insert poison into the tiny needle hole in Cosgrove's beer can, even if the aconite was in liquid form. Which means the poison had to be inserted in the tab opening, and it had to have happened at the poker table with all present. That's the stickler."

Hal grimaced. "We better report to Abrams."

"Let's check out Pedro's story first. Maybe he's telling the truth about the rat poison he bought. If he did, it will be one less complication to worry about."

"Now?"

"No time like the present." Karen smiled. "While we're out, we can check with Pedro's neighbors about rats in his apartment. What do you think?"

"Okay, but let's stop at the local beanery. I need to fix an upset stomach."

***

After watching Hal sip on a bowl of chicken soup, Karen remarked innocently, "How's the tummy?"

"Better."

"How about the rest of you?"

"Physically okay."

"And emotionally?"

Pausing, Hal looked at her, then replied, "I don't know." He slid out from the bench. "I'm done here. Let's check out Pedro's story."

At the Ace hardware store the manager was shown a picture of Pedro, but neither he, or any of his staff could confirm that Pedro purchased a canister of Durett rat poison. "That doesn't mean he didn't buy it here," the manager added. "We have no record of it. He could have paid cash. Sorry."

"Do you sell aconite poison?" Hal inquired.

The manager looked astonished. "Aconite is a poison that no one sells in its raw form."

"What do you mean raw form?" Karen asked.

"Every part of the pant can be toxic if ingested, but the root is the deadliest part of aconite. The roots are processed before it's used for heart disease. I used to work in a pharmacy. Aconite comes from a plant grown in the wild locally, with pretty blue flowers, but deadly if ingested. Animals have died from the poison in and around the foothills. It's only available by prescription."

"Poison is taken for medical purposes?" Hal questioned. I don't get it."

"The extract from the plant is used for cardiovascular conditions, such as arrhythmia, irregular heartbeat, and high blood pressure."

"The roots are far the most toxic and if ingested will kill a person within minutes.

"So, it's processed by a pharmaceutical company for patients with heart disease?"

"Yes."

Karen and Hal looked at each other.

"Is it available in liquid form?" Karen inquired.

"No, only capsules."

***

While the detectives drove to Pedro's apartment, they talked about the new information on aconite. At a signal light stop, Hal said, "Does it mean one of the players had heart disease?"

"Maybe. That would certainly alert the perp to the poison which has to be processed from the roots."

"We'll need to get everyone's medical record. Partner, our first good lead," he said, smiling, as he accelerated the SUV ahead.

At the apartment complex, they climbed three flights of stairs to interview Pedro's neighbor. After explaining they were investigating a murder, they questioned her about Pedro's alleged purchase of rat poison.

"He complained of rats in his apartment," she told them. "I had rats in my apartment some time ago, but I used a bait can—that way they don't wander away and hide in some unreachable area. Poor man, Jerry Cosgrove. Pedro told me he died." Her eyes ballooned. "I understand poison killed him."

"Pedro told you that?"

"Initially, he told me the man had died from a heart attack, then said he was poisoned, but didn't say how."

"The poison prompted his heart attack," Karen explained. "Do you know if Mr. Gonzales has heart disease?"

"I don't know. He's never mentioned it."

"What about Jerry Cosgrove?"

"He lives in the apartments here, too." Shrugging, she said, "He seemed healthy, never complained about his heart."

"Did Mr. Cosgrove show any signs of depression?"

"Sorry, I didn't see him that often. But Pedro mentioned just the opposite—that Mr. Cosgrove was usually in a happy mood, telling off-color jokes..." She smiled. "If you know what I mean?"

Karen leaned forward. "Pedro told you Mr. Cosgrove was in a happy mood?"

"Yes."

"So they knew each other here at the apartments?"

"Well, in passing, I suppose. I don't think they were bosom buddies. Pedro mentioned that Jerry insulted him often about his Mexican heritage."

"So, nothing was mentioned about Mr. Cosgrove losing a job?"

"No. To the contrary, Pedro said he was in good spirits, and expecting good news to happen soon, something about a big slew of money coming into Mr. Cosgrove's possession. Sorry, Pedro didn't say if he expected to win the lottery or an inheritance, or something else. But to answer your question about Mr. Cosgrove's health, Pedro said, he wasn't depressed, upbeat."

***

On their way back to the precinct, Hal reflected on the investigation. Most of the testimony was inconclusive, at best, iffy. At least they could rule out Cosgrove committing suicide. That in itself was good news—one less dilemma to address. If the other sources of evidence could be authenticated, reasonable doubt in the jurors' minds could be put on the back burner. He was learning a lot with this case because so far, there were no holes. He felt a smile cross his lips, thinking Cosgrove's killing had all the aspects of a perfect murder. Even so, prospects of solving the case were looking brighter. If only his marriage problems would take a turn for the better. *Not likely.* It surprised him that he was pleased with the second thought.

***

As soon as they sat down at their desks in the squad room, Hal's phone rang. Hesitating to answer it,

Karen picked it up. "It's your wife," she said, and handed him the phone.

"What?" Pause. "No. I'm working a case. Pause. "No, I'll be late." He hung up the phone.

"If you need to go home, I can cover for you," Karen offered.

"No, nothing important," he said, grimacing. The call was important, but he couldn't let his partner know. As a homicide detective, he knew the less she was aware of his personal problems, the better.

CHAPTER FIVE

LIEUTENANT ABRAMS GLANCED out the window, scowling at the drizzling rain, which added—In his opinion—continued frustration to the unyielding poker case. Shaking his head, he turned to Karen and Hal and said, "I should have known, bad news goes with the bad weather." He sipped on his coffee while Hal and Karen advised him of Pedro and Mark's interview.

"So far, all we have is a lot of hearsay, but no evidence," Hal said, crossing one leg over the other. He glanced at Karen, then uncrossed his legs, planting his shoes firmly on the rug. "Kinesics," he said to Abrams.

The lieutenant frowned.

"Just a personal thing," Hal replied with a slight grin, "between my partner and I. But we have nothing substantial to report. As it is, our players are all suspects."

"We can't charge everyone," Abrams said. "Not unless we can prove there was a united conspiracy involved." He glanced at Karen and Hal with a raised chin. "Do we have anything concrete that all of them were involved?"

"Only conjecture," Karen said. "I personally believe one, or at the most two, people were the instigators, but only one person could have put the poison in Cosgrove's beer." She glanced at her notepad. "We did find out that aconite is used as a heart medicine." She went on to explain the conversation with the hardware store manager. "We have feelers out to the players' primary care physicians and specialists to see if someone has heart disease."

"What significance does that have?"

"I'm thinking the one that killed Cosgrove knew about aconite if he had heart problems and was prescribed the aconite medicine. If so, he would have known about the plant having poisonous roots."

"Even so, "Abrams said, lifted his head in reply, "we'd have to prove the perp got the poison from the plant if there was only one of the players involved. Not a shoe-in."

"Right." Hal nodded. "And how he or she managed to extract the poison from the plant."

Abrams leaned forward in his chair. "Let's look at the facts. We know for certain aconite was in Cosgrove's beer can. The other cans were clean, okay? We know for certain that someone added the poison there at the poker table." Pausing, he glanced at Karen and Hal with a resolute expression. "So, if one person is responsible for the physical act itself of adding the poison, then let's concentrate on the doer."

Karen smiled, nodding. "Yes, sir, that's the brick wall we haven't as yet been able to break through."

"Is there any news from forensics yet about the hole in Cosgrove's beer can?"

"They're not certain how the perforation was made," Karen replied. "Not likely by a human. Their best guess is the can hit something sharp which made the tiny hole, a dubious reason at best," she added with a roll of her eyes. "Regardless, we've confirmed with a pharmaceutical company that Aconite medicine doesn't come in liquid form, only capsules, proving that the poison wasn't put into the needle hole.

"Capsules?" Abrams shrugged. "So the capsule had to be put in the top of the can after it was opened." With a lift of his chin, he said, "Mrs. Blydair was the only one who had the cans in her possession without the others being present."

"But everyone agreed the cans weren't opened until they were delivered to the poker table. Three saw the opening of the cans, the other three heard the popping sound of the tab as it was opened."

"That's correct," Hal added.

"Doesn't that rule out Mrs. Blydair?"

"Not really." Karen angled her head in an expression of uncertainty. "She, too, could have snuck in the capsule after the cans were opened. She was there like the rest of them."

The lieutenant frowned. "And someone would have seen her as the rest of the players testified, right?"

"Which supports the argument of a unified conspiracy." She sighed. "On a scale of one to ten, ten being total support, I give it a three or four. I can't imagine all six of them validating each other without a slip up so far in their testimony."

Hal's shoulder dropped. "I've been in homicide seven years, been through a lot of murders, but this is the first one where I feel completely stumped. No one is admitting anything against the others. They all have opportunity and motive by being at the table together; there's no smoking gun."

"Well, we'll have to find one." Lt. Abrams placed his palms on the desk. "The media is clamoring for anything positive in this homicide. We don't even have circumstantial evidence to take to the D.A. Thank god we have undeniable evidence of poison in Cosgrove's beer can." Abrams leaned forward in a pleading manner at Hal. "Do any of our players have heart disease suggesting he or she knew about aconite medicine?"

"Dead end there, too. Both primary care and specialists of our players reported no heart conditions."

"And knew about the plant's poisonous roots," Karen added. "That was my take on it, too. We talked with a farmer in the foothills where the plant flourishes. He has an incinerator in his back yard to get rid of waste. Using tree limbs, he grinds them up with a wood chipping machine which grinds the wood into sawdust. Extract from the aconite root can be acquired that way. The machine isn't rentable and costs more than a thousand dollars."

Abrams scoffed. "None of the players has a machine like that, right?"

"Nope," Hal replied. He looked at the lieutenant. "Not unless it was buried."

"At least we know the perp had to grind up the aconite roots somehow," Karen added, "but it could've been any of our players. The flowery plant in the foothills is widely known."

Abrams shook his head. "Our only option is to continue probing."

"And the suspects are getting antsy," Karen said. "Both Virgil and Mark expressed irritation about being questioned. They may lawyer up. We've been careful to mention they are persons of interest only, but they may lawyer up at any time."

"Anything else pending?"

Hal glanced at his notes. "Pedro said Cosgrove

was depressed to the point of suicide and could have brought the poison with him intent on killing himself at the poker party. He said Cosgrove lost his job."

"What job?"

"There's some confusion there also. It's true Cosgrove was working at a check cashing store." Hal paused. "You recall Cosgrove and the Blydairs had a check cashing store in business together a couple of years ago; anyway, the owner of the store said Cosgrove wasn't fired, he simply didn't show up for work giving no reason for his absence." Hal shrugged. "I don't know if we'll get much more from the players. Like Karen said, they could lawyer u p at any time."

"Then we'll have to do a little fibbing," Abrams said. "Maybe we can break out of this closet. Let's interrogate them all together and apply pressure suggesting we have a strong suspicion who the killer might be. One of them may say something that will give us a hint of who put the poison in Cosgrove's beer." Abrams gazed at Hal and Karen with heavy-laden eyes. "We'll need to be careful, we don't want them shutting down. I'll make arrangements to have the conference room available. We'll need to do this in the next couple of days. In the meantime, double check the lawsuit between Cosgrove and Virgil Blydair. Also whether there's any truth to Cosgrove's depression."

"We checked the lawsuit," Karen replied. "There's none pending."

"Check again. We know Blydairs had money problems with the victim."

Hal shook his head. "As to Cosgrove's depression, we've discounted that because all the other suspects said Cosgrove appeared happy. I think it was a trumped-up story to lessen his, and Lori's involvement."

"Everyone we've talked to confirmed that Cosgrove was in high spirits, not at all depressed. No suicide note, no evidence to support Cosgrove being depressed enough to kill himself."

Hal cocked his head to one side. "And yet, Cosgrove did have more opportunity to put a capsule in his beer without being seen than the others."

Karen added, "A good lawyer would surely use it as a defense tactic."

"How do you figure that?" Abrams questioned.

"If he had the poison in a capsule, he could've swallowed it at any time. According to the pharmaceutical company, a small dose of raw aconite, 200 milligrams like the size of an aspirin would be enough to kill him within minutes."

"You mean adding aconite dust in a capsule? But there was poison in his beer can. Besides, why would he wait to kill himself at the poker party? I don't buy it. As if we didn't have enough negatives in this case to worry about." Abrams' eyes widened. "What we need is a miracle."

Karen got up from her chair. "A good lawyer would surely use it as a defense tactic. I hope all future cases aren't this confusing."

The lieutenant waved his hand in the air. "Welcome to homicide."

Hal and Karen returned to their desks and busied themselves writing reports. While Karen was away from her desk, Hal hurried across the department hall. As he past detective Gillan's desk, Gillan said, "Where you going in such a hurry?"

Hal didn't answer and proceeded down the basement steps into the morgue of cold cases. He decided to rummage through some of the dead files hoping it might lead to a clue of how the poison got in Cosgrove's beer. He had searched the cold cases before and surprisingly, he would often run across clues unrelated to the current case under investigation. After looking through the index file he spotted a drowning case, which intrigued him. He opened the file and saw a picture of a small ladder angled against a Jacuzzi strikingly similar to his at home.

He read the file summary.

Cara Barton, a spokeswoman for the Middleton County District Attorney's office, said the medical examiner has ruled the death of six-year-old Timothy Chambers undetermined. EMTs arrived at the scene and began CPR, but were unable to revive the child. The mother, Gale Chambers, claimed her son had used a small stepladder to get into the Jacuzzi while she checked her mailbox for mail. She said she remembered moving the stepladder away from the pool before checking her mail. When the paramedics arrived they did find a small stepladder against the Jacuzzi, but believed the ladder to be too heavy for the small child to drag to the Jacuzzi siding. After investigators arrived, they interrogated the mother and family members. Mrs. Chambers said the boy had an obsession about climbing. Other family members disputed her claim, and said she had problems relating to the autistic child. With little circumstantial evidence, the D A decided not to indict the mother.

The case intrigued Hal because the investigation by the sheriff's office hadn't yet found any evidence the mother deliberately murdered her child. The case was ten years old. He wondered if she had gotten away with the perfect murder simply because the police didn't have solid evidence to indict her for the crime. The simple, but cunning explanation of the small boy putting the ladder against the side of the Jacuzzi couldn't be disputed. As he glanced through other files, he saw Karen approach.

"I wondered where you snuck off to," she said, her expression curious.

"I didn't sneak off. How did you know I was down here?"

"Detective Gillan told me."

Hal put the file folders away. "I was looking through some old cases hoping for a clue to help with the Cosgrove killing."

"Did you find anything?"

"No."

They both turned hearing Gillan's voice. "What are you two doing down her in the morgue?"

Karen looked at Gillan with an inquiring smile.

"Are you spying on us?"

"Is there a reason I should be?"

"None whatsoever," Hal replied. "What brings you down here, anyway?"

Gillan laughed. "Just taking a break from writing endless reports. "There's something about this dungeon that favors privacy, don't you think so?"

"What do you mean?"

Gillan shrugged. "Most of the time when I come down no one else is here like I said, the morgue. Except this time two people are here." His lop-sided grin showed arrogance.

"But this time you knew we were down here," Hal countered.

"True, but I was still surprised because of the rarity of the experience." He turned and headed for the stairs, and said over his shoulder, "You better not stay down here too long or someone might start thinking immoral thoughts."

Hal agreed with Gillan. He didn't want any suspicion reflecting a romantic union between him and Karen, not so much because it was forbidden by department policy, but he felt their partnership had to be impersonal in case anything happened to Evelyn. He stared at the boxes of files for a long moment, surprised that the thought of Evelyn's demise occurred to him.

"Are you finished looking?" Karen inquired.

"Yeah. Let's go."

***

After spending time at their desks, Hal and Karen left the department and visited numerous pharmacies to confirm that Aconite could only be attained by prescription. A doctor specializing in heart trouble also confirmed medicine with Aconite was only available in capsule form. The detectives headed for their car. Before Hal started the motor, he scribbled in his notepad, turned to Karen and said, "That confirms that the poison wasn't put in the needle hole of Cosgrove's can. You're a smart lady. Tell me, how can one be positive when all the leads dry up like a wet sponge in the sun?" He shook his head "Can I ask you a question?"

"I hope you do."

"Do you really believe it helps to be open with ideas, opinions...I mean with others?"

She looked at him. "Are you asking for yourself or is it a general question?"

"You sound like my wife—answers a question with a question."

She smiled. "In my humble opinion, yes, I'm convinced it helps. Expressing one's feelings allows others know where you stand and eliminates a lot of guess work."

He nodded. "I don't share things with others. I guess that's obvious by now. I've always been that way. It's gotten to be a problem in my marriage." He looked away, realizing he was getting far too personal.

Karen asked, "Do you have anything you want to tell me? I'm a good listener."

"No." He turned the ignition key starting the motor and drove ahead.

Hal shielded his eyes from a bright sun. He reached for the visor, then pulled his hand away. "I left my sunglasses at home. Do you mind if we stop by my house to pick them up? It's not far from here."

"Are you sure your wife won't mind?"

"She's not home. It's her weekly bridge party time."

They pulled into the driveway of a modest house in a cul-de-sac. He pointed to the overgrown front lawn. "I better mow before it takes over the house. This is the result of a heavy case load of homicides in the department and our nemesis, the poker party murder."

He got out of the car, and headed for the front door. "Come on in," he said, waving. "No need to sit out here in the hot sun. She got out of the car and followed him. When he entered, his wife suddenly appeared in the hallway. "What are you doing home?" he inquired, frowning.

"I should ask you the same question," Evelyn said, glancing at Karen.

"We were in the neighborhood. I stopped by to pick up my sunglasses. Aren't you supposed to be at your bridge party?"

"I told you yesterday it was cancelled." She held out a hand to Karen. "I'm Evelyn."

"I'm Hal's partner, Karen." They shook hands.

"He doesn't remember what I tell him," Evelyn said, then smiled. "Pardon me for being a bit snotty. Sometimes Hal gets on my nerves to be truthfully honest. She glanced at Hal. "Will you be home for dinner?"

"I don't know."

Shaking her head, she said to Karen, "He might as well move in the department because he's never home." She turned to Hal. "While you're here, two things—Thursday night is Rodney's school play. Don't disappoint him." She explained to Karen, "He's our Godson, Michael's son, Michael is Hal's brother."

"Yes, I've met Michael. He came to the precinct.

They were talking about their childhood."

"You mean Hal actually shared his feelings," she remarked with raised eyebrows.

Before Karen could answer, Hal interrupted. "Come on, let's get out of here," he said to Karen, "before she tells you what I had for breakfast."

He rushed into the bedroom and returned with his sunglasses. "I'll give you a ring about dinner tonight. We're on a tough case right now and Abrams is breathing down my back," he lied about the lieutenant, but wanted to look reliable in front of Karen."

"Are you married?" Evelyn inquired.

"No, not yet. But I'm not in any hurry. I was engaged at one time, however..."

"Come on, let's go," Hal said, and moved toward the door.

"Glad to have met you," Karen said to Evelyn, as she followed Hal out the front door.

Evelyn's parting words were, "Mow the lawn."

He didn't reply except for slamming the front door.

***

After a period of silence while driving back to the precinct, Hal apologized. "Sorry about the confrontation with my wife. I was surprised that she was home. She hardly ever misses her bridge party." He shrugged. "She complains that I'm gone most of the time and claims I don't share things with her."

"Not a huge problem. It's fixable." Karen continued, surprised that he seemed to be confiding in her. "From a woman's perspective, I think it would be nice to hear about my husband's thoughts *and* feelings. To

me it means a great deal to expect feelings from someone I cared about. I've always believed that two heads
are better than one facing up to the day's challenges.
Hal, I know you have some issues of working with me
as a partner, and as you said, you work better alone, so If
you'll pardon my forwardness, maybe that's the issue
that needs addressing in your marriage."

After a long moment without any reply, she
grinned. "You don't have to say anything, but a nod or
blink would be appreciated."

After pausing, he answered. "There's no problem
in my marriage, but I'll mull it over in my mind what
you said."

"Do you mind answering a trivia question?" Not
waiting for his answer, she continued, "Why do you hesitate or pause before you do anything or say anything?"

He glanced at her. "To avoid making blunders.
Thinking things out before stepping on the gas could
prevent a head-on collision, you know what I mean?"

"Yes, vividly clear.

"I'm a firm believer in planning—like words
squeezed against one edge of a bumper sticker that says,
PLAN AHEAD."

She grinned. "I got it."

At a signal stop, Hal went over the issues of his
marriage in his mind. Hadn't he listened to Evelyn's
complaints? Always, there was the issue of his being at
work too much, not being home with her or doting on
his Godchild. The one that stuck in his craw the most
was her disapproval of his lack of sharing his thoughts
and feelings. How often had he heard her say, 'I would
like to know what you're feeling,' ad nauseum. The
marriage had been a mistake. More and more, thoughts

of getting out of the marriage possessed him. And now he was saddled with a partner who reminded him too often of his loner attitude. He shrugged. *Something has to happen. But what?*

The honking of a car behind him captured his attention, and he pressed his foot on the accelerator moving the SUV forward at a rapid pace. Maybe it was true that he didn't broadcast his thoughts about the case, but it wasn't a character fault. He believed keeping his thoughts to himself actually helped consolidate in his mind what was and wasn't significant. Hadn't this ritual helped him on past cases? "I think so," he said aloud.

Karen glanced at him. "What?"

"Just thinking out loud."

She smiled. "That's good! You're alive." At the next signal stop, Karen's took on a stern expression as best she could. "I need to say something. Please hear me out. Hal," she began, if we're going to make any headway in this case, I need you to share more of your thoughts with me."

"What are we in now—a therapy session?"

"No, but maybe it should be. I need to know your thoughts and feelings about the poker players' testimony." He frowned. "Please, let me explain." She paused, then continued, "How we feel ties in with our logic about testimony presented, often difficult to separate our gut feeling from what we hear or see, not that thinking and feeling together is bad in itself, but we need to be aware of both."

He rolled his eyes. "Where did you hear that—the same place as body language? He didn't wait for her to answer. "Maybe I'll agree with gut instinct, but logic and feelings together seems way out of the ball park to me."

"Exactly my point. You've just explained your position, your feelings. It would help me if you shared both your feelings and your thoughts. If we're to work together as partners..."

"Wait!" He looked away from her intense gaze and focused his eyes on the road ahead. "My feelings are mine, mine alone, and I'll decide when I want to share them, end of discussion, okay?"

She didn't respond. Silence pervaded the SUV until Hal pulled into the precinct parking lot and turned off the engine. He turned to Karen, let out a sigh, then said, "Sorry for being an ass. I'm letting my personal problems interfere with my job, and with my relationship with you." He held out his hand. "Forgiven, partner?" They shook hands. He waited for her to say something, but she remained silent. Grasping the ignition keys in his hand, he said, "I'd like to ask you a question."

"Please do."

"What do you do when problems close in on you, and there seems to be nothing you can do to lessen the anxiety... seeing no light at the end of the tunnel?"

"Yes, I do. I've been there many times. My opinion—you have to be open to possibilities. For me I have to be positive with my thinking as well as with my feelings. Answers often do come from unlikely sources if one has an open mind. One time I fretted over what I thought was a difficult personal problem for days. At a checkout counter where I was buying groceries, I overheard bits of conversation between a couple ahead of me. Hearing their words, lo and behold, the answer to my problem came then and there."

"How probable is that?"

"Anything is possible with an open mind."

"And how does one get an open mind?"

"Sharing is one way."

He ran a hand through his hair. "I hear what you're saying. He looked at her with appreciative eyes. Thanks for your input. I'll see you tomorrow."

She exited the car, and waved good-bye. He headed home.

***

More than once of late, perfection loomed up before him, not too surprisingly because of the nature of the poker murder case, and he was enthralled at the possibility it might not be solved because of the cleverness of the killer. Putting himself in the killer's place of accomplishing the impossible, the thought crossed his mind, would show others of his brilliance. And yet, the paradox of the perfect murder resulted in no one knowing who committed the crime.

Hal put on his pajamas, sat on the edge of the bed, staring at the floor. "Think about something else," he said aloud. "Get some sleep. Be alert for tomorrow's interview of the poker case suspects. Think positive. You might even uncover a clue who put poison in Cosgrove's beer."

CHAPTER SIX

LT. ABRAMS, HAL and Karen stood around the periphery of a table which represented the poker table in the Blydair house. Abrams addressed the six suspects. "We appreciate your attendance and cooperation in this follow-up interview. Again, I remind you, no one is charged with the Cosgrove's murder, but we have strong evidence that at least one of you may be the killer. It behooves everyone to cooperate at this time, otherwise all of you could be charged as accessories." He glanced at the players. "I must inform you of your Miranda rights; the right to remain silent; the right to have an attorney present during the questioning, and if you can't afford an attorney, one will be appointed at public expense to represent you during this questioning. Do you understand each of these rights, and understanding these rights, do you agree to speak to us without a lawyer being present?"

The players looked at each other before Virgil spoke up, confidence in his voice. "Yes, yes, we understand and I for one agree. I've nothing to hide."

"Why do we all have to be present?" Mark Costello remarked, frowning. "We've already been interviewed to death."

"We're hoping it will jog someone's memory for a clue revealing the guilty person," Abrams said boldly.

Mark chuckled. "Then it would be wiser all us not

to participate."

"Except this…" Abrams glanced at each player. "Anyone wishing not to be a part of this interview will be a person of interest."

"Refusing to cooperate," Karen added, "presupposes guilt."

"I think I get the message," Mark replied. "Let's get it over with." The other players nodded in agreement.

"We'll go over the sequence of events as they happened on the night in question." He opened a file. "I'll start off by reading everyone's location in the living room at the poker table as you're now seated. Mr. Blydair facing the kitchen facing the kitchen in the Blydair home as it were. To his left, Tanya Costello. Next to her, Mark Costello, then Pedro Gonzales and Jerry Cosgrove across from Mr. Blydair." He smiled." Of course, the empty chair represents Mr. Cosgrove. Then Lori Evans next, and Mrs. Blydair sat next to her husband. Is this correct?"

Everyone looked around the table, then nodded their agreement.

Betty announced in a conciliatory tone, "Yes, I can testify to the seating, always the same, for the past eight months."

"You'll notice we have Budweiser Light beer cans in front of you, unopened," the lieutenant said, pointing, "and a can of peanuts in the center of the table along with a box of coins."

"Is this beer for us to drink?" Virgil asked, grinning.

"Yes, but it must be done according to the sequence of events which we will try to duplicate." He pointed to Virgil. "Begin just after your wife brings in the beer and peanuts."

"I shuffled the deck of cards and asked Betty to cut," Virgil said, motioning with his hands. "She did, then I dealt out five cards to each player for five card draw, then asked everyone to ante a dollar for the pot, and..."

Karen interrupted, "Wasn't change made first?"

"Yes, it was," Tanya replied. "Virgil pushed the coin box to the center of the table and we all took out change."

"Then we played out the hand," Virgil said, eyeing the can of beer in front of him, "and I'm sure I opened my can of beer and took a sip."

"So, everyone opened their beer cans at about the same time?" Karen inquired, scanning the group.

"Yes, I remember seeing Jerry and Lori open their can of beer," Tanya said, pausing. "And Virgil opened Betty's can after he opened his."

"When did you open your beer?" Hal asked, focusing his attention on Mark.

"Within the first two hands of poker, I'm sure" Mark replied. With a grin he added, "You can't mistake the characteristic *pop* of the tab.

"I saw Tanya and Pedro take a sip," Lori offered her opinion, "no later than the third hand of poker.

"What about Mr. Cosgrove?"

Betty spoke up. "He opened his can right away and took a drink."

"You're certain of that?"

"Yes."

"She's right," Mark said. "I saw Jerry taking a long swig of his beer even before change was made."

"I think we all took a drink," Virgil said, then added, "A toast, everyone, to a great evening of winning. That's what I said that night."

Tanya smiled. "Yes. I remember it well because I thought it humorous seeing all the cans tipped up to mouths like some kind of forced ritual."

Mark frowned. "There's nothing odd about drinking right away. There was beer before us and we opened the cans and drank from them, so what?"

Virgil spoke to Mark. "I think Lieutenant Abrams is suggesting that only Cosgrove had poison in his beer." He grinned. "Otherwise, we'd all be dead, eh?"

"Exactly." Lt. Abrams leaning forward. "Someone here had to notice the poison being placed into Mr. Cosgrove's beer."

"We think the poison, in capsule form, was hidden in one's hand," Karen remarked, "and inserted into the tab opening of Mr. Cosgrove's beer."

"Maybe Cosgrove did it to himself," Mark said, then grunted. "Suicide."

"That's been ruled out," Abrams replied. "We checked with neighbors and co-workers at his apartment complex," Abrams said. "Everyone we spoke to confirms that he had no complaints, worries or depression, and all of you in separate interviews said he was the life of the party."

Mark leaned back in his chair. "Maybe he was despondent due to losing at the poker games."

"Highly improbable," Karen replied. "All of you in separate interviews stated Mr. Cosgrove was in high spirits the night he was murdered..." She paused. "All except you, Mr. Gonzales. You disliked Mr. Cosgrove, and you had a reason to want him dead."

"I didn't kill him."

"Pedro didn't put poison in Mr. Cosgrove's beer. I would've noticed," Lori added.

"You also had reason to kill him because of his sexist remarks," Hal remarked to Lori. "And you were by his side at one point, correct?"

"Yes, I was," Lori said, defensively, "but so were the others."

"I wasn't near Jerry's beer can," Tanya said, glaring at Lori. "I was in back of him when I hit him on the head."

"But I remember Mark reached over and jiggled Jerry's arm."

Tanya shook her head. "Good Lord! Mark jiggled his arm when we learned that Jerry didn't reply to Virgil's request to ante in the pot for a new hand of poker," she said, defending her husband, "It was when we discovered him dead!"

"All of you were close enough to Mr. Cosgrove at one time or another," Abrams said, as he paced himself around the table. "I remind you," he said gently, "Unless someone comes forward and reveals the killer, all of you will be considered suspects."

"Yes, I fully admit I was angry enough to kill him," Lori said, glancing at her colleagues. "There were strong words between all of us and Mr. Cosgrove. "I didn't like him because of his sexist remarks, and he made bigoted remarks to Pedro, but hardly sufficient justification to kill him." With uplifted eyebrows, she said to the lieutenant, "Sticks and stones may break my bones, but words will never prompt me to violence."

Tanya pointed a finger at Pedro. "I'm not saying he did it, but Pedro was the closest one to Jerry.

"Yes, Pedro being left-handed and Mr. Cosgrove right-handed," Karen said, pointing. "Mr. Gonzales, you were close enough to sneak a capsule in his can. When did you do it?"

"I didn't."

Virgil shrugged his shoulders. "Hey, what about the suggestion that the beer already had poison in it when it was bought at Wal-Mart's."

"We checked that out," Karen replied. "We also received confirmation from the Budweiser factory. Contamination isn't possible because of the high security they maintain during the canning process." She glanced at Betty. "Even though we found a miniscule opening in Mr. Cosgrove's beer can, there's no way the poison could be inserted because it is only available in capsule form which must be attained with a doctor's prescription."

Lt. Abrams held up his hand. "All right, everyone, Detective Reiner, Detective Holmes and myself need to confer a minute outside. Relax while we're gone." He smiled. "We'll only be a minute."

In the hallway, Abrams asked Hal, "What's your thoughts?"

"Still thinking," he said, pinching his earlobe.

"In your opinion, who is the most viable of the suspects?"

"The Blydairs. The embezzlement charge against them is a strong motive."

"But Cosgrove didn't pursue any litigation, right?"

"According to the attorney we spoke with, yes." Karen glanced at Hal. "The only twist is we did receive testimony from the landlord that Cosgrove said he was expecting a windfall. Although that testimony can't be confirmed. The informant couldn't be located." Karen shrugged. "Maybe the one we least expect is the guilty one."

With a disapproving frown and hands on his hips. Abrams remarked, "They all have motive and opportunity, with the possible exception of Vigil Blydair. He's the only that wasn't close to Cosgrove, until he made change the second time around."

Hal glanced at Abrams before he spoke. "What did you say?"

"I said Virgil is the only that wasn't near Cosgrove, except when he made change the second time."

"Which is why I favor the Bydairs."

"Virgil couldn't have put poison in Cosgrove's can unless he had an extra hand," Karen replied. "Remember, he was taking medicine with a sip from his own can of beer."

"And all the others were watching." Abrams shook his head. "He's the least likely to be the perp."

Hal looked away thinking.

"But we're still left with all six possible suspects," Karen said, grimacing.

Hal tugged at his earlobe.

"What's on your mind?" Abrams inquired. "This is the time to share any ideas."

"Even if it seems ridiculous?" Hal replied weakly.

"Especially if it seems ridiculous," Karen replied."

"Maybe you're right. If I get it out in the open..." He paused. "What's been bothering me is how someone could have put the poison in Cosgrove's beer without being seen."

"Well, that's the mystery to be solved," Abrams acknowledged.

"We know that most of the suspects were close enough to Cosgrove to have slipped the poison in," Karen added. "But how it was done with five other people watching, including Cosgrove, is the stickler?"

Hal paused a long moment before speaking, then glanced at Karen. "Maybe the poison wasn't put in Cosgrove's beer can."

Abrams' posture stiffened. "What do you mean?"

Karen gazed at Hal. "Are you saying someone switched cans with Cosgrove?"

Abrams scowled. "We've been over this before. Cosgrove's beer was the only one with the aconite, and they were all drinking from their own can of beer from the get-go."

"Assuming there was a switch of cans, you may be on to something," Karen said, "but who could've done it?"

Hal rubbed the back of his neck. "I don't know." Hal motioned at Abrams. "Let's continue the interview; maybe something will be said to affirm my suspicion…"

"About what?" When Hal didn't answer said, Abrams rubbed his chin. "That's what I thought we were doing—looking for insight by their answers in a group setting. Okay, the ball is in your court. Let's go back in. We need to return to our guests before they lawyer up," Abrams said, turning the door knob. "What we need is a confession and soon."

When they entered the room, the suspects readjusted their positions in their chairs, showing agitation.

"How much longer is this witch hunt going to continue?" Mark inquired. "We've been over all these questions before."

"And we're almost out of peanuts," Virgil remarked grinning.

"We're almost done," Hal replied. "This question is directed to anyone. Did anything odd happen during any of the poker hands?"

After a moment of heads looking at each other, Tanya spoke up. "At one point, I remember seeing Pedro grabbing his beer and he hit Jerry's can, nearly knocking it over. Jerry caught his beer in time before it fell. That's when Jerry said, 'If you want my beer bad enough, you can have it in exchange for a night with Lori.'"

"And that was all there was to the incident?" Karen inquired, glancing at the other suspects.

Everyone nodded.

Hal readied his pen over his notepad. "When did this occur during the poker hands?"

"I believe it was during the second or third hand," Betty said. "Just before change was made."

"Karen spoke to Betty. "Demonstrate what took place in this regard."

Betty's eyes blinking momentarily, and she appeared eager to answer the question. "At the start of the games, Virgil pushed the coin box filled with nickels, dimes and quarters to the center of the table, and everyone took change."

"Tell me again why poker chips weren't used," Abrams questioned.

Virgil held up his hand. "The first night we played, I made the suggestion we play with real money, rather than chips." He grinned. "You have to admit, the feel of nickels, dimes and quarters compared to poker chips is more satisfying."

"And everyone paid for their change with paper money?" Hal inquired.

"Yes, mostly ones and fives, which were put into the box," Tanya remarked. "I remember Virgil kept the box on the floor by his feet when he wasn't making change."

"That's correct. When someone wanted more change I would bring the box up on top of the table."

Lori sat up in her chair. "Change was only made twice; at the beginning and then a few minutes later when Jerry requested change. That time Virgil took the box over to Jerry."

"Yes, I did." Virgil looked at Hal. "Jerry insisted I bring the box over to him because he didn't want to strain himself reaching for it in the middle of the table."

"How long were you by Jerry's side?"

"A few seconds, just long enough for him to grab a few quarters and dimes." He grinned. "Certainly not long enough to put poison in his beer, if that's what you're getting at."

"That's true enough." Betty remarked, nodding her head." I was watching. As soon as Jerry got his change, Virgil went back to his seat with the coin box."

Karen looked at Virgil. "You kept your hands by your side the entire time he was getting change?"

"No. but both of my hands were busy. I was taking medicine followed with a swig of beer."

"Yes, I remember him taking his pill," Betty said. A few others nodded their agreement.

Hal looked surprised. "So, you had your can of beer with you when you took the change box over?"

"Of course."

"That seems odd," Karen said, looking at Virgil. "Why did you take your beer along with you?"

"A simple explanation." Virgil replied. "While

waiting for Jerry to get his coins, I decided to take my thyroid medicine. Swallowing those capsules requires the presence of liquid."

"So, you took your pill with a swallow of beer?" Hal inquired.

"Yes."

"And then what did you do with your can of beer?"

"I took it back to my seat along with the coin box." He held up his hands. "The coin box in my left hand and the beer in my right. Doesn't that sound reasonable?"

"Is that the way it happened?" Hal inquired, scanning the group.

There was silence for a moment, then Betty said, "Yes, I can vouch for what my husband just said. Virgil took the coin box to Jerry, and sat it on the table in front of him while waiting for Jerry to make change. Virgil took his thyroid medicine at that time with a sip of his beer. I think Jerry was taking his time deliberately. Virgil held up his arm, and pointed at his wristwatch. 'We're all waiting impatiently,' I remember Virgil saying. When Jerry tossed a ten dollar bill into the box, Virgil picked up the coin box, and his beer and returned to his chair."

Virgil smiled at his wife. "My dear, you are irreplaceable."

Hal looked surprised. "What did you say?"

"I said her memory is outstanding."

"No, the one word you used."

"I said, irreplaceable."

Hal glanced at Karen. "Tell me, if you had a soda can in your hand, and you wanted to point at your watch which is on the other hand, wouldn't you put the beer can on the table first?"

"Yes, I would. I don't point well while holding a soda can."

Hal addressed Betty. "Ma'am, did your husband put his beer can on the table at any time while Mr. Cosgrove was taking change out of the coin box?"

"Yes, he did," she answered in a causal manner.

"Now I know how it happened," Hal said to Lt. Abrams. With handcuffs in his hand, Hal moved toward Virgil. "Mr. Blydair, you are under arrest for the murder of Jerry Cosgrove."

***

An hour later, after the other players were dismissed, Hal and Karen escorted Virgil into the conference room where they could have privacy. After seating themselves, Karen pointed at a document. "Write out your confession and sign your name at the bottom of the paper."

After writing his confession and signing his name, Virgil said with a wry grin, "I almost got away with the perfect crime."

Karen shook her head. "Sir, there are too many ways to make a mistake for a perfect murder. You are the perfect example."

"I thought I had planned ahead to avoid any mistakes. It was only by a fluke that you caught me. Taking my beer with the coin box over to Cosgrove was my only error. But I had to do it to be able to switch beer cans."

Hal nodded. "That's the only time the transfer could have been made because no one else's beer was close to Cosgrove's beer, except Pedro. I figured he didn't make the switch when everyone saw him nearly knock over Cosgrove's beer. Too obvious." Hal rubbed his hands together as a gesture of certainty. "I finally figured out your cleverness—setting your beer down, the one with the poison, next to Cosgrove's beer. You made the switcheroo at that time picking up Cosgrove's can."

"You drank from Cosgrove's beer while taking your medicine," Karen said, in a tone of inquiry, "clear of any poison."

"Yes, the others would naturally assume I had picked up my own can. It's all a matter of sleight of hand." Smiling, Virgil added, "I tipped Cosgrove's can to my mouth pretending to drink and swallowed my thyroid pill. Yes, a creature of habit as I did the same while I had the poisoned can of beer with me up until Jerry made change the second time. I took Cosgrove's can back with me along with the coin box to my seat." He grinned. "The can with the poison was left by Cosgrove's side."

"You are tricky. But when did you put the poison in your beer can? How did you manage that without anyone noticing?"

"Simple." Virgil curled one side of his mouth in a mocking expression. "As soon as Betty brought in the beer, I opened the tab, and then put my can between my thighs, out of sight from everyone, while the others opened their cans. I then took a capsule filled with the poison from my shirt pocket, dropped it into the tab opening with my left hand while I slapped the table with my right hand to get everyone's attention."

Karen smiled. "How did you know about aconite

poison?"

"A little research in the library and a few questions to pharmacists gave me the answers. The plant is grown locally in the wild about fifty miles north of here. When I found out it was fast-acting and attacks the heart when ingested, and that a spoonful of scrapings from the root would kill a cow, it was made to order." I journeyed into the foothills. Dug up a plant, they have a blue flower, sawed a branch of the roots and took it home to process."

Karen leaned forward with elevated eyebrows. "And how did you process the roots small enough to put into a capsule?"

"That took some time. But I simply sawed the branches, catching the saw dust into a bag. I bought an empty capsule and inserted the aconite dust."

"One final question," Hal said. "Why did you wait nearly three years to kill Cosgrove?"

He told me a week before the poker party he was intent on suing me on the embezzlement charge."

But he didn't pursue it." Hal nodded. "We checked with the law firm and verified that he didn't press charges."

Virgil looked surprised. "Oh?"

"And you didn't tell your wife about Cosgrove's threat of litigation," Karen said.

"I didn't tell her. She knew nothing about my plan of murder. But I guess you figured that out."

"We discounted her as your accomplice early on," Hal said.

"She was a prime suspect at first," Karen added. "Because she was alone in the kitchen getting the beer, but none of the cans were open at that time. And the perforation in Cosgrove's can was too tiny to accept powder."

Hal looked into Virgil's eyes. "If your wife had known about your plan of murder, she wouldn't have mentioned you setting your can of beer next to Cosgrove's."

Virgil glanced at the detectives with a resolute expression. "As the saying goes—the best laid plans of mice and men often go awry."

After eyeing Hal with an expression of wonder, Virgil said, "Tell me, specifically, what triggered your suspicion that I switched beer cans?"

"I owe that cleverness to Karen. I have a brother who could pass for my twin, and we were discussing antics we played on each other when we were kids. I told a date I didn't want to go out, and my brother took her out instead. Karen referred to it as a '*switcheroo.*' So when you told Betty she was *irreplaceable*, for me the word translated to *switch*."

Virgil nodded. "Ah yes, There's many a slip between cup and lip."

A uniformed officer escorted Virgil out of the interrogation room. Hal and Karen headed for Abrams' office. They briefed the lieutenant on the interview and gave him the confession.

"That wraps up this case. "Great job, you two. Good thinking on your part, Hal. Switching cans never would have occurred to me. How did Blydair know about the aconite poison?"

"He read about it and talked to pharmacists." Hal said.

"Well, he almost got away with it." Abrams laughed heartily. "While you're on a roll, let's put the

Christianson case to bed as well."

"I'd like to take a couple of day off to recuperate," Hal said. "I've got some things at home that need assistance."

"You earned it." The lieutenant looked at Karen. "Do you need time to recharge your batteries?"

"No, I'm fine." She glanced at Hal. "I'll check out some leads while you're gone. There's plenty to do."

They left the office and went to their desks. "How long will you be gone?" Karen asked.

"Two, maybe three days." He looked away momentarily. "You'll be okay."

"We're partners." She held up a thumb. "Okay, have a good time. See you soon."

He nodded, then extended his hand to her.

After caressing one another, Hal sat down at his desk. He picked up the phone and punched in numbers. As he waited, he grinned at Karen. After a moment, he spoke into the receiver. "Evelyn? Hi." Pause. "I'm coming home." Pause. "Yes, the poker case is closed. I'm taking a few days off." Pause. "Yeah, I knew that would make you happy. Yes. We'll tackle that problem together, okay?"

He cradled the phone and glanced at Karen again. He saw her nodding, her expression positive, indicating to him that she hadn't picked up on the fake chat with his wife.

***

For three days, Hal enjoyed his time off from the precinct. He managed to avoid time with Evelyn by mowing the lawn, replacing a couple of roof shingles and piddling in the garage. During the time they did converse, the subject usually ended in an argument. In one session he heard her mention divorce. He wasn't surprised. It hadn't been the first time.

Before in their discussions of family finances, the division of property was confined to a meager mutual fund, a small savings account and the house. But this time she hinted that his pension would be included. He couldn't allow that—he *wouldn't* allow that. The pension was his and his alone."

"Well I'm entitled to half of your pension, so plan on it."

"Over my dead body."

More appropriately, he should have said, "Over your dead body."

He made peace with her by suggesting they see a marriage counselor. It would give him time to think about his options. For the first time, Evelyn's death came to him as a viable goal.

CHAPTER SEVEN

ON THE OUTER edge of Beaverton's northern border, a large one story house spread out on an acre of land. A block wall enclosed the property, but a steel gate was always open to the dirt road that led to the house. Inside Edgar Buckingham sat in the easy chair in his reading room waiting for his niece to bring him her copy of the book, *Gone with the Wind.* He'd seen the movie years ago, but never read the book. With plenty of time on his hands now that he was retired from the brokerage business, he looked forward to enjoying the Civil War saga at his leisure.

He needed contentment of sorts to offset the eroding situation with his live-in nephew. The indolent young man was taking advantage of his good nature. Recent revelations suggested Jack was stealing from him despite a generous monthly allowance for tending to things around the house. His nephew's help had become willful disobedience. Edgar felt compelled to do something extreme to remedy the corrosive situation.

He heard the doorbell ring, then the familiar high-pitched voice of his niece. "Uncle Ed, it's Sheila. I'm coming in. He watched the thirty-year-old prance through the hallway that led to the library. Noticing the hallway light out, she flipped the wall switch, but nothing happened. She continued on into the library and placed the book on his reading table. "This will keep you occupied for a very long time. It's over 1000 pages."

He nodded. "I'm eager to get started. You know I'm a civil war buff. I have all evening to get through chapter one. I'm all set up here in the library with my reading table and cushioned chair and overhead light, except …" He angled his head to indicate the adjustable lamp behind him. "As you've already discovered there's a problem being able to switch from the hallway to the overhead lamp on my reading table. I'm hoping it's merely a matter of changing bulbs. Could you replace them for me?"

"Most certainly. Let me check out the switches under your table." She bent down, reached under the table and felt of the larger button, pressed it, but his reading table lamp didn't come on. She pressed the smaller button, but the hallway light didn't turn on."

"I've asked Jack to fix it numerous times, but you know him—he's always got some lame excuse."

"I know where the spare bulbs are," she said, pacing herself toward a nearby cabinet. Quickly replacing the bulb in the hallway, and the overhead reading lamp, she bent down again reaching under the table and pressed the larger button. The reading lamp came on. With a touch of the smaller button the light in the hallway illuminated.

"Good!" Edgar's amiable smile erupted. "I was hoping it wasn't the wiring gone bad. The two-way switch was a brilliant idea. I can turn either one on or off at my reading table without hobbling over there to the hallway."

"How is that leg of yours?"

"About the same. With the walker, I make it to my

bedroom slowly but surely. I do appreciate your concern and your help. Thank you, Sheila."

"Harry and I plan to have you over to the house soon. You can rest your leg in our sauna. I think it would ease the pain. Or join me in the pool. Harry and I would help you in. You can enjoy soaking in the warm water."

He smiled. "I would like that. You and your brother are like night and day when it comes to character. You're kind, considerate, always willing to help. Jack is arrogant, thinks he knows it all and helps only himself."

Sheila looked at her uncle with a sympathetic expression. "If Jack's not doing his job around the house, don't give him the allowance."

He nodded again. "I'm seriously considering asking him to leave. In the last six months he's become indolent, a free-loading lazy bum. All he does all day is play video games on the computer. He has no interest in a career, he's main goal in life is living off of me." With a rigid palm, Edgar raised it to his chin. "I've had it up to here!" The old man sighed. "I felt bad when your mother passed on. At the time it seemed like the least I could do—give you and your brother a home. Now Jack's 25 and amounts to nothing. I have to beg him to take me out shopping. Sheila, I plan on changing the trust fund Monday. I'm seriously considering disinheriting him."

Sheila hesitated, then said, "Jack won't like that. Have you said anything to him yet?"

"No. If he ever comes out of his room, I intend on telling him. Did you want to speak to him before you leave?"

"Yes."

"I'll ring him on my cell."

"No, don't bother. I'll go to his room."

***

As Sheila approached Jack's room, she noticed the door was ajar. She waited a minute before proceeding. At the door she was about to knock when Jack opened it with a flair. "Well, if isn't my beloved sister, scowling as usual. To what do I owe the misery of your presence?" He stepped aside and waved her inside.

"Listening to your nastiness as usual."

"Have a seat. Do you want a drink?"

"No to both questions," she said, and remained standing in a defensive stance. "I was just speaking to Uncle Ed. He's really ticked off by your attitude, especially not helping around the house. I should think you'd be happy to please him with the substantial allowance he gives you each month."

"Frankly, my dear, I don't give a damn."

"Well, you better. He's thinking of changing the trust fund, removing you from the inheritance."

"He's hyperventilating again. The trust fund says I get the house and property, the SUV, and half of the brokerage business when Unc breathes his last breath."

"If I'm not mistaken, the trust deed is revocable meaning Uncle Jack has power of attorney to make changes any way he likes, as long as he's not incapacitated, meaning he has the mental capacity. I read the trust deed recently." Sheila honed in on Jack's last words and with penetrating eyes, she remarked, "Uncle Edgar is in good health. He might outlive you."

Jack sneered. "I don't think so. So, you looked at

the trust deed. Are you afraid he'll disinherit you?"

"No. It's not me he's angry at." .She got up and walked to the door. "He really looks pissed this time. I'm only the messenger. I suggest you get on his good side. Little brother, you better change your ways because he has a mind to take away your allowance and kick you out of the house."

Jack snickered. "Are those his exact words?" Without waiting for a reply, he added, "Sis, come anytime with your exhilarating news." As he watched her leave, a scenario of murder popped in his head with familiarity as though he'd rehearsed it a thousand times. He stared at the desk top thinking. *Go to the movies, sneak out of the theater, return to the mansion, kill the old man, sneak back into the theater before the feature is over. Return home, call 911 and report the crime. Perfect alibi.* He Looked in his desk drawer, took out his hunting knife and ran a finger over the edge of the blade. "This will look good sticking in the old man's heart." He put it on the table, then got on the computer and began looking at theater movies and their schedules.

***

Sheila went directly to the library and waited for a moment while watching Edgar read from the opened book. "I can tell you're enjoying the story with your intense eyes focused on each page."

"Yes. Thank you again. Did you see Jack?"

"I did, and scolded him for being an ass."

"You mentioned that I'm thinking of disinheriting him?"

She nodded. "I did, but I think it went in one ear and out the other without pausing. You know Jack. He's good at showing complete apathy. I don't know what to advise you, except to do what you think is best."

Edgar sighed and nodding, he asked, "Do you want anything to drink?"

"No." She glanced at her watch. "I have to leave. I'm meeting Harry in town for dinner."

As she turned to leave, Edgar motioned for her to wait. He reached in his pocket and pulled out a thick roll of $100 bills. Removing a yellowish, wide rubber band from around the bills, he then peeled off a Ben Franklin and gave it to her. "This is for changing the bulbs."

She smiled. "I know you won't let me say no. Thanks for your generosity." She watched him stretch the rubber band onto the roll of bills with a half-hearted grin. "Do you get any comments about using a rubber band to hold your roll of Ben Franklins?"

"Once in a great while. I tell them it keeps the bills in place otherwise they would be loose in my pocket."

"But it does bring notice to a huge wad of money. I worry someone will rob you."

"It hasn't happened in over fifteen years."

"I'll take that as a positive note, and will say good-bye for now. I'll talk to later about a swimming date."

He watched her leave, then leaned back into his chair and started reading. A few minutes later as Edgar sipped from his wine tumbler, he noticed Jack standing in front of his reading table.

With legs apart, hands on hips, the tall, thin young man smirked. "I could've run you in with a knife."

"What do you want?"

"I ran out of cash. I need a retainer on my allowance for next month."

"That's exactly what I want to talk to you about," Edgar said. "Sit down."

"I like standing. So, Unc, what's so important suddenly?"

"I know you've been taking cash from the receipt box in the living room."

Grinning, Jack replied in a tone of caginess. "Me? Why not one of the many people who come in the house to service it?"

The old man placed his hands together. "Possible, but not probable. I remember putting a $100 bill in the cash box on Monday. There was only you and me in the house on Monday. When I checked the box Monday night the bill was missing."

"Obviously, your memory has taken a turn for the worse." Jack placed a palm against his shirt in the area of his heart. "I'm offended that you accuse me of this gigantic theft of 100 dollars. Of course, I deny it absolutely, completely and totally."

"I figured you would." Edgar gazed at his nephew. "You're good with words, Jack. You love to argue. And yes, and you're smart, but your know-it-all attitude is your downfall. You are a thief, you have no sense of responsibility, and you're no help to me around the house." Edgar sighed. "You have no redeeming qualities. That is why I've decided to disinherit you. There will be no more allowance, and I want you out of my house."

The stable grin on Jack's face dissipated. He pinched the bridge of his nose with forefinger and thumb. "Let me see if I'm hearing you correctly—no more allowance, you're kicking me out of the house and I lose my inheritance—is that what I heard?"

"Yes. I want you out of the house no later than Monday. Monday I'll speak to my lawyer about changing the trust fund. You're getting nothing."

Jack scowled. "Your declaration is almost funny. Wanting me out of the house is maybe negotiable, but no more allowance and disinherited... is...what can I say...is beyond the realm of possibility. Did it occur to you that you'll have no one to take you shopping?"

"I'll find someone, someone who's responsible."

Jack snickered. "Sorry, I can't let you interfere with my bonanza. The fact is, Unc, your time is up, old man."

With eyes of concern, Edgar stared at his nephew. "What do you mean?"

The nephew brushed red clumps of hair from his forehead. "It means you have just provided me with an excuse to end your sedentary life."

Edgar grabbed his cane and shook it at Jack. "You wouldn't dare! You'd be convicted of murder. Prison for the rest of your life isn't in your make-up. "

"Hey, you got that right. But I'll have an alibi. I won't be here when you're found with a knife stuck in your heart."

"You can't threaten me. You're not only a lazy bum; you're a liar and a manipulative lowlife as well. I've given you a place to stay rent free, a monthly allowance and you talk of taking my life. You are an arrogant and irresponsible."

"Is that all?"

"Twenty years old, no high school diploma, with little experience, and you think you know it all. If your father was alive, he'd knock some sense into that thick skull." The old man sighed. "No. You don't scare me with your threats. I want you out of this house. I don't care where you go—I'm done with you, boy. I mean it. Monday morning I'm calling my lawyer. You will no longer be a beneficiary of the trust fund."

"What about Sheila?"

"I have no quarrel with Sheila." Edgar raised his chin. I'm thinking of giving her *your* portion of the inheritance."

Jack remained silent for a moment staring coldly at his uncle, then with a shifty smile, he said, "Okay, maybe I would be better off on my own, I'll give you that. I won't have to endure your constant nagging, which is as painful as a cocklebur between the toes, you know what I mean, Unc?"

Edgar waved his cane in a show of irritation.

"Okay, you want me out of the house? Fine, but I have no money to move. I'm short of cash." He pulled his pants pockets out. "I'm broke. I'll need a hundred to rent a trailer for the move, okay? Do you think you can manage that?"

Frowning, Edgar reached in his pocket and pulled out his fist-sized roll of greenbacks. He delicately removed the rubber band from the roll, peeled off the top Ben Franklin, and handed it to Jack. "This is the last money you'll get from me ever, you shyster." The old man replaced the rubber band and shoved the roll in his pocket.

"I'd say thank you for the Ben Franklin, but it's seems inappropriate for the occasion."

"I'm done talking. Leave me be to my reading."

Jack sneered at his uncle, then left the room. He rushed to Edgar's bedroom, grabbed a pair of gold cuff links, and a box of Edgar's deceased wife's jewelry, dropped them in a bag, then hurried to the living room. He took a sterling silver teapot and a replica of Rembrandt's Mona Lisa painting. Sufficient items to represent a robbery, he told himself. He walked confidently to his SUV with the painting and bag of items. He felt assured that his plan of murder was fail-safe. He looked forward to answering any and all questions of the police; especially conversing with the detectives assigned to the robbery/murder. He reviewed the details of the scenario with a smile on his face. Killing his Unc while watching a movie—how clever! And the p*erfect alibi.*

***

The following Saturday, Hal and Evelyn arrived at the mental health clinic twenty minutes early and waited in the reception room, speaking only occasional with mundane bits of conversation. Hal glanced at his watch numerous times feeling guilty of participating in the hoax. At exactly ten a.m. the receptionist escorted them Hal and Evelyn into the therapist's office and introduced Dr. Brunner and quickly left the room closing the door behind her.

"Please be seated," Dr. Brunner said, motioning to chairs in front of her desk. She glanced at the data sheet in front of her while Hal and Evelyn seated themselves.

NAME: Hal Reiner

AGE: 37

MARITAL STATUS: Married seven years. Wife, Evelyn

OCCUPATION: Homicide detective

Having observed him entering the office, he seemed shorter than his five feet, eight inches. A prominent thick head of blond hair with blue eyes and no special features on his square face suggesting a man neither handsome or unattractive, someone easily forgotten. She noticed he sat in his chair with folded hands in his lap, perhaps in a posture of obedience. He wore a short sleeved striped shirt with a tie pulled away from his neck a few inches.

"I see you're a homicide detective, Mr. Reiner. Are you with the Beaverton Police Department?"

He nodded, then said, "Fifteen years, but only the last five years in homicide."

The therapist smiled. "You're my first homicide detective as a client." Pausing, she added, "No disrespect implied."

With no response, she turned to the data sheet.

NAME: Evelyn Reiner

AGE: 35

MARITAL STATUS: Married seven years to Hal Reiner

OCCUPATION: No employment history, home-maker

CHILDREN: None.

She gazed at Evelyn briefly. Brown eyes and neck-length auburn hair, soft facial features and petite. The woman sprouted a nervous disposition, clasping and unclasping her hands frequently. Perhaps of significance, she wore a white print dress with a neck line that completely covered the upper portion of her chest. Dr. Brunner glanced at them both. "How may I help you?"

"He spends all his time at the precinct," Evelyn remarked instantly. "When he *is* home, he spends most of his time in the den. We don't eat together and rarely sleep together. We 're no longer husband and wife."

The therapist looked at Hal, anticipating an answer. After a long moment, he said, "I suppose she's right. "I've been very busy at work."

Evelyn shook her head. "Because you don't want to spend time with me."

"Is that the core of your marital difficulties?

"Our relationship is fading away. When he's home, he's like a zombie, off by himself, stays in the den most of time."

"What about your sex life?"

"Non-existent," Evelyn replied smugly.

He wanted to defend himself, but realized arguing wouldn't show himself to be supportive of Evelyn. Above all else, he needed to appear receptive to the therapist's suggestions of a marriage on the mend.

Dr. Bruning leveled her eyes at Evelyn. "Let's get one thing straight at the outset. "Do you want to save the marriage?"

"Yes, I do. But…"

Dr. Bruning held her palm up. "We'll talk about the buts in a moment." She looked at Hal. "Do you want to save the marriage?"

He wanted to say absolutely not, but replied instead with a firm yes.

Mr. Reiner, would you be willing to make some changes in your work schedule to spend more time at home?"

"Yes. I think I better."

Even glanced at Hal, scowling. "I don't know if I believe him. We've been down this road before, but he doesn't change."

Dr. Brunner looked at Evelyn. "Would you be willing to make changes in your attitude toward your husband?"

Evelyn hesitated. "Of course. But I want him to appreciate me as his wife."

"Your ideas and his ideas of marriage compatibility may not coincide. What doesn't work is waiting for change to occur without compromise. I believe your marital problems can be worked through with the following recommendations." Dr. Brunner wrote on her notepad. "First, we'll get you both into group therapy sessions, and I would also like to see you individually for counseling. Would you be willing to accept this plan of treatment?"

Evelyn and Hal agreed. The therapist got up and quickly moved around the desk, offering her hand to Evelyn and Hal. "It's been pleasant talking with you both. I'll look forward to our next meeting. See the receptionist for appointment times."

They shook hands, then left the therapist's office and conferred with the receptionist. On the way home at a stop sign, Hal glanced at Evelyn and said, "Everything will work out okay."

Evelyn turned to him and said coolly, "I hope so."

At home, Hal's plan to pacify his wife included a lengthy conversation about commonplace subjects and he often complimented her. He felt in a good mood. With the poker case finished and reports filed and no new emergency meetings to attend, he decide to show her that he was changing his behavior.

"It's apple time," he said, with raised eyebrows. "I'm going to Nelson's Apple Farm and pick up a basket of your favorite apples— Granny Smith and Red Delicious—just for you."

"That would please me," she said simply. Although he expected more praise, he felt upbeat, waved good-bye, got in his SUV and drove along the main highway out of town until he came to the cobblestone road that led to the apple farm past the familiar Buckingham estate, a landmark of sorts, the only large dwelling leading to the orchard. He parked next to a small fruit stand, got out of his car, and waved his basket to a middle-aged man standing in the doorway. "I'm going to get some of your delicious apples."

"Well sure. We got a dandy bunch this season. But this may be the last time."

"What do you mean?" Hal inquired, stopping at the stand.

"Edgar Buckingham owns this land. His nephew, Jack, who lives with his uncle, told me his uncle was selling the property."

"The house, too"

"I don't know about the house, but the orchard is on half an acre. I rent the property from Buckingham. The nephew said they had a buyer for the property. Can't figure it—why they're selling the orchard. The old man is rich, he don't need the money."

Hal nodded. "Thanks for letting me know. I'll have to fill up my basket." He headed toward the apple trees, glancing east at the Buckingham house with its three chimneys high above the roof ridge appearing like battle stations of a fortress. He'd never met the Buckinghams, only heard that Edgar had made his fortune in real estate.

He paid for the apples and headed home. Entering the house, he sat the basket of apples on the kitchen counter near where Evelyn was standing preparing a dish for baking.

She glanced at him. "You got my favorite Granny

Smith's. I'm baking your favorite cake, with chocolate icing." Her eyebrows lifted. "And we'll have dinner together this evening, okay?"

He told her it might be the last time they could get apples at Nelson's orchard, explaining the Buckingham property was up for sale. He said he would spend the rest of the day working out in the yard, mowing the lawn, weeding and general clean up. He was surprised when she acknowledged his work tasks outside with a smile of appreciation.

While trimming the bougainvillea bush near the front door, he entertained the thought that his wife had suddenly changed her ways, maybe even feeling a fondness for him, but the grandiose idea evaporated when she opened the door and screamed at him. "I was just in the spare bedroom. My God! What a mess!" Shaking her head, she continued with her diatribe. "It amazes me how anyone can be so lazy. Your pants are on the floor, food particles on the nightstand, glasses on the desk. The room looks like a cyclone hit it!"

He didn't answer her, but felt like a victim again. There was no love in her heart for him anymore, no need to suppose things would be different with or without therapy. His wife was without a doubt bent on destroying him. The thought occurred to him in stark realism—in order to survive, he must destroy her first.

Leaving half the lawn un-mowed, Hal went into the garage, grabbed a hammer and began pounding the work bench with a fierceness that disturbed him. Laying the hammer down gently, he leaned against the workbench and wiped his brow with a handkerchief. "Don't be stupid," he said aloud. "Nothing good ever comes from frenzy. Plan ahead with calmness, you know it's

the only way to prevent mistakes." He didn't want to
wind up like his father, a man filled with hate and rage
unable to think things through. He relived the beating in
his mind again, gritting his teeth as he felt the belt smash
against his back repeatedly. The memory of his father's
rage cautioned him to think positive thoughts. After all,
he was a detective and had the experience and
knowledge to make perfect any plans of murder. He
took a deep breath. It was past time to sever his relationship with his wife of ill will permanently. Success meant
his willingness to be patient and plan for every contin-
gency.

CHAPTER EIGHT

EXITING THE HOUSE at 6:45, Jack headed toward the SUV with long confident strides. He glanced at his watch. And as expected, he knew the medical examiner would check the stomach for signs of digestion, establish body temperature, along with the degree of rigor mortis present, and the degree of body decaying activity, to estimate the time of death occurring between 7 and 10 p.m. precisely when it would have occurred—the time he was at the movie.

Jack tossed the painting and bag of items in the SUV, and then checked a five-gallon can of petrol in the tool shed. Nearly full, he set it aside to be used later. His plan for the old man's death seemed to be progressing effortlessly. He next mixed water and dirt together forming sticky mud which he pasted over the rear license plate of his Nitro. Tying the hood of his blazer tightly around his neck, which helped cover the sides of his face, he stepped in the SUV and started the engine with a determined twist of the ignition key.

On the way to a Harkins Theater, he made a detour a short distance to an apartment complex. He stopped at a parking space fifty feet from the apartment dumpster. Twilight had giving way to darkness, but he waited a few minutes more to make certain no one was passing by or watching him. Grabbing the bag which contained the gold cuff links, his wife's jewelry, and the sterling silver teapot, he walked briskly to the dumpster. Glancing at the bag, with an expression of resolve, he tossed it into the dumpster. He waited two minutes, looking around, and seeing no one in sight, he heaved the Mona Lisa picture into the dumpster.

The expensive objects from his uncle's alleged robbery had to go. He knew full well. Holding onto them for future compensation was far too risky having watched numerous crime dramas on TV. More often than not, retained property of that nature became evidence in a trial. Besides, any remuneration from kept objects would be chicken feed compared to the value of the house and property. *So long, nice knowing you,* he said under his breath, *indispensable just like my uncle.*

He returned to the SUV and checked the license plate to make sure the mud still obliterated the plate numbers. Wearing dark pants and a hooded blazer to cover his red hair, he felt confident no one could identify him as Edgar's nephew especially while traveling to the theater and the important return trip to his uncle's house during the time he should be at the movie.

He drove straight to the theater. Glancing at his watch, he noted the time. Only minutes away now; the movie Avatar would be starting soon. He'd already seen it, but a second viewing would refresh his memory of all the details during his interview with the police which was needed for his air-tight alibi. After parking in an adjacent lot, he hurried to the theater and gave the cashier a Ben Franklin apologizing that he had nothing smaller.

Midway through the movie, he went to the snack bar, bought a bag of popcorn, making small talk with the attendant. "You look like a friend of mine," Jack said. "I am amazed, sir, at the resemblance." The attendant smiled, shrugging his shoulders. Jack shook the man's hand, then made a motion he was returning to his seat eager to see the rest of the movie. He slipped out of the theater, dumped the popcorn into a trash can, then jumped in his SUV and headed home traveling the speed limit, cautious of all cars passing him. He couldn't allow an accident at this time.

Before leaving the SUV, he uncased his hunting knife, and held it firmly in his hand, then went directly to the rear of the house and kicked open the patio door with a bang, broken glass flying about. Jack stormed into the reading room stopping short of his uncle. Looking at the shocked face momentarily, he felt he must say something. With a devious grin, he hollered out, "Jack's here!" He stepped forward and thrust the knife into Edgar's heart.

He waited a few minutes then felt of the old man's pulse. Assured that his uncle was dead, he took the wad of bills from the old man's pocket, removed the rubber band, and tossed it on the floor. After wiping the knife handle with his handkerchief, he took his uncle's cell phone and dialed a fictitious number, part of the ruse to establish the old man was alive at 9:25 p.m. He waited until he heard an answering service, and hung up. Before placing the cell phone back in his uncle's shirt pocket, he smiled at his cleverness to avoid a common error by wiping his fingerprints from the cell phone, and planting his uncle's prints on the phone. He glanced around seeing the hallway light was off. The robbers would have turned it on, he reasoned.

Feeling a little rushed for time, he reached under the reading table and pressed both switch buttons by mistake; the large button which turned on the hallway lamp and the small button which turned off the reading lamp. He checked the patio doors and reading room to make certain it looked like a home invasion.

He fired up the SUV and returned to the theater, relaxing in a seat to watch the rest of Avatar.

It was nearly 10 o'clock when the movie ended. Before leaving the theater, he stopped by the snack bar and spoke to the attendant, expressing how much he enjoyed the movie. As soon as Jack got home, he removed mud from his license plate, and checked the gas gage. Three quarters full; exactly 1/4 of a tank had been used going to the theater and back home twice. He grabbed the gas can from the tool shed. Back at the SUV, he poured in the contents until he saw the gas gage peak between ¾ and full that would establish no more than the mileage to the theater and a return home. He entered the house and called 911, reporting his uncle had been stabbed to death. Within minutes a squad car arrived. Two police officers searched the house and took a brief statement from Jack. Soon, CS I officers arrived and began photographing the scene. Hal and Karen drove separate cars to the Buckingham estate after receiving a call from Lieutenant Abrams. Still groggy-eyed from sleeping, they spoke to an officer before going into the house.

"As far as I can tell, a stab wound into the heart is the manner of death," the officer said. "Looks like a burglary gone bad. As you can see, whoever it was broke through patio doors into the library. Victim is Edgar Buckingham. The nephew, Jack, found his uncle about 11 p.m. after arriving home, and phoned 911."

As Jack sat in the reading room waiting for detectives to speak with him, he looked forward to the interrogation with the detectives assured he would be able to answer all of their questions, maybe not to their satisfaction, but he loved to instill confusion in any debate. Amused at seeing the detectives enter the reading room; it became apparent they had come from their homes at the late hour. The man had obviously dressed in a hurry, his shirt not fully buttoned stuck halfway inside jeans, and one lacing of his shoes dragging on the floor. Karen followed Hal into the room, and he noticed she wore jeans and work shoes. Her hair appeared uncombed.

Karen spoke first. "We're sorry to interview you, Mr. Buckingham, so soon after your uncle's death. Can we talk to you now? Would that be alright?"

"Of course." He stood up, smiling at her and held out his hand. They shook hands. "I know the sooner you get information, the quicker you can find the killer." Sitting back down on a chaise lounge chair, he motioned for the detectives to be seated on a sofa across from him.

"I'm Detective Karen Holmes," she said, noticing Jack's posture in the chaise lounge. "And this is Detective Hal Reiner. We'll try to be brief. I understand you had been at a movie, and when you returned home, you found your uncle dead, is that correct?"

Jack clasped his hands together. "Yes."

Taking out his notepad, Hal inquired, "Does your uncle have any enemies?"

Jack grinned. "Correction. "*Did* my uncle have any enemies? Now that he's dead, you should reference him in the past tense. But to answer your question, none that I know of. Unc's retired. Made his fortune in real estate and from investors as a financial broker. But he was even-keeled, you know what I mean, pretty stable in his work, and made money for most of his clients."

"You lived here with your uncle?" Karen asked.

"Yes. I take care of the house, watched over him. Unc wasn't an invalid, but he had a bad leg, difficult for him to walk, but he got around pretty good with a cane and wheelchair."

Hal gazed at Jack briefly, then asked, "Mr. Buckingham, are you ..."

"Hey! No need to be so formal. Call me Jack."

Hal nodded. "Okay, Jack. Are you employed?"

"Right here. Like I said, I help out around the house. Sort of a Girl Friday in britches, you know what I mean? Unc gave me a monthly allowance which includes free rent. Can't beat that, right?"

After his parents passed away, his uncle adopted him and his sister, Jack explained. With unflinching candor, he told the detectives that he and his sister were beneficiaries of his uncle's trust fund upon his death. "I get the house and property, she gets the brokerage business." He watched them as they scribbled on their notepads. "Yes, I know—motive for murder, but it wasn't me." He smiled. "I was at a movie." Jack leaned forward in his chair, his forefinger extended. "So you won't be completely in the dark, detectives, I'll tell you what I think happened. Occasionally I take Unc shopping which I did late this afternoon. As is his custom, he carries cash in a big roll of $100 bills with a wide rubber band tied around the roll."

"Why the rubber band?" Hal asked.

"Why not? It's the perfect answer to contain his wad of bills, wouldn't you think so, detective?"

"If it were me, I'd fold them up without any rubber band."

"He usually carries too many to fold. His wad contains about fifty or sixty Ben Franklins at any given time. I've told him flashing that much money in a public place is stupid, but he says he likes the *feel* of a big wad in his hand."

"So the roll of bills is missing?" Hal inquired.

"Yeah! He kept it in his right front pants pocket. I asked the police officer to check it out, and he verified there was no roll of bills in his pocket. Other valuables are missing as well. I'll give you a list. So, it doesn't take a brain surgeon to realize this was a robbery. At the mall while Unc was buying a magnifying glass, paying for it with one of his Ben Franklins, I saw someone staring at Unc."

"Can you describe him?" Karen asked flipping a page of her notepad.

"Sure. Medium height. Early thirties is my guess. He wore a butch haircut, no facial hair, wore jeans and shirt without sleeves like a vest, you know what I mean?"

Hal nodded. "You saw just one man?"

"Right, but there could have been an accomplice. I was concentrating on the guy with the butch because he seemed like a statue gawking at Unc like he wanted to seize the wad of bills."

"Did you see anyone following you on the way home?"

"No. I stopped at a Chevron station and filled up the Nitro, then went on home." He shook his head. "Didn't see anything suspicious as I drove up the long driveway to the house." Jack pointed at the patio. "You can see where they broke in through the patio. Caught poor Unc by surprise. Although, Unc couldn't do anything to protect himself. I mean he didn't have the strength to fend off an intruder. He's an old man."

"I'm wondering why they had to stab him," Karen said, focusing on Jack. The burglar could have cleaned out the house without much interference with your uncle incapacitated."

"Unc was feisty with his words," Jack answered quickly. "He probably called the robber a few choice words, or maybe Unc tried to phone the police with his cell." Jack's grin widened. "What makes anyone resort to violence? There's motive in the madness, you know what I mean?"

Jack glanced at his uncle slumped in the chair, the hunting knife protruding out of his chest as though it were part of his body. "Probably the guy with the butch haircut killed him not wanting any witnesses to the robbery. That's my guess."

"Is the knife from your kitchen?" Karen inquired.

"No. Never seen it before. Whoever it belonged to brought it along."

Hal got up, moved closer to the victim and focused his eyes on the knife. "It has a unique handle with deep ridges on one side. Natural wood burnt finish in brown with white trim."

"You're very observant." Jack lifted his chin, grinning. "Maybe you can trace it to a store where it was bought, out of thousands of possible stores in the U.S. alone."

Hal glanced at his partner, then looked at Jack. "Assuming there were two intruders, wouldn't both of them break in, not knowing who might be here?"

"Not necessarily. For all we know, they looked in a window first to check out any other occupants. Detective, I'm supposing the accomplice waited in the getaway car while the killer subdued my uncle. It seems reasonable to assume the killer wanted to make a quick getaway after picking up a few valuables, don't you think?"

"Yes, good point." Hal glanced at Karen. "I'll make a note of your suggestion. Go on with your theory."

"Well, after they saw my uncle flash his wad of bills in the shopping mall, they followed us home and waited until I left for the theater." He pointed. "You can see the direct line from the door to my uncle's reading chair. The killer broke in and stabbed my uncle, took the wad of bills, quickly grabbed some valuables and fled. End of story."

"Except the killer had to search the house for valuables," Karen said.

"Yes, if he wasn't satisfied with the wad of Ben Franklins which could have amounted to upwards of $5,000. At any rate, it would only take a burglar a few minutes to look through the rooms for valuables."

"What were the items missing?"

"A pair of 24 carat gold cuff links, his wife's jewelry, an antique sterling silver teapot, and a Mona Lisa replica painting."

"An odd assortment of valuables."

"Well, when you're in a hurry, any port in a storm, you know what I mean?"

Hal rubbed his eyes. "You mentioned his wife."

"She's deceased. Unc keeps her jewelry as a memento."

Hal got up from the sofa and walked over to the reading table. He noticed something under the table on the floor. Hesitating before pointing at it, he asked, "What's this?"

"That's the rubber band that held Unc's wad of bills."

Hal called to an officer to take a picture of it. "Bag and label it" Addressing Jack, Hal commented, "Seems strange that the killer would take the rubber band off the roll. Being in a hurry, I would think he'd jam the roll quickly in his pocket with the band left on."

"Maybe he doesn't like rubber bands," Jack said, grinning. "I don't see that tidbit as anything significant, do you, Detective?"

Karen looked up from her notepad. "Well we don't know if it's significant until the lab checks it out. We have to weigh everything connected to the crime. It's evidence."

Jack cocked his head in an expression of ignorance. "What can anyone do with it, except look at it?"

"It's now part of this homicide case," Hal replied.

Jack made a motion with his hands. "Good luck with that. Anything else?"

"We'll need your fingerprints," Karen said.

"No problem." Jack held out his hands. "This will be a first for me. Never been arrested, or fingerprinted, you know, on account of my clean living."

Karen called for a CSI officer. The officer brought over a computer, set it on a table. "Sir, I'll be taking your prints with the computer. You won't need to clean ink from your hands, the process is digital. Place the palm of your right hand onto the glass platen and ..."

"I know how it works," Jack interrupted. "You scan my fingers onto the platen, then transfer the images to a high-tech program, right?"

The officer nodded and proceeded to scan Jack's fingers. After completing the procedure, the officer spoke to Karen. "Forensics is complete, evidence is documented and photographs taken."

"Well, we've taken up enough of your time," Hal said to Jack. "Your uncle will be taken to the morgue for an autopsy. We'll be in touch."

"As expected," Jack replied. "Anything else you want to know?"

"You don't seem too grief stricken of your uncle's death," Karen said.

"I admit we didn't get along well. We had an ongoing difference of opinion, you might say. But nothing to the level of violence." Jack pushed out his lips in a teasing manner. "To satisfy your curiosity, as I've said, I have an alibi. I was at the movies when my uncle was killed. When I left the house to go to the movie, Unc was alive. That's a true statement. Incidentally, I paid for the movie with a $100 dollar bill. Check with the cashier. I'm sure she will remember giving me change for the Ben Franklin. Saw Avatar. Did either of you see it?"

"Yes, I saw it," Karen replied, nodding. "Excellent movie."

Hal asked, "What was it about?"

"Sci-fi flick." Jack replied. "About an ex-marine who joins a mega company looking for minerals on the planet Pandora. But the minerals are under the home of Na-vi, a ten foot tall, blue-skinned native tribe who've been at war with the security arm of the corporation. The marine, Jake Sully, is recruited to try and negotiate with the Na-vi people using DNA to transform him into their likeness. Then he falls in love with a native..." Jack stops, then asks, "Do you want to know her name?"

Hal nodded.

"Neytiri."

"How does the movie end?"

The marine's conscience is torn between living with Neytiri in a sound body compared to a wheel chair bound life at the corporation, but he sides with the Na-vi people and battles the security forces until they are defeated in a spectacular finish."

Hal glanced at Karen with a questioning look.

"I couldn't have explained it better myself," she said, then held up one finger to her temple in a gesture of curiosity. "I remember this gigantic tree, a kind of holy shrine to the Na-vi people, but during the big battle scene it wasn't touched, why?"

Jack pointed his finger at Karen in a scolding manner. "Now I know you're testing me. The tree was in fact destroyed, set afire. Are you satisfied now that I saw the movie?"

Karen smiled, nodding.

"We'll be in touch," Hal informed Jack. "Sorry about your loss."

"Hey, no problem." Jack grinned. "But my ego needs to say I'm not sorry one bit that the old geezer is gone. Now I can enjoy the inheritance without hearing his constant nagging." Jack shrugged. "Hey, the truth is he was a crab, you know what I mean? Detectives, it's been a pleasure talking with you. I hope the rest of your evening is uneventful." He glanced at Hal with a wry grin. "Now you can go back to bed and maybe get a good night's rest."

***

After they left Jack at the front porch, Hal was a little more than surprised at Jack's arrogant manner, especially the unruffled admission disliking his uncle. It was beyond Hal's understanding why murder suspects invited suspicion. If the young man did kill his uncle, why wouldn't he hide any suggestion of involvement? Hal shook his head trying to understand this new person of interest in the stabbing death of his uncle. "He doesn't seem to care," Jack said to Karen, "whether or not we consider him a suspect."

Karen nodded. "Oh, yeah, got that. He doesn't hold back his feelings, that is, if he's being honest. The other possibility is he's testing us?"

"What do you mean?"

"To see how much we know about the murder, to gain information about any evidence we have." Karen angled her head to one side. "He's the kind of person that needs to be prepared at all times."

Hal nodded. "Being prepared. That I understand. We'll have to watch this guy."

***

Hal arrived home late in the evening and explained he was assigned to a new homicide case, that he was sorry he didn't phone. Evelyn didn't seem perturbed. She told him she saved his supper and would heat it up, but that he appeared exhausted, and suggested they relax for a bit in the Jacuzzi. Stopping short from shaking his head, he realized the opportunity to get on her good side with conversation and perhaps a friendly pat on her shoulder while in the Jacuzzi.

After he put on his trunks and met her at the patio door (she already had on her swim suit), Evelyn handed him a glass of wine, and he followed her to the tub. With drink in hand, he focused his attention on the Jacuzzi, recalling that Evelyn insisted on buying it two years ago. "It will sooth my body, *and my* nerves," she had told him. Evelyn pinpointed the installation in the backyard a substantial distance under the patio roof, where she could "breath the fresh air and still be protected from the rain." Despite his objections that the neighbors could see them, she won the argument. The design provided for three steps leading to the top of the tub including hand rails, and steps into the Jacuzzi but without hand rails. A person could slip and fall with nothing to grab onto, the possibility occurred to him.

As he followed Evelyn up the steps, his thoughts turned to the precinct basement, and reading about the six-year-old child drowning case. The cold case hadn't been solved because the police didn't have solid evidence to indict her for the crime. It surprised him he recalled the case, although at the time, he suspected the mother had gotten away with the perfect murder.

He had used the tub numerous times, but not nearly as much as Evelyn. In the past year, lounging in the tub in thirty minute sessions seemed to be part of her regimentation.

"You know, I worry about you using the tub alone," Hal remarked sitting next to her in the tub.

"After two years, now you're worried?"

"I've been concerned, but haven't said anything until now." He took a sip from his glass of wine.

She scoffed. "To ease your mind, Hal, I will be extra careful getting in and out."

"Thank you." He smiled. "The water temp is great. Is the temp okay with you?" He turned and glanced at the control panel. "It says 104 degrees."

"Yes, it's the way I like it."

"Then I like it too." Hal patted her on the shoulder.

He listened attentively as she told him about her visit to see their godson, Rodney. "They asked about you."

He rubbed his chin, frowning. "Sorry I wasn't able to go. From now on, I'm making a concerted effort to be a better godfather. Let's plan on having an evening at Michael's house soon."

After twenty minutes, he excused himself and stepped up to the platform, to the hand rails, then glanced back at the tile edging. A fall from the top would land one against the tile edging, then into the water, he surmised. Shaking his head, he stepped down to the patio floor and went inside the house. "Way to risky," he told himself, and yet, he liked the idea of Evelyn slipping and falling.

CHAPTER NINE

A FEW DAYS passed before Sheila Livingston could be interviewed. She agreed to meet Hal and Karen at the precinct station. Located off the main street, the precinct shared the facility with the county courthouse. Upstairs in the homicide department, five detectives and Lieutenant Abrams comprised the work force along with a secretary. Two interrogation rooms occupied one end of the elongated hall; both had adjoining viewing rooms. Abrams' office sat conspicuously in the center of the large hall. In one of the viewing rooms, Abrams watched Hal and Karen interview the niece through the one-way mirror.

Karen gazed at Sheila, studying her mannerisms. Pushing thirty, the petite woman, with a pleasant round face and auburn hair pulled back in a long smooth pony tail appeared at ease, although she fingered a silver and turquoise ring, suggesting nerves or simply a habit. Karen liked the woman's apparel, dressed in a white silk blouse and camel-colored slacks.

"We appreciate you coming in for an interview. Our condolences go out to you of your uncle's death," Karen said to Sheila, offering her to be seated at the interview table. "I take it you're employed with a busy schedule."

"Always busy, but I only work thirty hours a week. "It's no problem being here. I want whoever killed Uncle Edgar to be caught. "It's hard to believe he's gone." She paused and clasped her hands together. "I told him often that he mustn't expose his roll of $100 bills when he's out in public."

"Your brother told us the same thing about the roll of bills Mr. Buckingham keeps in his pocket."

"Yes, he held it together with a rubber band. He told me he likes the feel of it, whatever that means. He pays for everything with cash peeling off one of his Ben Franklins from the roll. Maybe that's the reason for the rubber band to keep the bills from flying away in the breeze."

"We interviewed your brother," Karen said. "He believes the reason for your uncle's death is robbery. He gave us a list of items taken—a Mona Lisa painting, gold cuff links, some jewelry and a sterling silver teapot. Are these items your uncle had?"

"Yes. The jewelry is from his late wife's collection. Did they take all the jewelry?"

"Your brother didn't specify the jewelry, but in his opinion the items mentioned including the wad of bills provided the reason for robbery.

"What other reason could there be of someone breaking in his house which is set back from the road some distance? The estate is out in the sticks so to speak."

"Did your uncle have any enemies?" Hal inquired.

"None that I know of. He had become over-conscious of his money during the past year."

"Why is that?"

"He thought Jack was sponging off him, which could be true. Even though Uncle Edgar is..." She stopped and lowered her head for a moment. "*Was* a wealthy man, he didn't like letting go of even a $100 bill. Whenever I took him shopping, he peeled off the Ben Franklins one at a time as though it was his last one."

"Sounds like your uncle and his nephew were at odds."

"He didn't get along with Jack, but that was an ongoing thing. I don't know of anyone in his business dealings that would resort to murder." Sheila searched Hal's eyes. "Do you have any suspects?"

"No... well, none identifiable. Your brother mentioned someone with a butch haircut ogling your uncle during a shopping spree at the mall. A police artist made a sketch of Jack's description, but the person hasn't been identified as yet."

"Of course, everyone's a person of interest at first, especially family members," Karen added. "That's the main purpose of this interview to eliminate family members so we can concentrate on viable suspects."

"I assure you, Detective, I wouldn't harm a hair on his head. I loved my uncle. I do have an alibi of sorts."

Karen held up a palm. "Before we get into alibis, tell us the sequence of events the day your uncle was killed."

Sheila nodded. "It was late afternoon, about five o'clock. I drove to Uncle Ed's house to drop off a book he wanted to borrow. I spoke to him briefly, then left to meet my husband for dinner in town. After dinner, Harry drove me home, then he went back to his office. He's a realtor. I stayed home the rest of the evening working on a photo album with my next door neighbor, Mrs. Turner. The only time I left the house was to make a short drive to the store to purchase needed bathroom supplies. I was gone no more than fifteen, twenty minutes." She smiled. "Poor Mrs. Turner was for a time without toilet paper. The store was Walgreens on Havenhurst Road. The clerk would surely remember me. So I was home for the most part during the time my uncle was killed."

"How far away is your home from senior Buckingham's house?" Hal inquired, posed to write on his notepad.

"A few miles. I'm guessing a fifteen minute drive, depending on the number of signal lights one has to stop for along the way."

Hal wrote on his notepad, then remarked with a bland expression, "According to the medical examiner, the homicide occurred somewhere between seven and eleven p.m. So you could've driven to your Uncle's house after the dinner date with your husband, is that fair to say?"

With raised eyebrows, Sheila grinned. "I don't know if it's fair, but it's reasonable, although it wouldn't leave me much time to kill him. Check with my neighbor, Mrs. Turner."

Karen got up from her chair and turned away toward the mirror. "We know that you and Jack would share a sizable inheritance upon your uncle's death, is that correct?"

"Yes. He took out the trust fund when he adopted us after our mother passed on some years ago."

Hal tapped a pen on the table. "How many years ago?"

"Jack and I were both in high school at the time. I'm 28 now, you figure it out."

Hal glanced at Karen, then back to Sheila with a slight grin. "I was never good at math."

"About nine years ago," Karen said to Hal. "You knew about the trust fund at that time?" she asked Sheila.

"Yes, Uncle Edgar made it clear the trust fund could only be used in the event of his death. He said he promised our mother he would take care of us."

Hal repositioned himself in the chair. "How long were you at your Uncle's house when you dropped off the book?"

"Fifteen minutes at the most. Uncle Ed was having trouble turning on the hallway lamp, but it was simply burnt out bulbs. I replaced the bulbs."

"The lamp has two bulbs?" Hal looked at Sheila, frowning. "Both bulbs were burnt out?"

"Yes, unusual. I need to explain," she said, motioning with her hands. "The hallway lamp and Uncle Ed's reading table lamp are on the same circuit, sort of a two way switch so he can turn the hallway lamp on or off from his reading table. It's a long narrow hallway leading out of the library into the living room which needs illumination."

"He does that from his reading table?" Karen inquired.

"Yes. There are two buttons located on the underside of the table, one for the hallway light and another one for the reading lamp."

"I'm heard of a two-way switch for stairwell lights, but confused that two separate switches are needed under his reading table. How does he know which button is for the two different lights?"

"Uncle Ed likes things easy and uncluttered, which is why he has the buttons under the table out of the way. One button, the larger one, turns on the reading lamp, the smaller button turns on the hallway light. They operate simultaneously—when one goes on, the other one goes off and vice-versa."

"Did you speak to your brother while you were there?"

Sheila nodded. "Briefly. Uncle Ed was very upset with Jack, and mentioned he was considering changing the trust fund, affecting the family inheritance. I told Jack to make peace with Uncle Ed."

"The trust fund is for both of you?" Hal asked.

"Yes, but Uncle Ed was referring to Jack's portion of the inheritance, not mine."

Karen leaned forward. "How serious was this rift between your uncle and your brother?"

"It was an on-going thing. Over the past year, their relationship worsened. As a matter of fact when I spoke to Uncle Ed that afternoon, he felt determined to discontinue Jack's allowance, and wanted him out of the house." Sheila sighed. "Uncle Ed gave him a fair allowance to help out around the house." She shrugged. "Although Uncle Ed's mood changed as quickly as the wind on a gusty day. At the time I didn't take him serious. He even threatened to disown me one time when he got his dander up. But it's true, during the past year, Uncle Ed and Jack argued often. My brother does have an ego; an arrogant attitude. Jack has it in his mind to take advantage of just about everyone to satisfy his need to feel superior."

"Do you think he was involved in your uncle's death?"

"I can't imagine him doing that. I don't know." She paused. "Jack can be very aggressive if he puts his mind to it."

"Did he threaten your uncle or you?"

"He told me one time during an argument to shut my mouth or he'd close it permanently. I didn't take him seriously. After saying it, he grinned. After all the years growing up together, I still can't tell when he's serious."

"This happened recently?"

"Perhaps last year. Sorry, I'm not certain when."

"Do you know if Jack threatened your uncle?"

"Physically?"

After Hal nodded, Sheila remarked, "Not that I'm aware; I don't think so, otherwise Uncle Ed would have said something to me. Jack likes to talk tough, but he's not violent."

Karen leaned forward. "Did you speak with Jack the night of the break in?"

"Yes, he phoned me."

"Did he sound normal other than being upset with your uncle's death?"

"Not really. As is his custom, he controls his emotion exceptionally well." Sheila intertwined her fingers. "He seemed normal on the phone. I was the one upset. It was a shocker to know someone stabbed Uncle Ed. But if you're thinking Jack had something to do with the murder…it's not my place to guess." She looked in Karen's eyes. "If Jack did kill Uncle Ed—I would gain Jack's part of the trust fund if he's found guilty and sent to prison." She cocked her head. "Yes, I know that's a strong motive for me to be involved, but I didn't kill my uncle."

Hal checked his notepad. "Mrs. Livingston, we'll need your fingerprints. Would you be willing to take a polygraph?"

"A polygraph?" After a pause, she added, "Yes. I

have nothing to hide."

"We like to eliminate family members as soon as possible so we can devote needed time for others in the investigation. It won't take long, only an hour of your time."

Karen glanced at Hal indicating she was done with questions.

Hal got up."Mrs. Livingston, that's all the questions for now. Come with us for the polygraph."

They walked Sheila to the testing room and introduced her to the examiner. After a brief explanation, the examiner attached probes to record blood pressure, cardiovascular and breathing activity.

"We'll begin now," the examiner said. "Relax and answer my questions as truthfully as you can. We've all done things in our past we're not especially proud of. Any of your comments are welcome. You needn't feel intimidated. Ma'am, is your name Sheila Livingston?"

"Yes."

"Your uncle's name is Edgar Buckingham?"

"Yes."

"Were you at your uncle's house the day he died?"

"Yes, late afternoon."

"Did you have anything to do with your uncle's death?"

"God, I hope not."

'What do you mean>"

Sheila didn't reply immediately. "I mean I haven't always been the perfect niece. I was with him constantly in his house from the time I was sixteen until my marriage—eleven years I believe it's been that long. There have been arguments..." Shaking her head, she added, "I don't know how to answer your question. It's confusing what you mean."

"Did you stab your uncle in the heart on the evening of ...?"

"Certainly not!"

The examiner continued to probing in detail Sheila's whereabouts between the hours of seven and eleven p.m. She related having lunch with her husband at about seven-thirty, then driving home. She also mentioned driving to the convenience store and back to her home at about ten-thirty.

"Did you travel to your uncle's house after having lunch with your husband or during the time you went to the convenience store?"

Sheila frowned. "I believe I said I was only at my uncle's house in the afternoon. Didn't I say the time was about 4:30 or 5 at the latest?" She shook her head. "I'm nervous."

The examiner watched the stylus as he said, "Then you're not certain?"

"All of these questions remind me of my dear departed uncle. Sorry, I'm not sure of anything at the moment."

The examiner turned off the machine. "We're done now. You may leave. The detectives are waiting for you."

Hal and Karen escorted Sheila to the interview room, then excused themselves while they stepped outside to speak to the examiner. Returning to the interview room, Hal spoke first. "You didn't pass the polygraph."

"I was nervous," Sheila said. "The questions he asked were confusing. I told him I didn't kill my uncle."

"Being nervous may have affected the machine," Karen advised." Frequently, that is the case during interrogation. Don't worry about it."

Hal glanced at Karen, frowning.

After sighing, Sheila asked, "Can I go?"

"You're free to go," Karen replied, not looking at Hal. "Thank you for your time. We may want to talk to you further."

At their desks, Hal questioned Karen. "Why did you let her go? The examiner said she failed the polygraph."

"He said the results were inconclusive, seeing only a few spikes on the graph indicating she lied. And he mentioned her nervousness. It can't be used in court anyway."

"Clearly she's not being altogether truthful. It puts her up there as a prime suspect."

Karen shrugged. "Okay, let's leave it like that then. Let's inform Lieutenant Abrams."

***

."The polygraph results are in question," Hal said. "The examiner said a couple of spikes were prevalent during questioning as to her location during the day of the murder."

"Nerves," Karen said. "During our interview with her, she answered all of our questions and appeared at ease talking about her uncle and her brother. I thought she was open and truthful."

"Definitely a person of interest until we can check out her story," the lieutenant replied. "She *does* have motive. Her inheritance is worth millions which she shares with her brother. Both of them are viable suspects."

"The problem is the nephew has a solid alibi. He

was watching the movie Avatar; witnesses confirming that he was there," Karen advised. "And there's the $100 dollar bill Jack cashed at the theater. The cashier remembers him giving her the Ben Franklin.

"Mrs. Livingston admitted that her brother was free-loading on Buckingham senior. She said the brother and uncle argued frequently. And just before the old man was stabbed to death, Buckingham senior informed his nephew of withdrawing the inheritance, according to her, stopping his allowance and kicking him out of the house."

Hal gazed at Karen, nodding, then grinned.

The lieutenant glanced at Hal with a look of confusion.

"I told Hal he needs to smile more," she said to Abrams.

Hal rolled his eyes. "Here it comes," he said to the lieutenant, "More of her kinesics."

Karen continued in all seriousness. "A smile is more than it seems. Actually, a smiling person is usually judged as more attractive, pleasant to be around, sincere, and *sociable*," she emphasized the word to Hal. "A smiling person invites others into the conversation." Karen continued with a smile, "A smile is a quick and easy way to tell others you are open to their comments, eager to listen to whatever they have to say."

Karen was about to say more, when Abrams held up his hand. "Interesting, but let's return to the Buckingham case."

Hal stifled an inner groan. "The sister gave us a bit if double talk in that arena. She said the old man was over-conscious of his money and even threatened to disown her at one time."

The Lieutenant glanced at Hal, surprised. "You're talkative this morning."

"I think he asked more questions of the Sheila Livingston than I did," Karen added, glancing at her partner.

"This case makes me think." Hal said with raised eyebrows, but without a smile. "Especially the sister and brother's open testimony. They don't seem to care whether or not we think of them as suspects."

"Good. Keep thinking." Abrams tapped a pen on his desk. "Are you suggesting they were in alliance with one another? What about her alibi?"

"It's iffy." Karen leaned her head from one side to the other. "We'll have to check with the principles involved, the neighbor and her husband."

"Lieutenant Abrams sighed. "It looks like what we have is heavy circumstantial and light physical evidence. Well, continue on. Bring in the nephew for another interview. See if we can get a polygraph."

***

Hal suspected that Jack deliberately delayed his appointment at the station house bent on delaying the scheduled polygraph examination, but when he showed up, he was all smiles, and gave a reasonable excuse for his tardiness. The polygraph examiner set up his equipment, ready to conduct the session when authorized to proceed.

Dressed in white, pleated trousers with a sleeveless purple shirt, monogrammed with his initials above a buttoned pocket, Jack moved into the interrogation room with a confident stride. Without a word, he sat down at the interview table, crossed his legs, placed his palms flat on the surface, then leaned back into his chair. "I'm ready for the hangman's noose," he said in a tone of smugness. "By the way, if you're expecting a confession, you're dreaming like Dorothy in 'Wizard of Oz'. I'm sure yours truly is a prime suspect even with my solid alibi." He grinned. "But even if I did kill old tight wad Edgar, you'd never be able to prove it." He patted the table with his hands in a drum beat, glancing at Hal then Karen.

Karen presented Jack with a welcoming face. "You seem very confident."

"Confidence is my middle name. Actually I'm looking forward to the examiner's questions. I *love* to debate." He lifted his chin in a pose of self-importance.

Hal acknowledged the comment with a nod. "Except this isn't a debate."

"Mr. Buckingham, you're not a suspect yet," Karen advised, "only a person of interest, but your comment does raise suspicion."

"I can't respond unless you call me Jack."

"We like to eliminate family members first..."

"Yes, I know about that. Family members do have a high degree of involvement in crimes of passion. I watch lots of crime shows, especially homicides where conviction depends on hard evidence." A subtle grin crept across his lips. "Allow me to inform you I'm knowledgeable of police investigation, but having said that, I intend to cooperate with your interrogation fully."

"Your frankness is recognized," Karen replied with a grin. "Together we can find the real killer of your uncle." She pushed a voice recorder to the center of the table. "Then you won't mind if we record this session."

"I would be disappointed if you didn't."

"Well, we'll get right into the meat of the meeting," Hal said, looking at his notes. Some of the information may be duplication, but just answer the questions as best you can. "What time did you leave your uncle's house to go to the movie?"

"About quarter to seven. I stopped in the library to ask if he wanted anything before I left. He said he didn't. Unc turned on his reading lamp and resumed reading 'Gone with the Wind'. I left and drove straight to the theater. Arrived there at 7:15."

Hal nodded. "We checked the cashier at the Harkins Theater. She remembers you cashed a $100 bill as payment when you entered the theater. And she verified that you spoke to her at about 9:50, at the end of the movie. Also the food attendant remembers speaking to you at about 8:30 during the middle of the film when you ordered a drink and popcorn." Hal cocked his head slightly. "So your alibi, although strong, is not flawless, meaning you could have left the theater, driven home, stabbed your uncle, and returned to the movie."

"Good, good. But you have no witnesses observing me leaving the theater, seeing me during the drive home or my return to the theater between the hours of 7:30 and 10:15. And I have both the concession stand attendant and the cashier verifying my presence at the theater." One cheek rose gently. "Am I correct about that?"

"Correct about the time." Karen looked into his eyes. "And you are right, we have no witnesses seeing you leave the theater from the time you got there and when you left."

Jack placed his hands together. "It doth appear ye have only circumstantial evidence. In a court of law, speculation without hard evidence amounts to reasonable doubt, wouldn't you agree?"

"Yes, but you have a motive. A million dollars worth."

"And I'm sure you've discovered that my dear sister has an even greater motive."

Hal nodded. "Yes, Sheila is also a person of interest. And her alibi isn't perfect, either."

Jack tilted his head with a teasing expression. "Just between you and me and the lamp post, she's too squeamish to stick a knife in Edgar's chest. If she gets a sliver in her finger she goes to the hospital. I remind you, our inheritance was conceived of years ago." He raised his chin with a big smile. "But having said that, you never know what someone will do in a moment of crisis."

Karen leaned forward. "The thought did occur to us that both of you, you and your sister, could be in partnership of your uncle's murder."

"Good thinking." Jack raised one eyebrow. "But keep this in mind, had Sis and I considered that probability of the inheritance as a motive for murder, the deed would have been instigated long before this time."

"We'll be back," Hal said, getting up."

Jack laughed. "You're going to consult with your supervisor."

"Can we get you a drink?" Karen asked.

"Yeah, a thick chocolate milkshake with a sprinkling of cashews."

"How about a diet Pepsi?"

"That'll work." He grinned. "Say hi to Lieutenant Abrams for me."

Hal and Karen entered the adjoining room observing Abrams shaking his head. "Arrogance beyond belief. He's enjoying himself."

They looked at Jack through the one-way mirror. Leaning back in his chair, legs spread wide apart, Jack gazed at the one-way mirror with a twisted grin.

They discussed the interview. All three agreed that both Jack and Sheila were prime suspects, but there wasn't enough evidence for the D.A. to indict either of them for murder, whether individually or together as accomplices.

"I favor Jack," Hal said. "He has the mindset of someone on a mission."

"No priors," the lieutenant added. "It's as if his goal is to pull off the perfect murder. He's smart. I think we're in for a tough fight."

"What we need is hard evidence," Abrams said. "Take another look at the crime scene photos. Interview anyone that might give us a clue. Let's hope the nephew fails the polygraph. It will give us some leverage to put on the pressure. Right now as it stands, the sister and brother are holding all the cards."

CHAPTER TEN

AFTER RETURNING TO the interrogation room, they asked Jack if he would take a polygraph. He agreed without hesitation, and told them he would take it easy on the examiner. They escorted Jack to a conference room where the machine was set up, and introduced him to Nathan McMasters.

"You're in good hands, Jack." Hal turned toward the door. "We'll talk to you after the test."

McMasters pointed to a chair next to the polygraph. "Have a seat and relax. I'll get you hooked up in short order, sir."

"Hey, we're friends. Call me Jack."

McMasters nodded. "Okay. I'll explain the procedure, and will ask you a few preliminary questions before we begin."

"Don't bother telling me about the procedure. I know all about it." Jack's grin showed a touch of pride.

"You've taken the test?"

"No, but all you've ever wanted to know about the polygraph exam is on the internet. Even how to render one's answers inconclusive."

"Really?" McMasters smiled. "Well then, Jack, it seems as though I'll need to be extra sharp when questioning you."

"By all means. I would be disappointed if you weren't. Just a friendly forewarning that this exercise is a waste of time." Jack replied, smirking, then added with a gesture of indifference, "But you have a job to do, I understand that, so let us get on with the game."

"I'll hook you up now. The leads will record physiological data—breathing, cardiovascular and sweat gland activity." After attaching the leads, McMasters asked, "Is your name Jack Buckingham?"

"Yes."

"Are you the nephew of Edgar Buckingham?"

"I've thought about that. Now that he's dead is he still my uncle? It's a situation of is or was, don't you think? I mean I can't very well say he *is* my uncle in now that he's physically gone. On the other hand speaking of him as a *was* appears to be a verbal misnomer since the old man is dead."

"Sir, no explanation, please answer the question."

"In a word, yes."

"Have you stolen anything from your employer exceeding the value of $50?"

"No."

"Since the age of 18, have you been arrested for drunk driving?"

"No"

"Have you ever had your driver's license suspended or revoked?"

"No."

"In general, how would you define the relationship you had with your uncle Buckingham—amiable or troublesome?"

"I only have two choices?"

"Please, sir, which is prevalent?"

"It depends on the situation." Jack glanced up at McMasters. "Sometimes I loved him; sometimes I hated him, you know what I mean?" Jack eyebrows lifted. "When he gave me money I loved him, but when he refused me money, I hated him."

"Please, no explanations, just answer the questions in a direct manner. One more preliminary question. In the last five years did you commit any serious crime?"

"Shaving with a dull razor."

"Sir?"

Jack spoke the words distinctly, "In my entire life, never, did I commit a serious crime, ever."

McMasters shrugged, adjusted the recorder volume, then turned on the polygraph machine. "We'll begin now recording. Relax and please answer the questions yes or no. I need to tell you the polygraph examination is voluntary. You'll be asked to sign a waiver at the end of the examination. Do you understand?"

Jack nodded. "Yes. Let's get on with it."

"Okay. Relax, be comfortable in your seat, and your first question is, "Will you reply to the questions truthfully?"

"Yes."

"Did you have anything to do with your uncle's death?"

"No."

"You claim you were watching a movie during the time of your uncle's death. At anytime, did you leave the theater before the movie ended and return to your uncle's house?"

"My answer is absolutely, unequivocally in the negative."

"Please, sir, answer yes or no."

Grinning, Jack said, "You mean the question you just asked me?"

"Yes, of course. Are you deliberately trying to confuse the machine?"

"Who me?"

McMasters shrugged. "Mr. Buckingham, during the evening of your uncle's death, did you take any of your uncle's possessions?"

"No."

McMasters paused for a minute, watching the polygraph needle as the paper moved along the track. "Did you stab your uncle with a hunting knife?"

"No."

McMasters turned off the machine and unhooked the leads. "We're finished."

"How'd I do?"

I won't know until I review the roll, but there was some unusual activity when asked if you would reply to the questions truthfully, and when asked if you stabbed your uncle."

"Hmmm, I don't recall the question relative to the stabbing. Did I answer it?"

McMasters didn't reply. He turned off the audio recorder. "You're free to go."

Jack got up and stretched. "So, there's nothing significant in my answers, I take it. In other words I passed the test, right?"

"Lt. Abrams will let you know."

"I'm sure he will."

"I'll escort you back to the interrogation room. Thank you for your time, Mr. Buckingham."

"It's been a blast."

Within fifteen minutes, McMaster joined Karen and Hal looking at Jack through the one-way mirror of the interrogation room.

"Did he pass the test?" Hal asked.

"He knows how to turn my questions into trivia eliminating the effects of lying," McMasters said, shaking his head. "I believe he killed his uncle. He's smart. All I can say is the results are inconclusive. He sees the polygraph as a game with only a few spikes, but in inappropriate places."

Karen leaned forward. "So whatever questions you ask him about the murder, his answers are make-believe to him—is that what you're saying?"

"Exactly. Based on that, he passed the exam. I'll fill in Lt. Abrams."

Karen and Hal joined Jack in the interrogation room. She gave Jack a waiver form to sign. Patting the table with one hand, he gazed at Hal and Karen. "Are you disappointed that I passed the exam?"

"Inconclusive," Karen said, glancing at her notepad. "But yes, you passed. Congratulations. There *was* some physical activity of the tape when asked about the means of your uncle's death."

Jack leaned back in his chair, hands behind his head. "I take it you think I lied, which means you suspect me of having something to do with the old geezer's death."

"Not just something," Hal remarked. "You are a prime suspect in the murder of your uncle."

"Ah, good. I was wondering when you would accuse me in person." He smiled. "But you're between a rock and a hard place. You have no proof, no evidence whatsoever. And there is the question of my sister's involvement. Did she stab Uncle Edgar with the left or right hand?" Jack laughed. "Allow me to remind you I saw a man staring at Unc when he peeled off a Ben

Franklin to buy a magnifying glass at the mall. Now there's your prime suspect—the guy with the butch haircut."

"We'll bring in an artist to sketch a composite of the man with a butch," Karen said, "based on your excellent memory, sir."

Jack stared at Karen for a moment. "Not sir, call me Jack." He laughed. "Interviewing mall employees with the sketch will keep you occupied for some time," he added, with a devilish grin.

"But the game isn't over yet," Hal said in a rare display of emotion. "This case will be given every advantage the law allows!"

"And we do have evidence," Karen added. "A chemical analysis was done on the rubber band and the $100 dollar bill you used as payment at the Harkins Theater. Both had the same chemicals confirmed by the lab's infrared-spectroscopy instrumentation."

Jack scoffed. "That only proves that I was at the movie."

"True. But it adds to the speculation that you took the roll of Ben Franklins when you killed your uncle."
"And did you find my finger prints on the rubber band?"

"No, only because the band is a mere half inch wide, highly improbable forensics would get an identifiable print of your forefinger or thumb."

"Then the rubber band is about as useful as tit on a bull if you'll pardon the expression." Jack's eyes rolled up. "There must be a hundred-thousand rubber bands like it—yellowish, half inch wide, of various diameters as rubber bands go." Jack gazed at Karen. "You should know about rubber bands since you ladies use them to tie back your hair, right?"

"We do, but our hair ties are much smaller, tubular and no more than an inch diameter if you want specifics. Are you looking for ladies' hair ties for yourself?"

Jack took a deep breath, then managed a sheepish grin. "Touché."

While Karen and Jack continued discussing rubber bands, Hal thought about the poker party homicide, recalling Virgil Blydair's slight-of-hand trickery. Replacing the poisoned beer can with the victim's beer can while redirecting everyone's attention elsewhere, could have been the in the hole for a not guilty verdict. But the deception failed to accomplish the perfect crime because Virgil didn't anticipate his wife's revealing testimony. *Mental note, Hal: If you're going to commit a crime do it without witnesses.*

The present case had a better chance of becoming an unsolved crime because of no witnesses and little evidence plus a credible alibi for the prime suspect. Hal mused to himself, enjoying the unfolding of events of the Buckingham murder. Not only were they challenging, but he anticipated the possibility of the perfect crime forthcoming due to the cleverness of the perpetrator—one Jack Buckingham. And yet Jack's arrogance could be his downfall. On the one hand solving the murder—a big plus in itself; on the other side of the coin, Hal's yearning to see the perfect crime realized struck a pleasurable note. Even more so, if it was Hal's perfect crime.

"Hal?... Hal?"

Hal raised his head, waved a hand, then got up. "That's all the questions I have," he said after a long pause."

"I have nothing more now," Karen said to Jack. "You're free to leave after the police artist finishes the composite of the man with a butch haircut. We'll be talking with you again, soon."

"I'm delighted to be of service." Jack bowed, smiling wide "A good day to you both. Call me anytime," he added, standing up to his full height in a pose depicting supreme confidence. Karen escorted Jack out of the room into the hands of the sketch artist and another detective.

***

Hal and Karen joined the lieutenant in his office. They sat down in chairs across from his desk. Abrams looked at a folder on his desk. "McMasters informed me of the nephew's polygraph, in effect, he passed it. So, where does that leaves us?"

"Behind the eight ball," Hal replied. "I'm convinced he did it. We're dealing with one smart jock."

Karen shrugged. "He has an alibi seeing the movie Avatar with witnesses confirming that he was there. The cashier at the theater confirmed that it was Jack she spoke to at the end of the movie at exactly 9:45 p.m. Also, an attendant at the food counter said he talked with Jack at 8:25, about the midway point of the movie. Substantiated when we showed him a photo of Jack."

"He could have slipped out of the movie at just about any time," Abrams said. "What's the distance from Buckingham's house to the theater?"

"About 20 miles from the Buckingham's garage to the Harkins' parking lot, a four lane road not heavily traveled." Hal pulled a small calculator from his jacket pocket, then started punching numbers. "It would take less than 30 minutes driving the speed limit."

"We checked the dealer where the Dodge Nitro was purchased," Karen explained. "Combined city and highway driving—14 mph. The tank holds 16 gallon."

The lieutenant frowned. "Only 14 mph?"

"According to the manufacturer, that type Nitro was a special order, eight cylinders, with extra power for towing, very low EPA rating."

Hal punched some more numbers. "So, four gallons of gas represents one-quarter of a tank. Which means a two way trip would amount to eight gallons."

"A CSI officer checked the gas gauge of the Nitro at the homicide scene." Karen added. "The officer said the needle was on the three-quarters mark. Jack said he'd stopped at a Chevron station on the way home from the mall and filled his tank, confirmed by a receipt."

The lieutenant shook his head. "Meaning he could have made an extra trip with his car?"

"Had he driven back to the Buckingham house during the movie, he would have used an extra four gallons," Hal said, punching more numbers on his calculator. "The gauge would have shown one-half full had Jack driven back home to kill his uncle during the movie."

Abrams smiled. "And according to the CSI officer, it only showed three-quarters, right?"

Both Hal and Karen nodded.

"So, it indicates an extra trip to the Buckingham estate didn't occur."

There was silence in the room as the lieutenant, Karen and Hal appeared in deep thought. Outside, detective Gillan looked in at Hal sitting with his head down as he passed by the room. He shook his head, then continued on to his desk.

"Unless," Abrams began, looking up. "The nephew made an extra trip back home and then added the four gallons from a gasoline can after killing his uncle."

"We think that's what he did," Karen replied, "but there are no witnesses that observed him on the road or at the Buckingham home during the time of the murder."

"And no gas can was found, either," Hal said."

"Another possibility. Maybe he stabbed his uncle *before* he went to the movie?"

"We checked the uncle's cell phone," Karen advised. "He made a three minute call at 8:55 p.m." She held up her hands in a show of irritation. "He was alive when Jack left for the movie, alive at least until 8:55. Jack would have been entering the theater at that time give or take five minutes."

"So we only have speculation," Abrams said, scowling. "Anything new on the Ben Franklin the nephew cashed at the theater?"

"The lab determined the bill was the one from Edgar Buckinghams's roll of Ben Franklins, and was used by Jack at the theater."

"The lieutenant frowned. "How so?"

"Forensics confirmed the same chemicals in both the rubber band and the Ben Franklin. That Jack used at the theater. That fact can go either way in a court of law to our advantage or Jack's. Unfortunately, it only proves Jack cashed the bill at the theater. Chemical analysis from the lab ties the $100 bill with the rubber band, but not the rubber band with Jack.

"Did they test for latent prints on the rubber band?"

"Apparently not. The rubber band is only three-quarters of an inch wide, not much room to get a print. I assumed they checked it out and found nothing."

Abrams angled his head to one side. "Have the lab test for prints on the rubber band, even partial prints. We need every tidbit checked. What about the sister; anything new?"

"Sheila admitted that her brother was free-loading on the old man Buckingham. She said they argued daily. And according to her, just before the old man was stabbed to death, he informed the nephew of withdrawing the inheritance." Karen paused to collect her thoughts. "But the sister was also part of the inheritance. She had motive, more to gain from the inheritance than Jack"

"Does she have an alibi on the evening of the murder?"

"Yes, and no." Karen angled her head to one side. "Her husband confirms that Sheila and he had dinner at a restaurant in town about seven o'clock, which we confirmed. The husband dropped her home, then he went back to work. She claimed she spent the rest of the evening pasting pictures in a photo album. Said that her neighbor, a Mrs. Turner helped her. I spoke with the neighbor. She confirmed she and Sheila's worked on the photo album, except for a fifteen or twenty minute window when Sheila left the house on an errand, but…"

"Don't tell me—this Mrs. Turner isn't sure when the niece left or returned," Abrams said, grimacing.

Karen smiled. "Almost her exact words. The husband got home about eleven that evening. We couldn't verify the whereabouts of the husband during the entire evening, but a co-worker thought he was at his office most of the evening."

"You suspect complicity of the husband?"

"Not really." Karen glanced at Hal, then back to Abrams. "He seems open, cooperative and willing to take a polygraph and submit to fingerprints."

"I agree," Hal said. "The husband isn't involved."

Abrams scoffed. "OH? You know that for a fact, do you?"

A mild grin erupted across Hal's lips. "According to his body language...and kinesics," He paused grinning mildly at Karen. "It's doubtful they were in league with one another."

Seeing Karen smiling, Abrams shook his head with an expression of futility.

Suddenly, Hal's thoughts turned grim as he recalled a meeting that evening at Michael's home to listen to Rodney's piano recital. Listening to his godson's mediocre performance had to be as desirable as the conversation at dinner time, always the same—Michael's accomplishments. Then on the way home, Evelyn's snide remarks comparing him unfavorably with Michael. He could predict with accuracy what she would say.

"He has a master's degree, works for a fortune 500 company and has an excellent salary. Michael volunteers his time as a high school tutor, helps at a local Red Cross facility and has a lucrative hobby as woodworking artisan."

Added to the nauseam, she would end with her favorite phrase, "And he spends time with his family."

"Okay. The niece definitely has opportunity and motive," Abrams said turning his attention to Hal. "She's a small woman. Do you think she has the strength to plunge a knife in the victim's chest? Hal, what do you thing? Hal? You're staring at the wall pic like it's a ghost."

Blinking, Hal nodded. "In a rage, yes. She's small, but her 100 pounds in back of a forward thrust could do it. The medical examiner concurs. Although Jack, the bigger of the two, would have more power."

"What about the chance the nephew and niece are co-conspirators?"

Karen nodded. "Could be. But no physical evidence to speak of, mostly speculation." She raised her eyebrows in an expression of disdain. "Jack seems to be the one who relishes his role as a prime suspect. It's as though he's trying to commit the perfect murder and proving it with his intelligence. "

Abrams rubbed his hands together. "The Assistant D.A. said we haven't enough to indict either one of them. If this case went to trial right now, the only thing we can be certain of from a jury is a not-guilty verdict because of reasonable doubt. God! I pray this case doesn't wind up in the dead file." The lieutenant gritted his teeth. "We have an iffy proposition of opportunity for either the nephew or niece, and only vague circumstantial evidence. Detectives, we got zilch!"

Karen leaned forward. "We got one big thing, sir, motive. Millions in inheritance."

The lieutenant nodded. "You're right. That should keep us engaged. Alright, check with the neighbors, anyone that may have seen something. And check with the lab. See if they can get any DNA from the rubber band to tie it with the nephew. What we need is solid evidence that one of them stabbed Buckingham senior."

Glancing out the window, Hal noticed two sparrows on a tree branch in what appeared to be a battle over territory, he guessed. More probably they were fighting over who was the more dominant. Instantly, the dark memory of his childhood surfaced again. He remembered it all too well. This time he felt forced to go into the details of the circumstances trying to understand if what he did was the cause of the beating—the legacy of his failure to speak out.

***

At the time, he thought he was doing good in school. He wasn't sure when his grades began to fall, but it must have been in fifth grade when his brother was praised for getting A's on all of his subjects. After receiving a reprimand from his teacher, Hal went home, his report card showing failing grades in the social sciences. He remembered the long walk home hesitant to see his father's reaction.

When he walked in the door, his father and Michael were playing chess. His father got up and patted Michael on the head. "Pretty soon you'll be as good as me." Holding out his hand, he said to Hal, "Let me see the report card. Your teacher called me about your grades."

Visibly shaken, Hal gave him the report card.

"What have you got to say for yourself?"

Hal tried to explain but was stopped in mid-sentence. Just two days before, he'd been hit across the head for mentioning his fear of speaking out.

"When I want an answer, I'll ask you, do you understand?" his father had said. A heavy blow knocked him backward against the wall. He knew Michael wouldn't come to his aid. He felt helpless knowing his father's unpredictable temperament. Why was he always the bad son?

In the living room, Hal's father continued scolding him because of his poor grades. But then the subject changed.

The father scowled. "Why are you so damned quiet suddenly? Thinking of revenge? After a pause, the father said, "Well speak up! Well, what have you got to say?"

Michael intervened, but not for Hal. "Hal don't know how to say things."

"He better learn."

Wanting to be free to speak out in his defense like his brother Michael, Hal opened his mouth, but paused for a moment. Then he tried to explain. "Father, I try to talk in class, but some of the other kids won't let me. The teacher doesn't …"

"Excuses! Lies probably. From now on, the rule is you're to be seen and not heard. Do you understand?"

In a moment of rare courage, Hal questioned his father's rule. "But Michael can say things and …"

"I said shut your mouth!" Hal recalled rage in his father's face, then the deliberate movement of his father taking off his belt, standing firm, legs apart with a full swing of his arm striking the body at random. Against the wall, Michael ducked his head and held out his hands for protection. The blows continued until his father stopped to gain his breath. The sting of the blows weren't half as bad as the pain he felt from his father's betrayal.

Exhaustion stopped the beating on Hal's back and he heard his father's words repeated over and over in his mind. "Go to your room. Don't come out until I say so."

***

He felt moisture in his eyes and closed them until he heard Abrams slap the desk top a few times. "Are you with us?"

Hal looked up. "Yeah. Just thinking."

"We're all done here," the lieutenant said. "You two can get back to the Buckingham case."

On the way to their desks, Karen asked, "Are you okay? You look a little flustered."

"I'll survive, I think."

"Do you want to talk about it?"

He paused, then shook his head. Talking about his feelings was the source of his affliction—a given like the rise of the sun in the morning sky. It seemed like the only solution would be achieving some miraculous goal and receiving the accolades that go with it. He sat down at his desk and glanced at Karen. "Let's go over Jack's interview one more time. Maybe something miraculous will pop up."

CHAPTER ELEVEN

JACK WALKED THROUGHOUT Edgar's house scrutinizing the rooms. Now that the large one-story dwelling would soon be his, he needed to determine whether to make physical changes to suit his fancy or sell it. The residence sat on an acre of land worth nearly as much as the house, including the apple orchard.

He felt slighted by his uncle because Sheila's inheritance was more than his. But money wasn't his only motive; always there was the challenge of accomplishing the improbable. He'd thought about it before—Sheila's death. Only thirty-years-old, she would not be dying of natural causes any time soon.

Concerning the money angle, he would only receive half of the brokerage firm if she died of natural causes or suicide, which was stipulated in the trust. And he would get zilch if her death was attributed to homicide. Unfortunately, suicide as a cause of her death would be hard to sell to a jury because there was nothing in her life suggesting despondency. Her husband and most of her friends could point out that Sheila enjoyed every minute of her existence; the very last thought contemplated would be ending her life by her own hand.

Which left her death by natural causes the only option. He cancelled his first thought, blaming a would-be burglary on her death. He needed something more challengingly intrigued with the idea of committing the perfect murder. Jack went to his room and searched the internet for causes of death. He pulled up a medical examiner web site and read through the numerous cases of death by drowning.

From a nearby water cooler, he poured hot water into a cup, dipping it in a tea bag. He watched the bag float on the surface of the water. He smiled. Death by drowning, yes, a common cause of death. Respiratory impairment from submersion in liquid. Air and oxygen can't get into the lungs and the victim suffocates. He sipped from his cup. Most of her friends knew she loved her heart-shaped pool, knew that she went swimming nearly every day.

There was a catch. What would cause her to be immersed under water for six minutes? There was only one viable possibility—a blow to the head, causing her to fall into the pool, unconscious. He'd found a case where a man slipped on the deck, fell, hitting his head on the edge of the decking and tumbled into the pool. His death was assigned asphyxia due to a slip and fall into the pool, rendering him unconscious where he perished by drowning.

Tasks went through his mind in repetitious order—get invited to swim in Sheila's pool, the meeting undisclosed to anyone else. Hit her with a rock to the forehead assimilating a fall on her head, rendering her unconscious. Put her in the pool, hold her head under until unresponsive. Check her pulse. Escape. The time would have to be in the evening, so he could escape without being seen by neighbors.

Jack stared at the far wall, thinking. What reason could he fib about meeting her alone in the evening at her house? The police investigation into Edgar's death, of course. He spoke out loud as though he were having a conversation with Sheila on the phone.

"Well, I haven't been swimming in a while. I'd like to take advantage of this warm weather we're having and get some exercise. The evening would be preferable, just the two of us to discuss something important." He paused for effect. "The police investigation. Something's come up of a serious nature. It's best I didn't say anything over the phone...what? Well the subject has to do with you and I as suspects and involves Howard. Don't say anything to Howard. Secrecy at this point is vital. I'll explain everything in detail when I see you."

"What evening this week are you available?" he repeated into the mouthpiece. "Why the evening time? Dear Sis, need I remind you of my ugly scars. At night they are less visible. Thank you." Pause. "Wednesday at eight p.m. is good. Will Howard be working? He won't be home, you'll be alone. Good. Hey Sis, will you be joining me for a swim?" Pause. "I'm relieved." He laughed. "Just in case you have to rescue me from drowning. Wouldn't that be the cat's pajamas—me dying in your pool? The police would have a field day on that occurrence of possible homicide."

Jack finished his tea. He'd have to plan everything down to the smallest detail. With two family deaths within a short time, and a large inheritance in the mix, the implication of his involvement would be like flashing railroad lights to the detectives. But the law was on his side. Even if indicted for murder, without eyewitnesses, he needed only reasonable doubt to convince a jury of his innocence. Besides, he loved the challenge of deception, and hoped Reiner and Holmes would be the detectives assigned to the case. It would give him exceptional pleasure in talking to them about Sheila's unfortunate accident.

***

Hal and Karen met with Lieutenant Abrams in his office. They sat down in chairs across from Abrams' desk. The lieutenant had his hands clasped. "I hope you have some good news... anything."

Karen nodded. "We spoke at length to the principle attorney of the law firm that set-up the trust fund. Edgar Buckingham had no children. He left his entire estate to Jack and Sheila, but not exactly in equal amounts."

"What's the total amount of the Buckingham's estate?"

"Well over four million dollars." Karen looked at her notepad. Jack gets the house and property worth one million in current pricing. Plus he gets one-third of the Brokerage business if certain conditions are met."

Hal nodded. "Here's where it gets interesting. If Sheila dies prematurely, her demise must be attributed to either suicide or natural death assuming Jack survives his sister, Jack would receive one-third of the brokerage business, but nothing at all if Sheila death is attributed to homicide. The business is worth about two and one-half million in current stock prices."

"Whoa!" Abrams leaned forward, frowning. "Am I hearing some sort of forewarning by Buckingham senior suggesting that his nephew might kill his niece?"

"There is that inference," Karen replied. "There is no such stipulation against the sister if Jack dies prematurely."

Abrams shook his head. "Give me the figures

again."

Karen referred to her notebook. "You'll probably want to write this down. It's a little complicated."

The lieutenant grabbed a pen and paper. "Fire away."

The trust fund total at current prices is a hair above $4,000,000. Jack gets the house and property worth $1,000,000 the SUV, and a small percentage of the uncle's brokerage business, 1/6 of $3,000,000, which comes to a cool $500,000." So Jack's total is $1,500,000.

"Sheila's portion of the trust is 5/6ths of $3,000,000 brokerage business or $2,500,000. These figures are basic to the trust when the uncle dies regardless of the cause of death."

Hal nodded with raised eyebrows. "Here's where it gets interesting. There's a stipulation in the trust if either sibling dies prematurely after the uncle's demise. Jack would receive 1/3rd of the brokerage business for approximately $1,000,000, providing Sheila dies from natural causes. That ups Jack's portion of the inheritance to 2 million. If her death is a homicide, Jack gets nothing of the brokerage business, zilch. But her demise must be attributed to either suicide, accidental or natural death for Jack to receive the additional brokerage money. The business is worth about $3,000,000 in current stock prices."

"What if Jack dies prematurely? What's the figures in that event?

"If Jack dies prematurely, Sheila inherits the entire estate. $4,000,000. Nothing is mentioned about a violent death, but in any event, Sheila would gain his portion of the basic trust, the house, property and all of the brokerage business."

"The niece is clearly the front runner in money incentive." Abrams said, tapping his pen on the desk."

"Yes, the sister has a lot more to gain," Karen added as a passing thought. "At this point in the investigation, either one could be a perpetrator or a victim.

Frowning, Abrams rubbed his head. "Does that negate the two as co-conspirators?"

"Not at all," Hal replied. "Both had opportunity and motive to kill the old man. It's reasonable to think they conspired together to kill their uncle."

"We're back to supposing that either one could now become a victim, due to the other sibling wanting more of the inheritance. Who do you favor in that circumstance?"

"I'm thinking Sheila," Karen answered quickly. "Only because she has more bucks to gain."

"I favor Jack." Hal paused. "He seems more devious."

The lieutenant scowled. "Devious? Is that a technical term, Detective Reiner?"

Hal shrugged, realizing the poor choice of adjectives.

"We haven't solved Edgar Buckingham's homicide yet," Abrams commented. "Here we are conjuring up more obstacles. Okay, let's put the possibility of the sister or brother as victims on the back burner and concentrate on what we do know for certain—Edgar Buckingham's murder. Double check their alibis and check with friends and neighbors if there were any suspicious characters seen at the Buckingham house around the time of the homicide.

***

While watching the news reports on TV, Jack put on dark-colored pants and his pull-over sweatshirt with a hood. He opened a handbag, dropping in latex disposable gloves, and jeans. He held a brick in the air and spoke to the reporter on the screen. "This is the murder weapon, my good man. What's that you ask?" Jack laughed. "Yes. I smack her a rock-solid blow to the head, and she falls to the pool deck striking her head on the tile. I rub blood from the wound onto the decking, which should convince the most methodical detective of her *accidental* death. How does she die? I hold her head under water until she's dead. Yes, thank you, it is a bit clever."

With flair, Jack dropped the rock into a cloth bag, turned off the TV, and headed out to his Nitro. After mixing dirt and water until muddy, he applied the gook to his rear license plate, covering the numbers. He fired up the SUV and drove out of the entrance road assured no one would recognize him. It was dark, but he took side roads to Sheila's house. Ten minutes to eight, he observed on the control panel. On schedule. And there was little illumination from the crescent moon. He parked two blocks away and walked lively along the sidewalk. As he approached Sheila's house, he saw a couple walking on the same sidewalk toward him. He stooped down pretending to tie his shoelaces as they past his position. He got up smiling, patting his back with a hand. "A bit of cleverness there, Jack," he said, continuing walking forward at good pace.

At the front door he pressed the door bell button and heard the familiar intermittent buzzing which he knew sounded out in the back yard. Soon the door opened. In her robe, Sheila stared at him. "Where are your bathing trunks?"

"In my handbag," he said with a dutiful grin. I'll change in your cabana at poolside, okay?"

She invited him in.

"Are you in your bathing suit?" he asked.

"Of course." She raised her eyebrows. "I usually wear a robe when I answer the front door. I've been in the pool taking my customary ten laps waiting for you."

He looked around. "Howard isn't here?"

"Correct. He's not here as you requested working at his office downtown." Scowling, she added, "You said you didn't want him present while we talked."

"Right. I'll explain the secrecy."

She led off toward the back door. "So what's this important information regarding Howard?"

"I'll tell you all about it at the pool," he said, walking quickly toward the cabana. "Hey! That water looks refreshing. You're coming in with me, right?" He mimicked a dry laugh. "I want you close by in case I have to be rescued."

Sheila rolled her eyes, then took off her robe, and stepped onto the pool decking. "Well, change into your trunks."

Jack pointed at the steps that led to the shallow part of the rectangular pool. "What's that there on the edge of the decking?" He followed her to the edge of the pool.

She bent down and looked. "What do you see?"

As she stood up turning her head, Jack already had the brick in his hand. With a full swing of his arm, he struck her in the forehead. She fell to the decking, unconscious. The blow caused bleeding. He wiped some of the blood on the raised edging to make it appear that she had slipped and fallen striking her forehead on the tile.

After Removing his pants and sweat shirt, he rolled her into the water, then jumped in, and held her head under the surface with both hands. He could feel her struggle to get free, but maintained sufficient force for what he thought to be over six minutes. He had read that amount of time was the minimum for asphyxiation. He checked her pulse. Convinced she was dead, he got out of the pool, put on his clothes and flip flops, then shoved the brick into his handbag.

Looking around the pool area, he checked to see there were no tell-tale signs of him being there. He moved swiftly into the house, to the front door, opening it a crack and observed the front and surrounding houses. No one visible. Locking the door from the inside, he stepped out, closed the door, then shoved the hood over his head, and proceeded up the sidewalk at a leisurely pace. He met no one on the way to his car. Glancing around the neighborhood one last time, he jumped into the Nitro. *Good job done,* he said to himself turning the ignition key. *Even Sherlock Holmes would be impressed by his ingenuity.*

***

Lt. Abrams stared at his laptop screen, shaking his head. "Unbelievable." He looked at Karen and Hal with an expression of astonishment. "It's just hard to fathom that the nephew, a prime suspect in the murder of his uncle, would have the audacity to murder his sister. He's either dim-witted or brash beyond belief."

"He's not dim-witted," Karen voiced her opinion. "He knows exactly what he's doing at all times."

"I wasn't surprised," Hal said. "Jack's arrogant enough to believe he can talk his way out of anything and smarter than anyone. I think the millions he would inherit with his sister out of the picture was too much to pass up."

"He may not have to say anything." Karen shrugged. "I mean we're looking at an accidental death according to the medical examiner. Death by asphyxiation, not the wound to her forehead."

The lieutenant rubbed his forehead. "I seem to recall the coroner's mention of a problem with the wound?"

"Yes, he did," Hal replied. "The wound, which has two gashes to the forehead is questionable, that it was caused by a fall on the edging along the periphery of the pool; the edging being curved. He recognizes that a hard object could have made the wound to the forehead. Although, DNA evidence convinces him that the blood on the tile was from the head wound. Unable to resolve some of his questions, he ruled her death accidental caused by drowning."

Abrams asked, "No object was found that could have caused the head wound?"

"Correct. That's not to say an object wasn't used and taken away. The coroner can't say it was a homicide even if he suspects foul play—no evidence." Karen clasped her hands. "The only reasonable conclusion—according to the chief medical examiner, Sheila slipped and fell, hitting her head on the edge of the pool, unconscious, then fell in the water and drowned."

"It sounds too perfect in my book," Hal said. "She's an agile young woman. What would cause her to fall, coincidentally close to the water?"

"She wasn't a drinker, and was sure-footed according to her husband," Karen replied. "And no furniture blocking her path to the pool."

Hal nodded. "Right. She didn't stumble or trip over her feet. My opinion—Jack killed her."

The lieutenant peered at Hal. "But how?"

"Karen's right. He used some hard object as a weapon and brought it along with him to Sheila's house concealing it until he struck her at the pool."

"Good theory, but some holes need to be filled." Abrams scratched his head, thinking. "He couldn't allow anyone seeing him at his sister's house. He would have to arrive and leave the scene without anyone seeing him, an incredible effort."

Karen nodded. "A good argument for saying Jack wouldn't put himself in that situation. And the two of them weren't exactly amendable to social visits." She glanced at Hal. "For what purpose would she see him?"

Hal managed a grin. "Right off the top of my head I don't know, but he's clever enough to have thought of something." Glancing through his notepad, he added, "There is the issue of the inheritance if either Jack or Sheila dies prematurely."

Abrams leaned forward. "Right. Assuming Sheila dies of natural causes. The nephew's portion of the trust increases."

Karen held up a finger. "But Sheila inherits the entire estate if Jack dies prematurely regardless of the cause of death."

"The niece is clearly the front runner in money incentive." Abrams said, tapping his pen on the desk, but she and her husband are comfortably well off, what possible reason would she have?"

"This is purely speculation," Karen said, "but Shelia may have been blackmailing Jack. Maybe she had some proof that he killed the uncle."

"Too much of a stretch," Abrams replied with a wave of his hand. "The sister doesn't need any blackmail money, and besides, as I understand his financial position, Jack's income left little for other needs."

"Lieutenant, there's no love lost between the siblings," Karen said. "Maybe she just wanted justice making him pay for her uncle's murder."

Abrams eyed Hal. "What do you think?"

After a pause rubbing his chin, Hal answered, "Hadn't thought of that possibility of either blackmail or her wanting justice. I would agree it's another alternative to consider as if we didn't have enough already." Hal shook his head. "This case is looking more like a dead file bound for the cold cases in the basement."

"Well, that conjecture is beside the point now. The sister is dead, and the brother is our only suspect." Abrams got up leaning on his desk, head down, frowning. "The nephew must have thought how her death would look to a jury so soon after the uncle's homicide."

"You can be certain of it," Karen replied. "It just emphasizes how arrogant he is thinking he can get away with murder so soon again."

Hal raised his chin in an expression of concurrence. "He's clever enough."

"Deviously clever," Karen added. "He's thought pretty much of everything for Sheila's *accident*. Somehow he managed to arrive and leave the scene undetected. But the crack on the head supports a fall against the pool decking, although he could've planted her blood on the decking to make it appear accidental."

"A lot of speculation," Abrams said. "You know what a jury would do with that."

Hal wrinkled his nose. "Reasonable doubt."

"As it stands we have nothing worthy of evidence to indict him."

Hal scowled. "It bugs me to think he'll probably get away with the murder of his sister."

"The husband found her when he got home," Karen said. "He's cleared, had nothing to do with her death. There's no one that would have a reason to harm her, except the nephew." Abrams scoffed. "Despite the high end motive, there's not a shred of evidence pointing to Jack."

"Are we going to call it quits on the investigation?" Karen inquired.

"Well, there's no point in investigating an accidental drowning." Boris raised his arms. "Unless some miracle from forensics materializes or the nephew confesses, our hands are tied. He may very well get away with the perfect crime. But he won't get away with his uncle's homicide. I talked to assistant D.A. Evans. They're going to indict him for the murder of his uncle."

"Even though we have only circumstantial evidence?" Karen asked."

"Yes. When added all up, the D.A. believes we can get a conviction."

Karen nodded. "I believe our strongest lead is the condition of the reading lamp turned off at the scene. Jack's phony burglars *wouldn't* have known about the light buttons under the reading desk. But Jack knew about it."

"The lab is checking on the rubber band to see if they can get a fingerprint," Hal added.

The lieutenant nodded. "Arrest him."

***

Busy fighting off the enemy with his laser gun on the computer game, Jack heard the chiming of the doorbell. As the sound continued in annoying repetitive intervals, he grudgingly got up and walked leisurely to the front door, hoping that whoever it was would be gone when he got there. He had on a t-shirt, under shorts and stockings.

Opening the door he saw detectives Holmes and Reiner and a uniformed officer on the porch. "What a pleasant surprise," Jack said smiling. "To what do I owe this unexpected delight?"

Hal spoke in a serious tone. "Jack Buckingham, you're under arrest for the murder of Edgar Buckingham."

Jack remained close-mouthed while Karen read him his rights, and ended with "Do you understand your right to remain silent?"

"Correction. I heard the words. Thank the gods you can't stop me from speaking. Actually I've been waiting for this arrest, expecting it with open arms. Now I'll have the opportunity to prove my innocence in a court of law. Accusing me of murder with only circumstantial evidence is like crawling along a high tree limb knowing it will break for you, you know what I mean?"

Karen smiled. "We'll enjoy a challenge. It's not often we get to prosecute a suspect as clever as you."

"Thank you, thank you. We both enjoy the enlightened conversation of interrogation even though we reside on different sides of the railroad track, so to speak." Smirking, he added, "It's invigorating to be at the center of attention. I love it."

"We'll need to handcuff you, Jack. The officer will take you to the precinct in his squad car. In a few days there will be a court hearing at which time you can give your plea."

"I do have one request. Before taking me into the dungeons, I would appreciate a little leniency to disengage my computer game and put on a pair of trousers and shoes. Is that too much to ask between friends?"

"We can allow that," Hal said. "Do it now. We'll follow you to your room."

After Jack removed his game cartridge and turned off the computer, he slipped on beige trousers and tennis shoes. "Would you all care for a drink?"

Karen arched her eyebrows. "No, but it was considerate of you to ask."

The uniformed officer handcuffed Jack and led him to the squad car.

Entering the car, Jack said to the detectives in a whimsical tone, "I'm requesting a hearing as soon as possible. Yes, I'll be charged with a first degree murder, but I have enough to make bond, a get out of jail monopoly card, you know what I mean? I want to get back to my computer game." He laughed. "Until then, come visit me anytime."

***

Three days later at his hearing with the help of his attorney, Jack stood before a judge. Charged with first degree murder, the judge asked for his plea.

"Your honor, I am innocent of the charge."

Assistant D. A. Evans spoke up. "The state believes Mr. Buckingham is a flight risk. We recommend incarceration until the trial date, with no bond pending."

Jack's lawyer, Miano addressed the judge. "My client is not a flight risk. He has every intention of standing trial wanting to prove his innocence."

Jack raised his hand mid-level with two fingers stretched as a V. "May I speak, sir?"

"Yes."

"Your honor, I would like to suggest wearing an ankle bracelet, in effect a house arrest in lieu of incarceration if it pleases the court."

The judge scowled. "Why a house arrest?"

"So I can take care of my pet dog who is incapacitated," Jack lied, his furrowed brow prominent."

There was a moment of silence, then the judge said, "You understand the ankle bracelet sends out a signal if you should try to leave the premises. Only excusable reasons to leave are religious practice, grocery shopping, and medical appointments. You may use your phone. You will be regularly visited by your parole officer. Is that understood?"

"Yes, sir. I have one more request, your honor. I would like to have a speedy trial. Within a six months time period if at all possible."

"Yes, you have that right under the Sixth Amendment of the Constitution. But I'll have to check my calendar. Alright, a condition of house arrest will be in effect tomorrow. In the meantime you will remain incarcerated in the county jail."

Jack thanked the judge and was hand-cuffed by a court bailiff. Before he was led out of the courtroom, Attorney Miano shook Jack's hand. "You're good. Very convincing. I would've been just as lenient had I been sitting up there on the bench."

"Wait until you see me at my best during cross examination by the assistant D. A."

"You intend on testifying? The prosecution *does have* a good argument with motive and opportunity."

"Speculation, you mean." Jack smiled at Miano as he was being led away by the bailiff. "Of course I want to testify to truth—right from the horse's mouth, eh, Officer?"

CHAPTER TWELVE

The courtroom filled with interested spectators, media reporters and the jury, all waiting to hear the assistant D.A., Evans to begin his opening statement. Saluting, Jack glanced at Hal and Karen who were in the back row of the gallery among the numerous spectators. Hal didn't return Jack's salutation, but Karen nodded her head.

Assistant D.A. Evans, tall and thin, whose facial features resembled Abraham Lincoln, faced the jury, his hands placed firmly on the lectern. "Ladies and gentlemen, it is our job to convince you that the defendant, Jack Buckingham, did willfully and maliciously kill his uncle, Edgar Buckingham, during the evening of June, 12, 2008 stabbing his uncle to death between the hours of eight and eleven p.m.

"We will detail the state's version of the horrific murder with witness testimony. We will show that all of the isolated incidents add up to the defendant's premeditated murder of his uncle. I know you will give justice to Edgar Buckingham by rendering a guilty verdict for the defendant, Jack Buckingham. Thank you."

As Evans returned to his chair, Jack gazed at him clapping his hands softly.

Defense attorney, Miano, short and heavy-set with his hands clasped behind his back. got up and strolled toward the jury. He shook his bald head slightly, then proclaimed, "Ladies and gentlemen, my client, Jack

Buckingham, has been accused of a horrendous crime—murder in the first degree despite the fact that the state has no verifiable evidence that connects the defendant to the homicide. We shouldn't be having this trial.

"The state's speculation and outright avoidance of any other suspects suggests that is why the prosecutor had avoided going for the death penalty because they can't prove the defendant's complicity. Instead, the prosecutor believes it will be easier to sentence my client to life without parole if found guilty. I remind you that we don't have to prove anything; that burden is for the state. The judge will instruct you about reasonable doubt, and remind you that if there are two opposing yet similar alternatives of fact by expert witnesses, you must choose the one favoring the defendant. I am confident you will render a not-guilty verdict after hearing the miniscule circumstantial evidence. Thank you." Attorney Miano returned to his desk.

The judge spoke to the court clerk, then motioned to the assistant D.A. "Call your first witness."

"Detective Hal Reiner."

Engrossed in his visualization, Hal didn't hear the prosecutor call his name. With his eyes half-closed, head angled down, his concentration centered on the scene unfolding in his mind. Hal clasped his hands and lowered his head in a position of reverence while standing with family and friends at the graveside funeral service for his wife. The inclement weather, cool and misty seemed appropriate for the occasion at the local cemetery. As a minister spoke a few words of endearment, Hal gazed at the open casket visualizing Evelyn's head propped up on a silk pillow. Beautiful fabric interior and liners with an adjustable bed. Both upper and lower containers featured hand-polished hardware in two-color mahogany. Her final resting place had to be perfect, and although expensive, he wanted to show the family the extent of how much he cared for her. Of course it was all a ruse to confirm her demise came by way of an accident of her own making. At the moment in his thoughts, he wasn't sure of the make-up of the accident or how it could be administered; sufficient now in his daydream to enjoy Evelyn's unexpected passing. Noticing the silence, a few scattered clouds and a slight breeze all of which had a pleasant effect on his mind, he experienced the scene as though real. After the close of the casket and a few words of endearment from the minister standing by, workers lowered the casket and began shoveling dirt in the cavity. Hal bowed his head and sighed. Walking away from the simulated setting by himself, he felt liberated. Now he could enjoy the life he wanted without her interference, and hopefully receive a little respect from his co-workers.

"Detective Reiner?" the prosecutor repeated.

"Here," he said, raising his hand. He got up and moved quickly toward the witness box. Hal gave his name to the clerk, affirming his testimony to be the truth, and then seated himself in the witness chair eager to be questioned.

"Detective Reiner, tell the jury your recollection of events on the evening of June 12, 2008."

"Detective Holmes and myself arrived at the scene at 11:15 p.m. We spoke to Officer Billings briefly, then entered the house and saw the victim, Edgar Buckingham, sitting in a chair in the library, deceased, a hunting knife imbedded on the left side of his chest. While CSI personnel were taking pictures of the scene, bagging and tagging evidence, detective Homes and myself proceeded to the living room to interview the victim's nephew, Jack Buckingham."

"What was the defendant's demeanor?"

"Composed. He appeared at ease, almost eager to tell us the events that led up to his uncle's murder. Without my suggesting that he was a suspect, the defendant said outright that he had an alibi."

"He claimed to be at a Harkins Theater watching the movie, Avatar, is that right?"

"Yes, he went into considerable detail about the movie and mentioned speaking with the food attendant and cashier. When Jack returned home after the movie, he said he found his uncle dead. He said the time to be nearly 10:15 p.m."

"Did the defendant reveal anything about his relationship with his uncle?"

"He admitted that he and his uncle didn't get along, they had disagreements about his work there at the Buckingham home where the defendant stayed."

"Did the defendant offer any reason for the cause of his uncle's murder?"

"Yes. He gave a detailed account of what he thought transpired during the late afternoon on the day of the homicide when he took his uncle shopping. The defendant said he saw a stranger watching his uncle when Buckingham senior paid for a small purchased item with a $100 bill. The defendant gave us a description of the man, a stocky male in his thirties with a butch haircut. A police artist composed a composite drawing, which was published in the local newspaper."

"Was there any response?"

"None whatsoever."

"That is all. Thank you, Detective." Evans returned to his seat.

Defense attorney Miano went straightaway to the lectern. "Detective Reiner, you or anyone assigned to the case didn't follow up investigating the man with a butch haircut, is that correct?"

"Yes, that's correct. We had no leads, no witnesses."

"But you did investigate the defendant's alibi, verifying that he was watching the movie Avatar, during the time of Buckingham senior's death. Is that correct?"

"Yes."

"And what was the result of your investigation?"

"We confirmed he paid a cashier with a $100 bill, entering the theater at 7:30 p.m."

"And what time did the defendant leave the theater?"

"At the end of the movie, exactly 9:50, confirmed by the food attendant who spoke to him at that time."

"Detective, tell the jury the time of Buckingham senior's death."

"According to the medical examiner, somewhere between the hours of 7:30 and 10 p.m."

Miano cocked his head slightly to one side. "Tell me, Detective Reiner, if the defendant was at the movies between the hours of 7:15 and 9:50 p.m., and there is no verifiable evidence that he left the theater during those times, isn't it fair to assume he *could not* have been at the Buckingham estate killing his uncle?"

"Well, we believe..."

"Sir, please answer yes or no?"

"Yes."

"That is all, thank you."

D.A. Evans called an expert witness for the state. "You are a crime scene investigator, is that right?"

"Yes. I evaluate homicide scenes for the police to determine possible scenarios of the crime."

"How long have you been doing this type of evaluation?"

"Twenty years."

Evans showed a picture of Buckingham library which included a portion f the hallway leading into the library. Another picture showed the underside of the reading table with the two buttons adjacent to each other. Pointing with his laser at a large screen, he mentioned the larger button turned the hallway lamp on and off while the smaller button turned the reading lamp on and off; both on the same circuitry. Evans explained to the jury that Buckingham senior had trouble walking and used the two-way switch buttons to light or extinguish the hallway or reading lamp. "Sir, did you review testimony of CSI officer Billings that the reading lamp was turned off at the time of Buckingham's murder?"

"Yes."

"According to the defendant's testimony at the time, Buckingham senior was reading a book with the reading lamp on when the defendant left the house to go to the movie. Is that correct?"

"Yes."

"Explain to the jury your evaluation of why the reading lamp was reported off when the police arrived at the scene."

"Apparently the defendant turned the reading lamp off by mistake after killing his uncle because he was in a hurry to leave the premises to go to the movie."

"How did you arrive at that conclusion?"

"The defendant's account of the suspect with the butch haircut killing his uncle is not probable because the stranger would not have known about the two-way switch buttons on the underside of the reading table. The defendant was the only other person who knew about those buttons under the table."

"Your witness," Evans said to defense attorney Miano.

Jack leaned toward Miano and whispered something in the attorney's ear. Miano remained seated at the defense table and spoke to the witness. "Just one question. Sir, is it possible that Buckingham senior turned off the lamp himself, perhaps tired of reading?"

"Anything's possible..."

"Yes, or no, please."

"Yes."

"Noting more for now. Thank you."

Assistant D.A. Evans stood up and spoke to the judge. "Your honor, the state may or may not have additional evidence. We expect an answer at any time. So as not to delay the trial, the state agrees if the defense wishes to call their witnesses."

"Mr. Miano, any objections?"

Miano glanced at Jack, then said, "No objections, your honor."

"Call your first witness."

"We have only one witness, the defendant."

Jack got up, pressed down the beige suit, then ran a comb through his red hair, all the time smiling at the jury. He took his seat in the witness box, gave his name and agreed to tell the truth."

"Regarding the testimony of the expert witnesses about the reading lamp having been turned off, tell the jury what you recall about your uncle's reading habit?"

"I've been in the library with him countless times while he was reading. Almost invariably after reading for fifteen minutes, he would turn off the lamp and take a snooze."

"This was a commonplace thing with him?"

"Yes indeed." Jack raised a hand in a gesture of amazement. "He would repeat this process during a two or three hour reading period. Every fifteen minutes he would turn off the reading lamp and would doze for fifteen minutes, then switch the lamp back on and start reading again in a repetitive routine."

"That would explain why the lamp was out when the police arrived."

Jack scanned the jury with piercing eyes. "Yes. As God is my witness, I'm positive that is what happened."

"You and your uncle didn't get along too well, is that correct?"

"Correct. We had disagreements about the details of my work and schedule." He turned to the jury and said with focused yes, "I admit this in all honesty—there were times when our discussion amounted to name-calling and shouting. But allow me to say unequivocally I did not kill my uncle."

Miano referred to his paperwork. "Explain to the jury the details of the shopping spree with your uncle during the afternoon of the day he was killed."

"I took my uncle shopping during the late afternoon, which I did often. He couldn't drive and I wheeled him around in a wheelchair during his shopping bouts. He has...had a bum leg. We stopped at the Electro-optics store in the mall. He wanted to buy a magnifying glass."

Jack lowered his head for a moment. "Unc picked one he liked and paid for it with one of his $100 bills he carried in a roll. As he removed the rubber band holding the bills together, he handed a Ben Franklin to the cashier. During this time, I noticed a man staring at my uncle." Jack gazed at the jury with a sullen expression. "I'll never forget that face. As God is my witness, I'm positive that man and his accomplice murdered my uncle." Jack paused, then said, "How? They followed us home, waited until I left for the movie, then broke through the patio door and stabbed my uncle, taking his roll of Ben Franklins and other valuables." Jack lowered his head again.

"Mr. Buckingham, do you need a minute?"

Wiping his eyes with a handkerchief, he replied in a gentle manner, "No, I'm alright."

"Explain to the jury the sequence of events on the night of your uncle's death."

Jack nodded, then scanned the jury, stopping momentarily on each juror, his expression friendly. "I stopped in the library and asked if my uncle needed anything before I left. He said no. He turned on his lamp and resumed reading. Leaving immediately, I arrived at the theater, gave the cashier a $100 bill, the only cash I had on me, and took a seat. It was 7:05 when the movie started. About 8:30 I went to the snack bar and got popcorn and a soda. Spoke briefly with a food attendant, retuned to my seat and continued watching Avatar.

"The movie was over at 9:45. I arrived home at exactly 10:10. He glanced at the jurors. "I glimpsed at my watch while driving into the estate wondering if one of my favorite TV shows had started. Once inside the house I noticed the hallway lamp on and went directly to the library. That's when I found my uncle…" Jack put a hand to his head for a moment covering his eyes. "Sorry. Even though we had our disagreements, it was a shock to see him…motionless, a knife sticking out of his chest. I knew his was dead. There was a stiff breeze coming in from the patio open doors, where the intruder broke in. I immediately called 9-1-1. The police arrived within minutes, and I told them the burglars had taken valuables, expensive cuff links, a silver teapot, a painting and jewelry and my uncle's roll of $100 bills."

"How did you know his roll of Ben Franklins was taken?"

"I saw the rubber band that contained the bills on the floor. I told the officer, and he searched my uncle's pockets and didn't find the roll, of course. Unc always kept the roll in the right front pocket of his trousers. The burglars had taken it."

"How do you answer the charges of the prosecutor's suggestion that you killed your uncle during the showing of the movie?"

"By the state's own testimony, my uncle made a phone call at 8:55 p.m. which proves he was alive at 8:55 well after I had left for the movie. There is also testimony that I was at the theater speaking with the food attendant at approximately 8:30 pm in addition to speaking with the cashier at the end of the movie at 9:45. They would have no reason to lie." Jack shrugged his shoulders, then with a slight grin to the jury, he commented, "The fact is a person can't be in two places at the same time."

"Please tell the jury your state of mind during this time of tragedy in your household."

"It's been like a nightmare. I've been depressed to the point of complete exhaustion. Unable to think, almost unable to function. I had thought about seeing a therapist for my grief." Jack looked at the jury, with a deep furrowed brow. "Then I was arrested. I couldn't comprehend why the state would accuse me of killing my uncle with no physical evidence. They didn't pursue the burglar with the butch haircut. In my opinion the state disregarded all the evidence of my innocence."

"Jack Buckingham, did you have anything to do with your uncle's death?"

Jack placed his palms together as though in prayer. "As God is my witness, I did not."

"That is all."

Jack glanced at the jurors, with a look of gratitude, then returned to his chair at the defense table.

The judge motioned to assistant D.A. Evans. "You may cross examine the witness."

The prosecuting attorney stood up. "Your honor, we have just received additional evidence..."

"Approach?"

The judge waved the two attorneys forward. At the side bar, prosecutor Evans handed the judge a document. "Your honor, this is a fingerprint comparison chart which shows the defendant's thumb print on file and a thumb print on the rubber band. They are a match. It's proof that the defendant handled the rubber band after Edgar Buckingham was stabbed. If the defendant admits to the killing, we'll consider the possibility of parole in the sentencing." The judge handed the document to Miano. After reading it, he said, "I need to look this new evidence over, and speak to my client."

At the defense table, Miano showed Jack the document. "I'm afraid it's physical proof of your complicity."

Jack glanced through the document quickly. After a moment he shook his head. "How did they get my thumb print off that narrow rubber band?"

"Forensics has come a long way in identifying latent prints. According to the document a comparison is 100% for certain, and your DNA makes it proof positive. Jack, there's no way we can refute this evidence. My recommendation—take the plea bargain when it's offered at sentencing. At least you'll have a chance at parole."

Jack nodded his agreement.

After Jack and Miano stood up, the judge asked, "Jack Buckingham, are you entering a guilty plea of your own volition?"

"Yes, your honor."

After dismissing the jury, the courtroom cleared of spectators, except detectives Reiner and Holmes. They approached Jack as he was being hand-cuffed.

"I think you finally made a wise decision pleading guilty," Hal said.

"Well, at some point in my life, I'll get out of prison, and can resume my life of excitement and wonder." He laughed. "One good note, detectives. I escaped being tried for Sheila's death."

"So far," Hal replied.

Smirking, Jack said, "Correction. I'll never be convicted of Sheila's murder. Her death was ruled an accident."

"You've been a worthy adversary," Karen said. "If it hadn't been for your thumbprint on the rubber band, it may have gotten away with the perfect murder."

Jack took a breath of air, expelling it slowly. "Ah yes. Technology is the winner." He glanced toward the ceiling. "And all the time I thought my Unc was stupid when he stretched that rubber band around his wad of bills. Outwitted by a rubber band. Here I thought I had achieved the perfect murder." He lifted his eyebrows high. "But I'm confident Sheila's death will be the perfect murder."

"The case isn't officially closed," Karen advised. "Even though the coroner said it was an accidental drowning, we're still hoping to find evidence of wrong doing. So, you're not off the hook yet."

Jack's grin widened. "You may need help with that."

Karen turned to Hal. "Do we need his help?"

Shaking his head, Hal answered, "No, if the case is to be solved, we alone want recognition."

As he was led away, Jack had the last word. "You know where to find me."

***

A week later, Hal and Karen confronted Lieutenant Abrams outside his office. Karen didn't hesitate to tell the lieutenant in front of a few other detectives seated nearby her amazing news. "We found an expert witness that will testify that Sheila Buckingham's fall was no accident."

"Doctor Goodwin, a pathologist," Hal added.

How did you come about this?" Abrams asked Karen.

Karen glanced at Hal. "My partner found him after a little research."

The seated detectives nearby stared at Hal with expressions of doubt.

"But does it point to Jack?" Abrams inquired, frowning his disbelief.

"Yes. Expert testimony from a pathologist. And we found hard evidence as well. Along with a strong motive, I think we'll have a doable case."

Karen handed Abrams a document. "Sheila's husband has a solid alibi. With no other suspects, I believe a jury will find Jack guilty of murder one."

Abrams nodded. "Okay, I'll speak to Assistant D.A. Evans. "Good work, Karen," he said, nodding, then turned quickly and headed for his office.

Hal didn't say anything as he and Karen returned to their desks, but the expression on his face revealed his displeasure. Once again he was not given any recognition for his efforts.

CHAPTER 13

DESPITE THE UNRULY wind that seemed to be blowing in every direction, Hal and Karen made their way with some difficulty up the courthouse steps to attend the arraignment of Jack Buckingham who was charged with first degree murder of his sister. Taking seats inside the courtroom with a few other curious attendees, Hal noticed Jack's had a blasé appearance unmoved emotionally. With no bond pending, Jack pled not guilty, requesting a speedy trial. The presiding judge had an opening in his schedule within a few months. Both the prosecuting and defense attorneys were available, and with the rapid acceptance of 12 jurors, the trial would commence only months away.

As the months dwindled away, Hal was eager for the trial to start, wondering if Jack's perfect murder would win out or if the best planner of murder he'd ever known could usurp justice.

The trial began as scheduled. After the opening statement, Prosecutor Evans called his first witness, detective Karen Holmes. Wearing a flowery pink dress, she passed the defense table, and glanced at Jack, noticing his demeanor—slouched in his chair, head held high with a smug smile. Hal sat in one of the back rows with other spectators. As agreed with the prosecutor, Karen would be the police spokesperson of the investigation.

Hal's real purpose attending the trial provided him

the opportunity to picking up any particular that might come in handy at some future time. As he listened to the opening statements, Hal assumed Jack's frame of mind questioning the planning of the murder. Most definitely, he wouldn't use a brick to strike the forehead of the victim as Jack had done. Whatever he chose would be disposed of promptly after use, and he would have a better alibi. And above all, he wouldn't appear antagonistic toward the witnesses; which could influence the jury in a negative way.

After Karen was sworn in, Assistant D. A. Evans approached the podium. "Detective Holmes, did you speak with the defendant during the investigation of Miss Livingston's death?"

"Yes, I did."

"What were the circumstances of that conversation?"

"Detective Reiner and myself spoke to the defendant after he pled guilty to the murder of his uncle, Edgar Buckingham. When we asked him about his sister's accidental death, his words were, 'she could have been murdered.' He went on to say the blood on her forehead could have been caused by a sharp blow with a hard object instead of a fall on the cement edging of the pool."

"How did he come by that information?"

"When asked, he only shrugged with a smile. I think he was taunting Detective Reiner and myself. It was his usual method of confrontation, enjoying any kind of debate." She noticed Jack nodding in agreement."

Evans glanced at his paperwork. "So he wasn't serious when he made that statement about the head wound?"

"His exact words were, 'the wound was obviously caused by contact with a flat surface.'"

"He didn't mention the severity of the wound?"

"Only that it appeared to be a skin deep, and caused blood-letting."

"This conversation took place at the inquest?"

"Yes, it did.

"Did he say anything to you when his sister's death was ruled an accidental drowning?"

"Yes. His exact words were, 'the perfect murder.'"

"Did he elaborate on that statement?"

"No."

"What did you infer from his statement…?"

Miano stood up promptly. "Objection, your honor, speculation."

"Sustained."

"Thank you, Detective Holmes. That will be all." Evans sat down.

Hal thought about the conversation he and Karen had with Jack. It amazed him why Jack would suggest an alternative to his sister's manner of death. Why even mention a sharp blow to the head of his sister inferring a hard object with ridges to cause the laceration on the forehead?"

Jack's attorney, Miano, asked Karen from the defense table, "When he said 'the perfect murder,' he was joking… smiling, correct?"

"I don't know if he was joking."

"But was he smiling when he said it?"

"Yes, I believe he was."

"No further questions, your honor."

The judge motioned to the assistant D. A. "Call your next witness, counselor."

The expert witness, a gray-haired elderly man, sat down in the witness chair and was sworn in. His demeanor and relaxed composure suggested a scholarly man. He opened his briefcase and took out numerous papers.

Defense attorney, Miano stood up and addressed the judge, waiving verification of the doctor's credentials and a stipulation of his many years of a specialty in pathology. "We acknowledge Dr. Goodwin as an expert in pathology, your honor."

Assistant D.A. Evans approached the podium. "Dr. Goodwin, you inspected Mrs. Livingston's head wound, is that correct?"

"Yes, but not during the autopsy."

"Alright. At some time soon after the autopsy, did you look at the victim?"

"Yes. I conducted a thorough examination of the wound to the forehead of Mrs. Livingston."

Evans pointed to a video screen near the jurors which showed an enlarged picture of the wound. "Doctor, please tell the jury what you discovered during your examination."

The doctor aimed a laser pointer at the wound, then spoke to the jury. "You'll notice a recess, a gouge in the middle of the wound, a laceration."

"What does that suggest?"

"The laceration had a depth of nearly one-half inch. A gash that deep would have to be made by a sharp object."

"A sharp object?"

"Yes." The doctor aimed his laser pointer on the viewing screen at the wound. "If she had fallen and hit her head on the pool edging according to the alleged theory, that circumstance *would not* have caused that deep of a laceration."

"Why is that?"

"Because of the roundness of the tile edging that is essentially flat could break the skin, but *wouldn't* have caused a laceration with any depth."

"In your expert opinion, doctor, to what do you ascribe the cause of the wound?"

"A blow to the head by an object with sharp protrusions such as a rock. I'm of the opinion it's highly unlikely a fall had caused the wound, that her death *was not* due to an accident."

"You're suggesting her death was a homicide?"

"Yes."

The prosecutor glanced at the jury, then sat down.

Miano spoke briefly to Jack, then addressed the doctor. "Sir, just one question. I wish to clarify your testimony about this sharp object you mentioned. Sir, are you aware of any testimony that a sharp object was found at the scene?"

"None that I know of."

"If no sharp object was found at the scene such as a rock, doesn't that imply the victim's wound to the head would've been caused by a fall against the tile?"

"Well, the object could have ..."

With his palm held high, Miano interrupted. "Yes, or no, please?"

The doctor shrugged. "Yes."

Miano glanced at the jury with an expression of certainty. "Thank you, that is all."

Evans stood up and addressed the judge. "Your honor, I would like to recall Detective Holmes." As soon as Karen sat down in the witness box, the prosecutor asked, "Did you and Detective Reiner conduct a search of the pool area at the Livingston residence?"

"Yes, we did after reading Dr. Goodwin's report. We found an object in the evidence room that had no significance at the time of the death."

"What was the evidence?"

"A thumb-sized piece of red cement."

"You mean like from a brick?"

"Yes, a small piece that appeared to have been broken off from a larger piece."

"Did you find any brickwork in the backyard of the Livingston residence that would match the broken piece?"

"No."

Assistant D.A. acknowledged her answer. "Okay. Then what significance would it have?"

"None at the time, until we read Dr. Goodwin's report concerning a sharp object causing the wound to Mrs. Livingston. Detective Reiner got a search warrant for the Buckingham residence on the probability of finding brickwork there that would match our evidentiary piece."

"And what did you find at the Buckingham estate if anything?"

"We found two halves of a brick in a flower bed alongside the front entrance. The red bricks were used as a border around a flower bed. Inspecting the two halves that were placed together, we found one of them had a notch in it the size of our piece of evidence. We took the pieces back to the forensic lab. Technical specialists confirmed that the piece found at the Livingston residence near the pool was from a broken brick at the Buckingham residence."

"Was there anything else the specialists discovered during the examination?"

"Yes. A dark smudge on one of the bricks."

Evans pointed at an overhead screen. "Detective Holmes, please tell the jury what you discovered?"

Karen pointed her laser at an enlarged picture of the brick halves, and spoke to the jury. "The dark smudge on the left brick half is Mrs. Livingston's blood."

Evans glanced at the jury, then asked Karen, "What did you conclude from this information?"

"That the broken brick caused the laceration."

Without warning, Jack stood up and clapped. "Bravo! Bravo!"

The judge hammered the desk with his gavel. "Restrain the defendant," he said to Miano.

Miano nudged Jack. "Sit down and don't say anything more." Jack complied, smiling.

Hal shook his head at Jack's extravagant behavior applauding the prosecution's witness.

"Do you have any questions for the detective?" the judge asked Miano.

"None at this time, your honor. I'd like to call my witness, Jack Buckingham." Jack took his time standing to his full height, all the time smiling at the jury, as he strode confidently to the witness stand. After affirming to tell the truth, Jack raised his arms as though permitting the judge to continue.

At the podium, Miano asked Jack, "Hypothetical question: If a person is being struck in the face with an object, wouldn't he or she raise their hands to protect themselves from the blow?"

"Of course. My sister was very sensitive about anything in her face, and would often shield it with a hand at the slightest disturbance."

"In other words, her hand would have deflected the object in that sort of scenario and therefore, she would not have been knocked unconscious?"

"Absolutely correct. The only realistic appraisal of her death is a slip and fall onto the decking, striking her head."

Miano glanced at his papers. "Let's talk about the laceration on the wound. Dr. Goodwin has suggested that the deep gouge in your sister's forehead was cause by some object with sharp protrusions insinuating that someone struck her. Mr. Buckingham, would you care to comment?"

"Yes, I would." He turned and looked at the jury, then said simply, "He's mistaken." Jack raised his arms to the air. "He wasn't there when it happened so he's only guessing that some object struck her in the fore-head. It seems more likely that when she struck her head on the pool edging, it was on a tile groove which caused the half inch laceration."

One more question, Mr. Buckingham. "Explain to the jury your thoughts about the physical evidence of the brick found at the Buckingham estate, and the broken piece of brick discovered at the Livingston pool with her blood on it. It does sound incriminating."

"My answer—a conspiracy. Detective Holmes claims they discovered the thumb-sized piece of brick in the police evidence room long after Sheila's death. How convenient. Both detectives Holmes and Reiner have been after me from the get-go. The truth is they got one of my planter bricks, broke off a thumb-sized piece, took it to my sister's pool and planted it there. They broke my planter brick in two pieces, even smeared Sheila's blood on one of the halves and placed it in the flower bed at my house." He raised his eyebrows at the jury. "This is the perfect example of the police scheming to convict me of a false murder. But I'm one step ahead of them. I have an alibi."

Many of the jurors leaned forward, attentive. The spectators stared at Jack. Hal listened closely with pen ready in his hand to take notes.

"Continue, please," Miano said, glancing at the jury. "Tell them."

"At the time my sister fell to her death, which has been documented to have occurred between the hours of 8 and 10 p.m., I was on my laptop searching the web for storage units." He paused for a moment, "to contain my uncle's material goods for safe-keeping until such time that I could dispose of the personal belongings prudently."

On cross, the assistant D.A. remarked, "We checked your computer. Yes, you were on line between the hours the victim's death occurred at the Buckingham residence, but that doesn't prove you were physically there the entire time. Your testimony is… strictly speaking, only your opinion, isn't that correct?"

Jack laughed. "My opinion is all I need." He placed his hand on his chest and looked at the jury pausing for a few seconds at each juror. "Ladies and gentlemen, on my mother's grave I plead innocent of this outrageous murder charge. The prosecutor has only a smattering of circumstantial evidence, and I remind you the state has to prove me guilty." He grinned. "Which they have not done. If there is reasonable doubt such as I've described in detail of the detectives planting evidence, I implore you to find me innocent."

Miano gave his closing statement. "Ladies and gentlemen of the jury, as my client has suggested, the prosecutor's case is based on circumstantial evidence most of which has been obtained by inaccurate and misleading investigative techniques. There is no evidence that Jack Buckingham was at the Livingston residence on the night of her death. Allow me to remind you of the rule of law—if there is reasonable doubt, you must find the defendant innocent of the charge of murder."

The assistant D.A. concluded his closing statement stating that the buildup of circumstantial evidence points to the defendant as the perpetrator of the homicide. "With motive, means and no viable alibi for the night the victim was murdered, you must find Jack Buckingham guilty of first degree murder as charged. Thank you, ladies and gentlemen of the jury."

Deliberations took only three hours. The jury returned with a verdict of guilty. Before Jack was handcuffed by the bailiff and taken away, he spoke out with an expression of resignation.

"It has to be fate. First I was defeated by a rubber band and now a broken brick has done me in."

Hal made a notation in his notepad, <u>ALIBI!</u> He marveled at Jack's desire to plan his sister's murder almost to perfection, but he had made the one mistake that is inexcusable—using a brick as a weapon from his planter at the Buckingham estate. His downfall was not expecting the brick to cause a sharp wound on the forehead. And when he hit his sister with the brick, he didn't foresee the possibility that the brick would break inflicting the deep laceration. Obviously he didn't notice Sheila's blood on the brick half. Hal made a notation in his notepad. TOP OF THE LIST! PLAN FOR UNEX-PECTED EVENTS!

***

Hal and Karen returned to the precinct and were ushered into Lt. Abrams office by two other detectives. "Gillan and Sikorsky are joining us to hear about the Buckingham trial. As witnesses, they have one coming up soon."

Karen gave a verbal report of the trial explaining in detail her testimony of rebuttal questions from the defense attorney.

"You didn't testify?" Abrams asked Hal.

Hal shook his head.

"Why not? You were the lead detective."

"He wanted to observe the proceedings," Karen remarked. "And the assistant D.A. agreed to use me."

Gillan looked at Hal with a wry grin. "You didn't want to screw up the testimony so you gave the job to your partner."

A few seconds passed before Gillan's dig registered in Hal's mind. He caught himself from reacting in a negative way and grinned. Underneath his calm appearance, Hal felt the full brunt of yet another disrespectful rebuke from his colleague. A similar traumatic event dominated his mind on his 16th birthday. He, his brother, Michael, and his father were having lunch at their home for the celebration such that it was without a birthday cake and no gifts by comparison to Michael's birthday two months previous with birthday cake and presents. The discussion centered around a traffic accident he and Michael had witnessed in front of their house.

"Well, you were both there," the father had asked both boys. "Who was at fault, the truck or the station wagon?"

Michael had answered first. "It looked to me like the truck swerved into the station wagon."

Hesitant to say anything for fear of being judged, Hal recalled his father's piercing eyes insisting he speak.

"Father, I don't know for certain."

"I didn't ask for proof, did I? Just tell me who you think was at fault."

"I thought the station wagon turned into the truck."

"But why did he do it?"

After shrugging with no comment, his father said, "Just as I thought, Hal, you don't know what you're talking about. His father then complimented Michael on his interpretation of the accident. Another criticism unwarranted from his father which was at the time like a slap in the face.

***

Seeing Hal staring off in the distance, she attempted to defend Hal, but Abrams spoke up. "Let's not be arguing over who should have been testifying. I, for one, am grateful we put this case to bed successful."

Discussion of Gillan and Sikorsky's upcoming trial continued for the next ten minutes. Hal remained closed-mouthed, and only nodded his head when ideas were presented. As difficult as it was for him to hold back his anger, he grasped his hands, and sat upright in his chair, almost holding his breath, feeling crushed at Gillan's unsavory comment. He was good at holding off deeply-felt emotions, and would react at a later time.

***

After the meeting, Hal excused himself, informing Karen and Abrams he wasn't feeling well and went home. Thankful that Evelyn didn't meet him at the door, he went to the spare bedroom and sat on the edge of the bed recalling Gillan's disreputable words. He grabbed a bottle of brandy from the night table, gulped down two mouthfuls and stared at the far wall. In a rare moment of searing hatred, he grabbed a chair and threw it against the wall. The loud *whack* seemed to reverberate throughout the house. Hal was not only surprised but felt responsible for his atypical behavior when he saw Evelyn walk into the room, her mouth open as she stared at the chair on the floor with a broken leg.

"My God, have you gone crazy?"

He grimaced. "I don't know what happened."

"It's not like you..." she stammered, "openly displaying hostility. "What's going on with you? I've had it. It's not safe here anymore. I think you should leave the house permanently!"

She stormed out of the room.

While standing with arms to his sides thinking for a long moment, finally in a relaxed stance, he picked up the chair. He said to himself, *Maybe I can fix the leg, glue it back on.* He glanced around the doorway, and saw Evelyn making a phone call. He heard her address the person on the other end of the line, one Theodore Brewster, a divorce lawyer. He sighed, but was relieved. The time had come to put his plan of murder into action.

Not wanting to disrupt his work schedule, he convinced Evelyn to allow him to stay at the house. Maintaining that he still cared for her and wanted desperately to make amends of their failing marriage, and his pledge to attend counseling sessions became the deliverance to give him the extra time he needed to formulate a plan of action to kill his wife.

CHAPTER FOURTEEN

IN THE FOOTHILLS of Beaverton, north of the county line, John Kepler negotiated the rocky path down a steep slope from the summit of the mountain. He surveyed the surrounding landscape, rugged terrain all around, but he felt energized by the experience of traversing the wilderness all by himself. How much more invigorating would it would have been living in the wild during the California Gold Rush in 1849? He took off his back pack and sat down on the ground. Taking out a photo, he stared at the wallet-sized copy of his great-grandfather, Joshua Kepler, standing in a stream with gold pan in hand. A man had to be strong in character to survive the harsh environment of the gold diggings; definitely a time of excitement and adventure, life was meaningful. John glanced at his watch. Time to start back home, taking his time and arriving late, so he could hopefully miss a confrontation with his wife.

When he got home, he left his equipment in the garage, took off his shoes and tip-toed into his bedroom. He turned out the light and got into bed continuing his fantasy of living the life of Joshua Kepler.

***

The next morning John took a sip of orange juice while studying his class notes at the kitchen table. With peripheral vision, he detected his wife strut into the room with quick short steps typical of her Type A personality. The less he saw of her the better.

Opening the bread canister, she said over her shoulder, "It must have been late when you got home last night, I didn't hear you come in."

"Yes, it was," he said, deliberately not giving her further explanation.

"Did it ever occur to you that I might be worried?"

He looked at her. "Not about my safety. If anything, you would be concerned about losing control."

"You creep!" she yelled, recognizing his dig had struck an exposed nerve once again. "Give me a break!"

He knew her standard outburst didn't require an answer, but within her furor he sensed her sarcasm about his passion for history.

She spread jelly on a piece of toast, and then gazed at him. "I see you're not having breakfast."

"Correct." He inspected her angular face, and a furrowed brow that stood in place as though permanent. Her brown hair that terminated in a bun; the perfect exterior to go along with her acid tongue. "I'll get something at the school cafeteria."

"We have food here. Why do you need to go to a cafeteria?"

"Because it's doing something different, do you mind terribly?"

"Oh, are you suffering from too much routine again?" she asked, sneering.

He didn't answer.

"I'm going shopping this evening," she said in a tense voice. "I thought you might accompany me to the mall?"

She knew what his answer would be, but she delighted in taunting him. "Gertrude...you know very well shopping is one of my least favorite things to do, unless it's looking at camping equipment. Fortunately for me that store is across town, not at the mall. No, tonight I will be busy here at the house."

"Watching your civil war movies on the boob tube, no doubt."

"No, I'm reading about the California Gold Rush."

"What on earth for?"

"Because it interests me." John opened his billfold and pulled out the photo of his great-grandfather. He looked at it fondly. "I should have lived in Joshua's time. Plenty of excitement then during the California Gold Rush."

Gertrude gasped. "My God, that was ages ago." She pointed at a calendar on the wall. "Look! Today is Thursday, February, 28, 1991. We live and work with modern conveniences. We don't have to kill a bear for our sustenance."

"Maybe that's the problem—things are too easy."

She rolled her eyes. "Of course they're too easy because you never finish a job." She groaned. "I should have picked up on your procrastination when we first got married. It's a major defect in your warped personality."

Still looking at the photograph, he nodded. "You're right. I do put things off, but I suspect it's because you never cease reminding me. For once I would like the option of deciding for myself when to accomplish a task. I do have other things that occupy my mind."

She scoffed. "You mean daydreaming about living in the past."

He nodded. "Fantasizing about living Joshua's life allows me needed personal freedom."

"From me?"

He put the photograph back into his billfold. "Sorry, no time to discuss the issue with you now."

"Oh yes, that's always your excuse." She waved a hand through the air as though shooing away a pesky fly. "Well, go then."

He got up and stuffed papers into his attaché case. "My parting words of wisdom to you, my dear — patience is a virtue."

"It doesn't work for me."

"Accounting skills and cunning logic are your coping strategy."

She groaned. "You're impossible to talk to." She went on elaborating on a list of his inadequacies.

He peered at his wife as she reminded him repeatedly of forgetting household chores. Nagging him of insignificant details had become a major flaw in their relationship. But most of all, her closed mind to his great-grandfather's adventure put a strain on their seven-year marriage.

"Yes, yes, I'll get to it," he interrupted, walking out of the kitchen, but heard her last salvo.

"Jonathan, don't forget to change the air-conditioning filter when you get home. I get tired reminding you constantly..." She continued on, he guessed, babbling into empty space; her way of showing she had the last word.

***

The drive to the Osborne Community College took him past a string of small business shops. He observed the huge signs advertising their products and services. At a signal stop, he reminded himself, *No gain without pain* as he recalled swishing the gold pan in the icy stream of yesterday's adventure. He drove into a parking slot, and sauntered into the school.

Walking down the hall toward his classroom, he sensed another person's presence. "Oops," he said, as he turned the corner, stopping within inches of a student. He noticed she was at ease. He smiled. "Thank you for avoiding a run-in?"

"I sensed someone was coming."

"Ah, a clairvoyant."

Shaking her head, she answered promptly. "No, I think I heard your footsteps, Mr. Kepler. I don't believe in fate or happenings preordained by gods or devils."

He laughed. "What about intuition? Those ideas that come from out of the blue, so to speak, could they be from some unknown source other than your own mind?"

"I don't know," she said, shrugging her shoulders. "Maybe."

"Good. Then that other world of mystery and metaphysics is not completely closed to your mindset. We'll be discussing dreams in today's lecture." Glancing at his watch, he added, "See you in class."

Extra long steps carried John's small frame into the classroom. He reclined into a chair, dropping his briefcase on the desk, then inhaled deeply, letting it out slowly. Another boring day lecturing beginning psychology to young college-age students. The only positive thing to look forward to was the subject of today's lecture—dreams. The mystery of dreams intrigued him. He wrote them down and filed them away according to the subject matter. Most of his dreams centered on traveling back in time. His thoughts were interrupted as students entered the classroom.

He stood up, appearing shorter than his five and a half foot height. "Good morning!" Brushing at his beard with his hands, he continued, "We've been studying the chapter on memory and cognition: perception, attention, memory, mental imagery and comprehension. Today we'll take a side trip and talk about ..." He paused, then went to the blackboard and wrote in large letters: DREAMS. Turning, facing the students who were arranging books and writing instruments on their desks, he asked, "Are dreams useful, or are they random thoughts, having no significance?"

A male student shot a hand in the air. "Sigmund Freud proposed that dreams are the means that one has of expressing unconscious wishes. He said that bad dreams allow the brain to gain control over the feelings that are a result of distressful experiences."

A female student shook her head. "I don't think dreams have any use. Dreams are merely about our experiences that have happened in the past. It's a bygone event."

John glanced around the class. "Is it important to know about the past?"

Another student spoke up. "Sure. Dreams can help us sort out why we do things."

John looked at the student who denounced dreams. "Various theories on dream interpretations exist, but the real purpose of dreams is still unknown. Research shows that during an average lifespan, a human being spends about six years in dreaming which is around two hours every night."

Another female student shrugged her shoulders. "I think dreams are based on one's interpretation. I think it's paranormal."

"Yes. The term is usually taken to mean unusual experiences that lack a scientific explanation." John glanced at the sober expressions of some of the students, then walked to a window overlooking the campus. He said almost in a tone of reflection, "There is something strange and intriguing about the paranormal. Maybe people who have near-death experiences possess something beyond our explanation of reality. Dreams are often a mystery." He moved back to his desk and faced the students. "Question: The five senses; sight, touch, hearing, taste and smell—are they our only means of reality?"

"Intuition is something," a student remarked. "You know, an idea that comes to you from out of the blue."

John paused momentarily waiting for someone to comment, then continued. "Maybe most mysterious of all is time. We rely upon time to function in the world, but time is an invention of man. What is deemed past or present could be altered, even interchanged. What do you think?"

A male student raised his arm. "You mean like time travel to a place in the past?"

"Yes, Even the scientific community cannot claim it's impossible. If time is an invention of man, maybe the past and present could be interchanged." He smiled. "Doesn't it sound intriguing to be able to travel back in time and experience life in a bygone era?"

A female in the front row frowned. "Not for me, sir. I don't think I want to experience outdoor toilets or horse and buggies or life without air-conditioning."

Another student raised his hand. "I don't know anything about my great-grandfather, but maybe a personal experience would be interesting... for a while."

"And exciting," John replied quickly. "The possibilities are limitless. Perhaps one could even change history. Anyone, what do you think?"

A female in the front row asked, "Wouldn't you have to have a time machine? How else could you travel to a different time?"

John rubbed his beard. "Good question. Experts say we've only seen about ten percent of the mind's capabilities. Perhaps time travel to the past using one's mind may be our next scientific breakthrough."

Glancing at dubious faces, he realized the students had little interest in his discourse on time travel. He finished his lecture on how to better understand dreams, explaining, "If you want to know the significance of your dreams, write them down as soon as possible after they occur. You can then capture the accuracy of images and emotions felt." When he asked for questions or comments with no response, he dismissed the class early.

The rest of his classes were of like manner, most of the students unresponsive to his lecture about dreams and time travel. It had become a lackluster day at school, and he stopped at an outdoor specialty shop looking at camping equipment to forestall going home to hear more ridicule from his wife.

* * *

In the Beaverton homicide department, Karen and Hal spent a good deal of time sifting through their files during the debriefing in Lt. Abrams' office. Hal made notations as he listened to the lieutenant's summary of the Library murder case. "Happy to close this one down," Abrans said. "You solved a potentially perfect murder."

Karen made a gesture of surprise. "Do you think there is such a thing?"

Hal spoke up. "Oh yeah. But the term is a misnomer." He raised his arms. "Because in order for it to be a perfect murder, we wouldn't know about it."

"Well said." Abrams closed his file. "Continue with your present cases until the next *almost* perfect murder challenges our abilities."

***

It started raining as John Kepler drove home thinking about the conversation he had with his students. As the heavy downpour obliterated his view ahead, he turned on his windshield wipers. Almost instantly the rain stopped and his view was clear again. He smiled at the apparition. Was the change due to time or was it time that made the change? His reverie shut down immediately as soon as he walked in the house. Gertrude confronted him. He walked past her and plopped on the sofa.

"Do you have any plans this evening other than sitting on your butt watching TV?"

"That depends."

"I'm reminding you to change the filter in the air conditioning unit instead of sitting there like a zombie."

"That's what I feel like." He wiped his brow with a handkerchief while staring at his shoes. "It's the same thing day in and day out. I get up, shave, go to work, come home, watch TV, go to bed, and get up again. It's the same routine over and over again." He pulled the wallet-sized photo of his Great grandfather from his bill-fold, looking at it affectionately. "Yes, Joshua's time had plenty of excitement then during the Gold Rush."

"You keep harping on that nonsense." A wry grin crossed her lips. "If you want excitement, put the garbage bags in the container," Gertrude said with hands planted on her waist.

He wasn't sure how to answer. He preferred the truth—saying he disliked her annoying chatter—but he hated confrontation and simply said, "I'll get to it, eventually."

"I figured as much. Well, I'm going out."

He shook his head. "You have no respect for my love of the past."

Her eyes ballooned. "Your fixation on the past won't change the present."

"The present? What enjoyment is there today with all the conveniences of technology? There's no chal-lenge. Joshua was on his own, surviving from day to day with only his bare hands. Life was hard, but it was meaningful."

"You can't live in the past."

It irked him that she threw the reality in his face at every opportunity.

"I don't want my friends thinking I'm unable to handle my marital challenge," she said, eyes leering at him. "Someone has to keep you focused on the here and now."

"And you enjoy it—reminding me constantly about daily chores." He looked at her, and held up a fin-ger. "But I have a plan to escape the present," and in a lower tone, he added, " and away from you."

"I heard that remark. I wouldn't allow it." She waved a hand through the air. "Of all your fantasies, time travel is the most bizarre." She rolled her eyes. "You're crazy."

"I'm seeing a hypnotist about past lives regression. I firmly believe I can be transported back in time, out of the present, away from you."

"I wouldn't allow it."

"What are you going to do—kill me?"

When she didn't answer, he noticed her staring at him with a far-away look. She turned abruptly and left the room.

John went into the den, manipulated the combination of the wall safe, opened the door as he had done hundreds of times before and took out the photo album.

He carefully picked up a daguerreotype and looked at it longingly. He was thankful there was a record of Joshua's adventure in the gold fields back in 1849. The pictures had been taken with his friend, Emmett Hodges, by a passing photographer during their early days of prospecting. Joshua had sent them to his wife. She in turn had kept the pictures in safe keeping. The photos and letters were handed down from grandfather to father to son. The scene of the two bearded men in rocky undulating terrain revealed their purpose: gold-panning for nuggets in a fast-flowing stream. Both men were smiling. He removed a protective plastic sheet from the album, then carefully took out a letter his great-grandfather wrote his wife while he was still in the gold fields. He read it slowly in silence.

Dear Maude,

Me and Emmett's been panning out of Yuba River in Placer County. We figure to stake a claim soon. How you doing? And my boy? I know you can't answer. Soon as we strike our bonanza, I will come home. Rough out here in the wilderness trying to locate food and shelter from the weather. Had to fight off a couple of filchers trying to steal our nuggets. And a bear attacked the camp. Shooed it away with a shotgun blast. Always something going on here in this desolate country. Lots of tall evergreens and rocky terrain, but we had good luck panning nuggets from the river. Excitement every day. I am well, feel good. Good-bye for now.

He put the letter in the plastic bag. "That's the life for me," he said aloud. He held the picture of his great-grandfather comparing the daguerreotype with a photo of his face. John smiled. "Looks like me, too," he said aloud. "I got his eyes and nose, and the beard." He chuckled. "Hey, Joshua, we could pass for brothers." After glowering over the picture for a minute more, he stroked his beard, smiling. *Keep the faith, John,* your *plan of time travel will work.* He cocked his head to one side. *Are you believing or hoping?* He put the album away, turned off the overhead light and got in bed; the best time of day when he could reflect on his fantasy without interference.

While adjusting his pillow, he noticed a glow from the wall socket light. He closed his eyes; no light visible. Then opening his eyes again, he saw the glow. Repeating the sequence a few more times with eyes closed, he imagined seeing the glow, bright enough in his mind's eye to get out of bed and walk to the bathroom by the illumination. Opening his eyes, he confirmed the socket light on and grinned at his foolhardy experiment. But who is to say what is real or imaginary? The mind is a powerful instrument he argued to himself. Research has shown what we anticipate happening in our thoughts can become a physical reality. How true it is in a court of law when eyewitness testimony seeing a defendant at a crime scene has often been proven false.

In one of his psych classes he recalled a student's behavior as she argued against the idea of déjà vu. "Thinking that one has been oneself before, perhaps in a past life at best is a coincidence." Suddenly, looking around the room, she gasped and put a hand to her forehead. He remembered her next words of shocking admittance: "I just had an experience of déjà vu." She pointed at the blackboard. "I'm writing numbers, there are other students nearby, where I don't know, but my feeling is like it happened a hundred years ago."

A short discussion followed, and although he favored her revelation, the majority of the students discounted the happening.

John turned on his side staring at the opposite wall in his bedroom. After closing his eyes, he thought about time travel, troubled that most people claimed it to be fantasy. It occurred to him that if traveling back in time was feasible, certainly someone would have done so. Perhaps Gertrude was right, his desire to live in the past revealed only his emotional whimsy. He needed something tangible to give him hope of his dream experiencing a past even in real time. John renewed his aspiration feeling the excitement of panning for gold in the California hills back in 1849 as he drifted off to sleep.

***

The following day after school, John Kepler headed back home, listening to the radio. The program was interrupted with the news. The newscaster got his attention when he heard a brief report on the power of the mind. John pulled over to the curb and stopped to listen. According to Dr. Bernardo Vincetti, a renowned hypnotherapist, not only one's past can be revealing, but past lives of relatives are accessible with the mind. Dr. Vincetti's book, Mind Power, explores the subconscious mind, including his research with children's memories of departed relatives.

John made a mental note of the man's name and headed for a book store at the mall. He purchased the book and was impressed seeing the unique cover, which showed a depiction of the brain superimposed on an hourglass half-full of sand.

He rushed home believing this was one of those moments of intuition. Passing Gertrude on the way to the den, he smiled at her, holding up the book. "I think I've found the answer to my quest—a serendipitous occurrence."

She shook her head at him. "Whatever that means. Don't forget to change the air-conditioning filter."

In the den, he read the book from cover to cover pausing occasionally to review the ideas presented. His hope had suddenly become fruitful. He must visit the learned doctor. Researching the man's address, he discovered Dr. Bernardo Vincetti lived only an hour's drive from Osborne Valley. He dialed the phone number listed and talked with a secretary. Enthralled that the learned man still did past lives regression sessions with new clients, he made an appointment for the following Thursday.

CHAPTER FIFTEEN

JOHN COULD HARDLY wait until his last class on Thursday when he could see Dr. Vincetti. On his way to the hypnotherapist, a sudden mist forced John to turn on his windshield wipers as he drove down the unpaved road. He hoped it wasn't an omen of bad news to come. Approaching a small house nestled among walnut trees; he observed a sign which read HYPNOTHERAPIST. Dr. BERNARDO VINCETTI. He parked in front of the house, got out and rang the door bell numerous times, eager to meet the man who could put him in touch with his great-grandfather.

A short, pudgy man in his forties opened the door. John immediately noticed the full head of black hair, but with graying temples and penetrating green eyes. "Bernardo Vincetti?"

"Yes. You must be John Kepler. Come in."

After John entered the living room, it surprised him to see austere furnishings. Two easy chairs and a sofa sat in the middle of the elongated room. A small desk stood off to one side. Two large pictures depicting a black and white symbol in each frame hung on the opposite wall. John pointed at one of the framed Yin-yang pictures. "I like your pictures—cosmic duality?"

Bernardo nodded. "Yes. A reminder to my patients of mutual dependence. Yin, the black side, and yang, the white side within the circle, originally represented two sides of a valley, one in a shadow and the other in the sun—contrasts such as dark and light, male and female, positive and negative, active and passive, heaven and earth, but also completeness within the circle." He paused, clasping his hands, then continued on as though speaking to students in a lecture hall. "The small dots of opposite color in each field symbolize mutual dependence, such that light and shadow are not in conflict but rather depend on one another for completion."

"Do you use the symbology in your therapeutic sessions?"

"Yes. To heighten one's awareness and the symbolism facilitates a deep hypnotic state." Please be seated. My secretary said you have an interest in past life regression of departed relatives. May I ask how you learned about me?"

"Purely by accident." John talked fast, feeling excited about his visit. "So far everyone is telling me I'm wasting my time trying to time travel to the past." John felt a comradeship with Bernardo. "My main interest is my great-grandfather's life. He, Joshua Kepler, was a prospector during the California Gold Rush, an exciting time." John eyes brightened. "I crave that kind of adventure. Dr. Vincetti, from reading your book, I noticed you have investigated time travel to departed relatives."

"Refer to me simply as Bernardo, please." He clasped his hands together. "Yes, most of my research has been with children. Nearly three-quarters of the subjects described the mode of death of a departed relative. It's proof to me that we have a link to past lives of others, and with mind power, we should be able to access it physically."

John rubbed his hands together. "Yes, that's what I got from your book. I wasn't too clear on how that's achieved, Bernardo."

"Simply put—with intense concentration powers and a strong belief system."

"I suppose my ignorance is showing, but how does one physically time travel to the past using mind power?"

Bernardo peered into John's eyes. "Auto suggestion is like an affirmation. If you were to say, 'I am now traveling back in time to 1920,' that would be an affirmation. Saying the same thing as an auto suggestion becomes more powerful because of the high energy field it produces in the mind during a past lives regression."

Glancing at the Yin-yang picture on the wall, Bernardo continued. "It's only in recent years that advanced thinkers are making it known that we become what we think about. One of the major secrets to success with anything at all, be it wealth, health, fame or even a desire to enter another life, is to bypass the conscious mind in order to access the immense powers of the subconscious. The subconscious is about 90% of your total mind power as opposed to the 10% of mind that you usually use in your normal daily waking state." Leaning forward, Bernardo raised a finger in the air. "And we can influence the subconscious with auto suggestion. The subconscious mind is pure; it will accept anything you submit to it without question, and will then act upon your instructions thereby enabling you to experience your heart's desire in full measure."

John took a deep breath and expelled it with gusto. "I would be deeply committed to traveling back in time. I've had numerous dreams about my great-grandfather and the life he led. It's all I think about. My wife says it's an obsession, but I disagree. It's something I desire, and after I've had that experience, I think I will be satisfied."

"Well, regressing back to a child is standard therapy for those patients who need the awareness of problems in childhood, but regressing beyond one's birth to an older relative's life..." He paused, smiling. "That would require total faith in the process." Bernardo held up one finger. "Returning to the past even before you were born and connecting to a relative will require numerous sessions of deepened attentiveness." Bernardo pressed his lips together. "You need to be aware of unforeseen hazards."

"You mean during the hypnotic sessions?"

"If and when you are living the past life."

John leaned forward. "Like what?"

"The grandfather paradox: If you travel in the past and murder your own grandfather before he sires your mother or your father, do you instantly pop out of existence before you were born?"

"So you're saying I might not come back to the present when I want to? Or I might end up dead. Isn't there some way around getting caught up in any unforeseen events of harm's way?"

Bernardo looked down in contemplation. He glanced at the Yin-yang symbol on the wall, then pointed to the coffee table. "You'll notice the Yin-yang symbol embedded on the brooch here on the table." He picked it up and handed it to John. "I have used it as a post hypnotic suggestion to return to consciousness in some of my own sessions. Believing in the power of the symbol is critical." He shrugged. "What you think about intensely, you can bring about as long as you know for certain, emotionally, it is achievable." He put both hands on his knees. "You will need to keep the brooch with you at all times during the hypnotic state, and also during your travel back in time."

An uneasiness appeared on John's expression. "What if I run into a bear during my adventure? There's bound to be danger I would encounter in the wilderness, although it *is* what I crave—excitement."

Bernardo nodded. "Dangerous encounters can happen, and the brooch will be a safety reminder. Sort of like an eject button on an aircraft. When confronted with a hazardous situation, grasping the brooch and saying a keyword aloud, a post-hypnotic suggestion, will allow you to move instantly forward to the present." Waving a finger from side to side, Bernardo added, "Doubt will be the one thing you must avoid feeling."

"What is this keyword you're talking about?"

"Any word would do. *Believe* seems appropriate in your case."

John nodded and took a deep breath. "*Believe.* Okay. I want to do it. What's the next step?"

"Well, get comfortable. We will go through a practice session now to show you the procedure of self-hypnosis which you can accomplish on your own at your convenience at home. Three sessions should be enough for you to reach a state of heightened awareness so you can make the transition to the past."

"I'm eager to begin my journey."

Bernardo moved closer to John, focusing on the eyes. "I'll put you in a relaxed state of mind, then we will go deeper into past lives regression. There, you will concentrate on reliving his life in 1849 as you believe it to be. And I'll give you the post-hypnotic suggestion, *believe.*"

"When can the real adventure begin?"

"As I've said, after three or four sessions of self-hypnosis in the convenience of your home. After you've reached an alpha state and have feelings of your great-grandfather's presence, you can make the crossover into his life. You will know it when you arrive."

John raised his eyebrows. "Will I also be aware of my present life as John?"

"Yes, most definitely. Now, hold the brooch in your hand, concentrating on its power. When you feel yourself dozing off, visualize yourself entering into your great-grandfather's life. You will have arrived after seeing different surroundings. When you want to return to the present, speak out the word *believe,* holding the brooch in your hand." Bernardo clasped his hands together. "Are you ready for a session now?"

"Yes, I'm ready."

Bernardo pointed at the Yin-yang brooch. "Grasp it with a closed fist. Relax." After a few minutes of silence, Bernardo instructed, "You are now entering the subconscious."

During the session, John could see himself in the wilderness. Although he was alone and didn't experience his great-grandfather's presence, he felt the excitement. What he sensed the most was a feeling of freedom. He marveled at how refreshed he felt after being awakened from his adventure when Bernardo told him to speak the word *believe.*"

Bernardo gave John a hearty handshake at the front door and said, "When you return from your adventure, call me. I want to know all about it." On the way home, John couldn't help but feel an exhilaration of mind and body. His dream of excitement and adventure would soon become a reality.

***

At the precinct, Karen and Hal had finished writing a lengthy report on their visit to the landscape business. Karen got up from her desk. "It's time for a break. "I'm going to grab a bite to eat downtown. You want me to bring you back anything?"

"No. Take your time," he said, grateful that he'd have some time to himself. *I've got some thinking to do about a killing,* he said to himself. The words reverberated in his ears. There was little doubt in his mind what he must do—kill his wife. And it would have to be before she filed for divorce. With little time for planning, he would have to be meticulous in selecting the best possible scheme for the perfect murder. Fortunately, the last three cases had given him food for thought; especially the Library murder. The coroner had ruled Sheila's death an accident, but the truth had finally surfaced that the homicide was premeditated.

The ideal situation would be having someone find Evelyn dead in the Jacuzzi, but that scenario seemed improbable, unless he could arrange the numerous events that had to be timed perfectly. He considered Karen finding Evelyn's body, which would give more credence to an accidental death. But that involved too much finagling to arrange for Karen's presence at his house, and the reason for his absence. He knew it was unwise to depend on someone close to him that knew him well.

A hit man was out of the question. He quickly discounted his brother, Michael, as an accomplice. Not possible. He was all too familiar with betrayal in the best of families. Besides, Michael was a saint, not nearly enough brotherly love to agree to murder. Involving anyone other than himself was certain to be catastrophic mistake. But he had to consider all options.

The only foolproof method of killing his wife had to be a drowning, a slip and fall near the Jacuzzi hitting her head on the tile edging. Achieving the scenario would be tricky. He must include every possibility of unforeseen events before, during and after the commission of the act to eliminate suspicion. He reaffirmed in his mind Evelyn's accidental drowning to be the only viable method.

Not being at the scene was a top priority for any kind of plausible alibi. But who would find Evelyn's body? His next door neighbor, Mrs. Annette Greenville? He nodded his head at the sudden insight. How to accomplish the improbable task? He went through the steps of capability—talk with Annette over the slated fence that separated their property on the ruse that one of the slats needed replacing. Fortunately, the fence was low enough so the neighbor could see in his backyard, and see Evelyn alive and well. Evelyn would see him speaking to Annette and may even wave. He would explain his wife had vertigo, and worried about her getting into the Jacuzzi when he wasn't there, and asking her to check on Evelyn while he was at the precinct, a sudden trip of necessity. After the short conversation with the neighbor, he would then need to get Evelyn near the Jacuzzi before the next step of killing her. But how to accomplish the killing?

Questions ran through his mind. How to simulate a slip and fall? And he had to hold Evelyn's head under water for at least six minutes assuring her death, then leave the scene quickly before Mrs. Greenville checked on his wife. There was only one way to render Evelyn unconscious—a blow to the head with a hard object. What object? Right away he discounted a brick remembering the fiasco of Jack Buckingham's weapon of choice. A better weapon would be a piece of two by four with jagged edges. Hit Evelyn with a short piece, smear blood on the edging, drown here in the Jacuzzi, check her pulse to make certain she's dead, and dash to his car. He would then head out to the precinct.

The blow would have to be hard enough to break the skin. He needed a little bit of blood to smear onto the deck edging validating the wound. He would explain to investigators that his wife had vertigo. Karen could attest to that. Wait! What's the reason to get Evelyn into the Jacuzzi? After a moment of staring at the far wall, he had his answer. Call in a service man to fix a fake malfunction of the heating element. After the repairman's service call, he would ask Evelyn to join him in the tub to check the water temperature. Anticipating her response, "Why can't you do it?" and he would explain, "I'm not a good judge of water temperature. You're the one that uses it the most. But the two of us together can tell if the temperature feels like 90 or 100 degrees." It's what the repairman had suggested, he would tell her. If needed, he would entice her by offering to talk about sharing his pension.

Having his neighbor find the body was a risk he'd have to bear. What if she forgot to check on Evelyn? There were a lot of ifs. But eliminating as many ifs as he could became part of the challenge. Timing had to be perfect. Still, he needed the alibi of his neighbor finding the body for added credibility. He felt excited planning and committing his improbable mission. Smiling, he said aloud, "My plan is far better than Jack Bucking-ham's."

A nearby detective looked at Hal. "You talking to yourself again?"

He didn't answer. Mastering the perfect crime and killing Evelyn seemed to be a good match; killing two birds with one stone, achieving something on his own, and getting rid of his wife, but his perfect murder would have to address the three pillars of homicide—means, motive and opportunity.

He wanted to be rid of Evelyn. The marriage had been a mistake. He knew that from the start. Divorce wasn't an option now that he knew she would want have of his pension. His pension was his and his alone, hav-ing toiled countless hours during his fifteen years of po-lice work. Needed money for his retirement was a side issue, of course, but more than anything it was the prin-ciple involved.

One thing in his favor—killing her over money wouldn't be considered a motive. They had very little life insurance, a small savings account, and even a smaller mutual fund. The only thing of substantial value was his pension; sharing it with her was not an option. Keeping all of his pension and getting rid of his mar-riage, he told himself, were the real reasons for her de-mise. Behind it all, he knew full well, the desire of achieving the perfect murder.

Begin planting seeds with his partner to ward off any suspicion of wrong-doing on his part, just enough, however, for Karen to know crucial information. He needed to discover a hobby of Karen's that would be a good match for Evelyn. A bogus demonstration of Eve-lyn's vertigo fit the mold nicely. At a signal stop, Hal glanced at Karen. "Are you a thinker or a doer?"

"You mean in my spare time?"

"Yeah."

"A little of both but more a thinker. One of my hobbies is writing poetry."

"Really? Evelyn dabbles at writing short stories. But she needs help—encouragement mostly." He paused, thinking. "I just had an idea. Would you be interested coming to dinner some evening? You and Evelyn can exchange ideas on writing. I know she would appreciate any guidance you can give her."

"Great idea. I'll bring along some of my poems."

***

On Saturday, in a good mood, John Kepler chose to think his wife was being helpful when she made her suggestion "Easter week-end is coming up." She forced a smile. "If you want to fend for yourself out in the wild, spend a few days next weekend in the local mountains with your pup tent and gold pans."

"An excellent idea. I think I will be ready for my excursion to 1849," he said nodding.

She sighed. "It will be a welcome relief not hearing your complaints about routine and monotony." As she left the room, she said over her shoulder, "But before you go, replace the air-conditioning filter, and while you're making yourself useful, put the garbage in the dumpster. The heaping pile of bags are taking over the garage."

For the remainder of the week John had two practice sessions regressing into his past using Bernardo's procedure of self-hypnosis. The second time he regressed to his childhood, during the session he thought he saw his great-grandfather wink at him. It was a sign he was getting closer to his goal. John said the word *believe* and returned to the present. He waited a few days before he attempted another session.

Thursday evening, he felt eager to experiment one last time, and got comfortable in his upholstered chair holding the Yin-yang brooch in his hand. He concentrated on the image of his great-grandfather, noting the man's features. After achieving a deep regression, he saw Joshua swishing the gold pan around in a stream, hearing the sound of water rippling over the rocks, and there was the sense of freedom. John felt drowsy, but concentrated on keeping the image in focus. He suspected entry into alpha rhythm. The next stage would be the auto suggestion to his sub-conscious if only he could maintain a heightened awareness of his great-grandfather's presence. For a moment he could feel a tingling pressure on his arms. As the scene became vivid in his mind's eye, he heard a door open, then a voice.

"There you are," Gertrude said. "What are you doing?"

He shrugged. "Nothing."

"Are you still going up in the mountains Saturday morning?"

"Of course." He glanced at her. "Right now I'm attempting a past life's regression if you'll please leave me alone."

"Well, you'll need plenty of rest for your trip hiking through the mountains." She laughed then closed the door. The interruption convinced him to wait until he was up in the local mountains to hypnotize himself one last time before crossing over the time gap. The wilderness environment would give his mind that extra sensitivity to reach a heightened state of awareness and travel back to Joshua's time.

***

At mid afternoon on Friday, the Osborne Community Park contained only a few scattered empty cars. Gertrude waited in her station wagon tapping out a beat on the steering wheel when she heard a knock on the passenger door. Looking up she saw a man in dark glasses peering at her. "Are you Gertrude Kepler?"

"Yes."

"I'm Utah."

"Yes, yes," she replied, waving him inside the car. "I thought you'd never come. I hate to be kept waiting,"

After occupying the passenger seat, he continued glancing around the park. "Is it a go?"

She looked him over. "I'm pleased you come right to the point. Well, I won't bore you with details, only to tell you I am a person of reason and logic, keeping my emotions on the back burner most of the time. My husband, John Kepler..." She took a photo from her pocketbook and gave it to him. "This is what he looks like. He no longer serves my purpose, and I want him out of the way. Divorce is not an option. A lucrative life insurance policy is."

"The reason you want him out of the way isn't my concern," he said looking at the photo.

She shrugged her shoulders. "Fine. I'm very particular how the job is done."

He turned facing her. "What do you have in mind?"

"John's going camping this Easter weekend up in the local mountains. He'll be alone. I want him shot dead up there."

"That can be done, but why up in the mountains?"

"I'm a stickler for details. I want a clean killing, no evidence of foul play. As far as the police are concerned, his death will be due to an accidental shooting by a hunter scouting for mountain lions. You will be the mountain lion hunter."

He gazed at her before speaking. "You want me to tell the police I shot him?"

"Well, of course. You can tell the authorities it was simply an accident. Make up any story you want, but a reasonable one would be you were hunting mountain lions and saw one dash out from behind a bush thinking it was the mountain lion attacking, and shot my husband by mistake. There is nothing to tie you to me or John other than being in the vicinity of the shooting."

"Too risky. I've done time for armed robbery."

"But nothing on him will be stolen. You have no motive."

He shook his head. "Too close for comfort. I don't like it, and it's kind of sudden. Tomorrow?"

"I am prepared to pay you extra for your trouble."

"How much?"

"How does seventy-five thousand dollars sound?"

"I don't know. I'm taking an extra risk."

"Alright, I'll up to one-hundred thousand, but that's my final offer."

"Cash?"

"Yes, I can arrange that. Is it a deal?"

A full minute went by before he answered. "Okay, deal."

"You know my address." She paused. "He'll be leaving in the morning so stay hidden until John leaves, then follow him into the mountains. Shoot him dead at your convenience, but make it appear as an accident."

"Yeah, yeah, I got the picture. After the job is done, where do we meet for the money exchange?"

"Here at the park. One week from today, agreed?"

"Yeah, yeah." Not looking at her, he got out of the car and left.

***

Saturday morning, Gertrude stood at the front door and watched her husband load his station wagon with a pick, shovel, pail, a gold pan, his back pack and bedroll. John brushed off his hands, looked around, then opened the car door. Waving to her he said, "I may not be back."

"Good. I'll have a little peace and quiet. I hope you have a miserable time. It deserves you right for not going with me to my parents' house."

"Tell them hello, but I have a date with destiny in the California gold fields of 1849."

She shook her head. "This nonsense about traveling back in time is beyond my sensibilities. I won't miss you."

He laughed. "As much as you would like to come with me to maintain your control, I can't allow it. Sorry, you'll have to wait for my return, if I return. Hey, don't worry, should anything happen to me, my life insurance payments are current." He waved, got in the car, fired up the engine, then headed down the street.

Some distance back, Utah followed John's car.

Following an unpaved road, John continued up a hilly terrain until he came to a dead end and parked in a cleared area. He began assembling his gear. His backpack bulged with a tent, gold pan and small shovel. Grunting, he put it on, then moved out among the evergreens. There was coolness in the air, and he felt excited as he marched higher into the back country. He came across a swift-flowing stream. A huge boulder sat adjacent to the stream, part of it immersed in the water.

Some distance to the rear, Utah hid behind thick underbrush. With a rifle strapped across his back, he waited for the right moment to take a bead on his victim.

***

John swiped sweat from his brow with his arm. *This is good. No gain without pain.* But the spot didn't feel right for his last hypnosis session, and he decided to climb higher in the rugged terrain. Continuing his trek along the same stream, John stopped by another large boulder, took off his backpack to rest for awhile. He observed the peace and quiet of the surroundings. He swept up a handful of pine needles and sniffed them, then stuck his hand in the swift-flowing stream. He felt alive. He reached in his pocket and felt the brooch. He wanted to begin his journey to Joshua's time among the peaceful surroundings. Here he would make camp, and begin his hypnotic regression.

***

Utah kept one hundred yards to the rear of John's position at all times, and was now behind a tree, resting the barrel of his rifle across a small limb. He sighted through the scope, the crosshairs on John's body.

***

After taking off his backpack, John got into a

comfortable position sitting next to a tree, clasping the brooch in one hand, and closed his eyes. He focused his attention on an image of Joshua. As he went deeper into his visualization, he could hear the sound of water rippling over rocks, the singing of birds in the trees, and there was a feeling of adventure in his heart.

***

Closing in, Utah could see John against the tree. It was a good place to make the hit. He had a clear shot. In a prone position, he steadied the rifle and took aim. To his rear he heard crackling of pine needles. Turning, he saw a hunter a good distance away, moving up a steep embankment, heading toward John. It had to be one chance in a million that another person would be in the same area this high in the mountains.

Utah moved to a new position to keep hidden, his eye on the hunter. To his dismay, the hunter set up his tent and made camp. Utah waited throughout the night hoping the next morning the hunter would break camp and head downhill. At sun up, the hunter did break camp, but stayed in the area. The situation became intolerable. Utah decided to abort the mission. Too risky with a hunter nearby popping up at the wrong time. Utah headed down the mountain.

CHAPTER SIXTEEN

JOHN CLASPED THE brooch in his hand focusing his attention on an image he'd seen in one of the pictures of his great-grandfather and Emmett Hodges. He felt a noticeable silence as he went deeper into his visualization, drifting off into an alpha state. The letter his great-grandfather wrote to his wife appeared in his mind. He could hear Joshua's voice reading the letter.

John felt himself moving, floating toward his great-grandfather as though suspended in space. A tingling sensation pervaded his entire body. Looking down, he noticed a thin layer of snow on the ground, then a chill surged through his body. John looked around the landscape to find himself standing in a swiftly-moving stream, a large pan in his hand, wearing soiled coveralls, boots and a denim jacket over a wool sweater. Had he made the crossover to the gold fields of 1849? He shoved his hand into his pants pocket. He felt the brooch. Afraid of losing it, he quickly put it in a small pocket of his backpack. *But John, what if you need it in a hurry? Joshua didn't have a Yin-yang brooch, he told himself.* He straightened up, sticking out his chest. "You've made the crossover. Live adventurously!" he said aloud.

"What's that you say?" grumbled a voice from behind.

Turning around, John could plainly see Joshua's

prospecting partner, Emmett Hodges. The short, stout man, with red hair cresting his shoulders looked every bit the part of a prospector.

"Hey, Josh, you gonna stand there all day day-dreaming?"

The realization had come to him that his experience was genuine, that he had become his great-grandfather. But he also knew of his life in 1991. His dream of excitement had come true, at least for a time. He would enjoy it to the fullest now being a part of history. "Just taking a breather," he said to Emmett, stepping out of the stream and tossing his pan to the ground. "What's up?" he asked.

"Dark soon." Emmett motioned with a nod of his head. "We best git back to the tent. The bend in this stream is played out, anyways. You find any yella?"

John shook his head. "Nope. Not a sliver. Okay, go ahead and start back. I'll follow."

"Don't forget your gun." Emmett motioned with a nod of his head at the muzzle-loader leaning against a tree. John shoved his pan in his backpack, put it on, grabbed the gun and headed out.

"Keep your eye peeled fer grizzlies," Emmett cautioned, climbing through dense vegetation.

The excitement of confronting a bear brought on heavy breathing as he glanced around, while pacing himself cautiously.

"A grizzly could get the jump on us real easy among these trees," Emmett called back over his shoulder.

John tightened the grip around the stock of his gun. He'd seen pictures of Civil War re-enactors firing a muzzle-loader, although in an emergency, would he have the presence of mind to successfully go through the numerous steps? *Not to worry: otherwise you wouldn't be alive this moment.* He plunged forward scanning the wooded area, blinking as light snow struck his face. He didn't feel cold, perhaps because of the excitement, but it added to his fantasy of adventure. A surge of exhilaration filled his body. He pushed out his chest. *Come on, grizzly. I'm ready for you.*

Looking ahead, John noticed Emmett had increased the distance between them. Occasionally, Emmett would disappear from sight as they continued along the undulating terrain. Suddenly, John sensed something in back of him. Turning his head to the rear, he saw a bear move out from behind a large boulder. Startled, but not frightened, John stood still, fixed in place, waiting to see what the bear would do next. Any movement on his part might be a challenge for it to attack. But that's what he wanted—to make his fantasy more real.

Standing the rifle butt on the ground between his feet, he groped inside his coat. Surprised, but yet reassured, he pulled out a paper cartridge. He tore the paper with his teeth and poured powder into the barrel. *Wonderful! Just like he remembered it on TV.* The bear rose on hind legs, growling. John took a cartridge from his belt, tore off the paper, stuffed the powder and mini ball into the rifled chamber, then quickly removed the ramrod from its casing and jammed the ball down into the barrel. In that instant he sensed from peripheral vision the grizzly charging toward him at full speed. John glanced at the gun. *What are you waiting for? Cock the rifle?* His hand shook. *Don't panic. Aim the barrel and squeeze the trigger. Was there time to get the brooch in case? But it's in the backpack!*

John felt the force of the bear's front paw smash against his chest. He was knocked to the ground. The gun fell a few feet away out of reach. He looked up to see the bear standing over him, mouth open, growling, huge claws in the attack mode. *Don't feel fear.* Alarmed, but with a sense of excitement, John wondered if he should fight or run. He raised an arm to defend his head. The bear grabbed him, shook him like a rag doll, then slammed him to the ground. He thought it strange he didn't feel any pain. He saw the grizzly rise up ready to pounce on him for the kill. Convinced now he was in danger, even though he didn't have the brooch in his hand, he would call out the word *believe.* As he opened his mouth, he heard a musket shot. The grizzly turned away as Emmett reloaded his rifle and fired again. The bear jerked, then dashed off the trail into the thicket.

"You okay, Josh?" Emmett inquired, helping John to his feet.

"Yeah, I think so."

"Come on, let's git moving 'fore he comes back. He's wounded and mad as hell."

As twilight darkened the landscape, they made camp in an open area, surrounded by a cluster of pine trees. John could hear the frigid gusty wind sweep around the trees striking his cheeks like the sting of ice held against the skin. *Exhilarating! What a wonderful change from the thermally-controlled atmosphere of his home.* He turned his back to the wind while he helped Emmett assemble the tent. Emmett tried to build a fire, but the wind, overpowering, quenched any flicker of flame before it could heat up wet branches.

"Dang! We're gonna freeze in this here storm," Emmett said, stomping his feet on the ground for circulation.

John nodded. "Must be near ten below. The tent will protect us."

"Fer a spell, I reckon. Let's git in."

When they settled inside the tent, Emmett handed John a biscuit.

"What's this?"

"Hell, can't you tell hard tack when you see it? Enjoy, there ain't no more."

"Nothing to drink?"

"Eat snow. Storm should let up by daybreak. Then we move on."

After a few hours, the sleeting snow stopped. Darkness pervaded the landscape. He could barely make out Emmett's form only a few feet away. The silence became noticeable. He felt pain in his legs. "You got pain in your legs?" he asked Emmett?"

"Sure 'nough." Emmett rubbed his ankles. "Swelling in the joints from standing in water. That's the cause."

Smiling at the realism of his adventure, John patted his cheeks to keep them from freezing. But the pain was doable; part of his fantasy. The world of the 20th Century he recently left with its conveniences seemed far away.

***

The next morning at daybreak, John and Emmett folded the tent and squeezed it into John's backpack. Emmett flung an arm in a westward direction. "This way. Follow me. Keep close. And keep your eyes peeled fer varmints... and grizzlies," he added with a wink.

Following Emmett, John trudged on, feeling emptiness in his stomach. He would gladly eat a rat, even uncooked, he told himself. *John, you're in the wilderness and loving it.* They struggled up a steep hill, then entered a valley and came upon a swift-flowing stream. Beyond a small waterfall, they stopped at a clearing near an outcropping.

"Damn! Lookee there—black sand," Emmett said, pointing. "Where's there's quartz, there's gold. We done found ourselves a spot." The excitement engulfed John as they made camp. John watched Emmett shovel a portion of dirt and rocks into his pan, then added a scoop of water, observing how Emmett jiggled the pan in a revolving motion.

John did his best to copy his partner. After a few pans of dirt, John yelled out, "Eureka! Emmett, I got some nuggets."

"Got me some, too," Emmett replied, nodding. "Looks like this basin is loaded up, some the size of my thumb. "Sure 'nough, we've got ourselves a find."

John danced in the stream, happy that he had found a bonanza. They panned for the better part of the morning collecting three pouches of nuggets.

After taking a few minutes rest, John raised his arms in the air doubling his fists. "Awesome! My fantasy is everything I hoped for," he said, looking up at the sky.

Emmett frowned. "What's that you say?"

"I am a happy man, Emmett." John reached over and took a bag of nuggets, tossing it in the air, then catching it. Smiling, he was about to say something more when he sensed someone entering their campsite. Turning, he could see two men approach with drawn rifles. The bigger of the two, heavy-set, near six feet tall, with shoulder-length hair and a beard jerked the rifle to his shoulder. "All we want is your gold, mister."

John looked at the big man. "You're going to steal our gold?"

The big man glanced at his partner. "We got ourselves a holdout."

"I worked hard to get these nuggets," John said, wanting to delay the excitement of his fantasy. "They're mine. Sorry, you can't have them."

"I'll shoot you dead," the big man said without hesitation, then cocked his rifle.

Unafraid, John smiled at the stranger. "It won't do you any good. I'm from the future."

The big man leveled his gun at John.

The sound of a nearby waterfalls splashing over rocks could be heard in the following silence. A brisk, cold wind blew in from the North. The stream flowed fast, without impediment during the spring of 1849 in the California gold country.

***

Monday morning Gertrude fidgeted in her lounge chair, wondering if she should call the police, and report John missing. Thinking he could have gotten lost or had an accident, she decided calling the police the more prudent thing to do.

At the Beaverton precinct, Lt. Abrams called Hal and Karen into his office. After explaining the call he'd received from Gertrude, he told them to take her statement. "She said her husband had gone camping in the mountains over the week-end and should have been back Sunday." Abrams shrugged. "I told her he may have decided to stay another day, but she said he had to come home Sunday because he was a teacher and would never miss his classes. Get her statement. I don't anticipate problems."

"You mean the case or the person?" Hal asked, with a serious expression as if it was a reasonable question.

"Either one is fine with me." Abrams frowned. "Hal, I think you're just bored, after having solved the testy Buckingham case."

"No, I've just got a lot on my mind at the moment."

***

Hal and Karen arrived at Gertrude's house. They gathered in the living room. Karen leaned forward, and introduced Hal and herself. Gertrude motioned for them to be seated on a sofa. She explained that her husband left Saturday on a camping trip in the mountains, that he went by himself. "John's a loner. He has this fascination about living the life of his great-grandfather." She pointed to a picture on the wall. "That's the great-grandfather, Joshua Kepler, on the left. The man with him is his prospecting partner."

Hal and Karen looked at each other.

"How old is that picture?" Hal inquired.

"At the time of the California Gold rush. "It's been in the Kepler family the entire time, passed down to each generation."

"Does your husband go hiking often in the mountains?" Karen asked.

"Only lately. He says he likes to be on his own in the wilderness. He pans for gold."

Hal grinned. "Does he find any?"

"I don't think so." Gertrude looked askance. "He has this fantasy of time travel to the California Gold Rush, living the life of his great-grandfather."

"So, he was supposed to be back Sunday?"

"Yes. He's a teacher at the community college. He wouldn't miss one of his classes. I'm positive about that."

"Tell us a little bit more about his fantasy of time travel," Karen inquired.

"John's obsessed with living a life of his great-grandfather. He's been seeing a therapist who gives sessions in past life therapy. I don't know the details, but John believes in the man."

Hal looked at Karen. frowning. "Past lives therapy? Is that possible, Mrs. Kepler?"

"I certainly don't believe so. I told him he was crazy, but it seems to drive him harder to accept such nonsense."

"Ma'am, are you and your husband having marital problems?"

"Like any couple, yes, but we're able to settle most of the minor issues."

"What's the therapist's name?" Karen asked.

"Bernardo Vincetti. I can give you his address."

"Hopefully, your husband will return home soon," Hal replied. "Anyway, we'll be in touch with you."

***

Three days later, Hal phoned and made an appointment to see Gertrude at her home. After being seated, Karen spoke up. "We didn't want to tell you over the phone, but we've called off the search for your husband in the mountains. There is no trace of him or any of the equipment you mentioned, but we did find his car."

Gertrude's jaw dropped. She didn't say anything for a long moment. With no sign of emotion, she said to Hal, "Do you think he's dead?"

Frowning, Hal replied, "It doesn't look good. We've covered the river pretty much from the source down in the valley. Used a police helicopter, and hundreds of volunteers, but no evidence of him."

"I wouldn't be surprised if he was attacked by an animal," she said, frowning. "John isn't careful. He's clumsy, you know." She got up. "Well, what should I do?"

"The case will stay open," Karen advised. "It's a waiting game now for any news of someone finding his body. Sorry. It does seem unlikely he would survive the rugged terrain."

Gertrude almost smiled at the woman's comment. Maybe she was rid of her despicable husband by natural means.

Getting up to leave, Hal said, "If anything comes up we'll phone you. You have our number. Good day."

***

Thursday evening, Utah called Gertrude, and demanded that she meet him in the community park. After parking next to his truck at the end of the parking lot, Gertrude waited as the large man walked over to her station wagon. He tried to open the passenger door but it was locked. He banged on the window, until she lowered it. "What do you want?"

"I want to sit down. Unlock the damn door!"

After she unlocked the door, he opened the door and dropped in the seat. Turning, he gazed at her. "Did you bring the money?"

"No, I told you I'm not paying. Your job wasn't finished."

"What the hell do you care? He's probably rotting up there in the mountains. Look, I did the hard part traipsing through the mountains following your husband for a day and a half. A hunter showing up wasn't my fault. Besides, you got what you wanted—he's gone, right?"

"No help from you." She looked at him with contempt. "I only pay for services rendered providing they've been accomplished."

Scowling, he demanded in a threatening tone, "I'm not asking, Lady, I'm telling you—give me the money we agreed on."

She held onto her purse a little tighter. "No. I'm not paying one penny. Obviously, you are as stupid as my husband," she went on belittling him. "I'm not paying. Get out of my car now!"

Utah lunged at her, grasping her throat with both hands, squeezing with all his might. She scratched his face and arms with her fingernails in an attempt to fend off his attack, but the struggle soon ended. He felt her pulse. Dead. After glancing around the parking lot, he grabbed her purse, jumped out and ran to his truck. Looking through her purse, he found no money. He tossed the purse out the window, started the engine and drove off.

***

Hal and Karen looked through the mirrored window at the large, heavy-set man seated in the interrogation room.

"You ready?" Hal asked.

"Let's do it."

They entered the room and sat across from Utah at a table.

"Max Akers..." Hal paused glancing at his notebook. "I see you have an alias, Utah. Do prefer being called Utah?"

"Yeah."

"I'm Detective Reiner and this is Detective Holmes," he said, pulling a scrap of paper from his shirt pocket. "We're investigating a recent homicide at Beaverton Valley Community Park. We're hoping you can help us."

Utah shrugged his shoulders. "Who was killed?"

"Mrs. Gertrude Kepler," Karen answered promptly.

Hal handed the scrap paper to Utah. "This AVO was found in Gertrude's purse at the scene. Read it."

"It says Utah, then Eight p.m., then community park."

"Could you tell us why the victim has a reminder note for a meeting at the community park with your name on it?"

"Oh yeah," Utah said, nodding, thinking, then muttered, "I met her in the park a few weeks ago to talk about doing some work for her. Painting her husband's den."

Karen looked in her notebook. "I see you recently did time for a burglary."

"Yeah. I do odd jobs like painting, trash removal, that sort of thing."

"Why meet her at a park at eight p.m. in the evening?' Hal inquired.

A long minute elapsed before Utah spoke. "Oh yeah, I remember; she didn't want her husband to know. The paint job was to be a surprise."

"Did you paint the room?"

"No. We couldn't agree on a price. She's a tight-wad."

Hal glanced at his partner, then gave Utah a business card. "Here's my phone number. If you can think of anything else, give me or Detective Holmes a call. Thank you for your time."

They escorted Utah out of the room.

***

At their desks, Hal and Karen talked about John's fixation of time travel, wanting to live the life of his great-grandfather during the California Gold Rush."

"Do you think he was crazy?" Hal asked.

"I don't know, but the husband seems confused about reality, assuming his wife was telling us the truth."

"About the disappearance?"

"Yes. The note to Utah suggests something more ominous than painting a room."

"Something to do with the husband's disappearance."

"Exactly."

"Maybe we can unveil scuttlebutt at the county detention center. What we need is one of Utah's cell mates willing to admit Utah's involvement."

***

Two days later at the county prison, Jose Mendez, a jailhouse snitch, revealed to Hal that he had shared a prison cell with Utah. "Just before Utah was released, he said he'd been offered money to kill John Kepler."

"By Kepler's wife?"

"Yeah. Gertrude Kepler. Utah told me in detail how he'd followed Kepler up in the mountains, but he didn't go through with it."

"Did he say why?"

"Nope. That's all he told me."

Mendez's testimony provided good reason to get a warrant, but the search of Utah's apartment contained no incriminating evidence. Coupled with the disappearance of John Kepler and Mendez's testimony of the wife's possible involvement, the D.A. told Lt. Abrams to arrest Utah. He would be charged with manslaughter. The trial began a year later. The defense attorney, a public defender appointed by the court, gave a hard-driving defense, pointing out the prosecutor had no tangible evidence, with only a jailhouse snitch who made a deal with the D.A. to reduce his incarceration time.

Hal focused his attention on the prosecutor's closing statement, and the judge's instructions to the jury. He wanted to gain as much information as he could to avoid being charged with Evelyn's murder. As the trial progressed, it became apparent that the circumstantial case against Utah was losing ground. Then a surprise witness came forth that turned things around. On the stand, she explained that on the night of the murder, she had taken her dog to the community park for his nightly walk.

"And what did you see?" the assistant D. A. asked.

"I noticed a white older model Dodge truck parked next to a newer model station wagon."

"And did anything happen?"

"Yes," she said nervously, pointing at Utah. "That man at the defense table got out of a truck and got into the station wagon."

"And what time was it when you observed the defendant?"

"A few minutes after eight in the evening on the night of the murder."

"And then what happened?"

"Well, it was dark, but I could see a woman in the driver's seat. No more than five minutes passed when the defendant got out of the car holding something in his hand, and he rushed to his truck and got in. Soon after, he drove off."

The defense attorney asked the judge for a short break to speak to his client.

Because of the damaging testimony of the eye-witness, Utah took a plea bargain reducing his sentencing time.

Hal made a mental note realizing there could be no unforeseen witnesses sabotaging his perfect murder. As the Assistant D. A. and Hal left the courtroom, Prosecutor Markey said, "You never can be certain of anything. Life seems to be a continuous series of random events."

Markey nodded. "I think John Kepler is the only one in this case that got what he planned for."

"What's that?"

"Well, for one thing, he got away from his wife."

"But he's probably dead."

Markey nodded with a grin. "Hey, man, you can't have everything."

Hal laughed. "My last three cases have been mind benders, reminding me that nothing's for certain. Life continues to be a mystery, right? For all we know, John Kepler might be having a ball living his great-grandfather's life during the California Gold Rush."

"If you believe that, I think Lt. Abrams will be looking for a new homicide detective. Well, one thing's for certain—Utah or Kepler's wife didn't get away with the perfect murder."

Hal nodded. Thinking ahead, he told himself it was time to set his perfect murder in motion. Returning to the precinct, Hal briefed Karen on the trial. As he got up from his desk to go home, he reminded Karen of the dinner date at his house. "Bring along your poems and an empty stomach. Evelyn has prepared a sumptuous feast."

CHAPTER SEVENTEEN

KAREN ARRIVED PROMPTLY at Hal's house, and greeted her partner and Evelyn, and then they moved into the living room, Karen and Evelyn sitting on matching sofas across from one another. Hal excused himself. "Need to make a pit stop, will be back soon."

"Good to see you again," Karen said to Evelyn. "How are things going?"

Evelyn shrugged. "Hal said he wanted to make our marriage work. He wants to see a counselor."

"Well, that's good."

"I'm not sure I believe him. We've been down this path before." Evelyn waved a hand through the air. "He's a different person of late. I don't know what occupies his mind; he's off in some other world most of the time. The other day he threw a chair against the wall, and it wasn't because of me. I wasn't even in the room. When I asked him why, he gave me some cock and bull story about the chair not being level. Something is on his mind, but as usual, he won't say what it is. Does he ever get violent at work?"

Grimacing, Karen replied, "I don't know if I should be talking to you about Hal. He *is* my partner.

"I know. Karen, you're very open. I trust you. I need someone to confide in. Please, this is strictly between the two of us."

"I don't remember him ever displaying anger at

work. He's like a lamb. But you're right; he is off in his own world. Getting his opinion is like pulling teeth. When he's in one of his moods or whatever, I have to prod him to answer me." Karen put a comforting hand on Evelyn's arm. "I'm sorry to hear about your marriage problems. What are you going to do?"

"I don't know." Evelyn sighed. "Enough of my disheartening news. "I'm so glad that you've come to dinner. I made a seafood casserole and tapioca pudding for dessert."

"Yummy. We can talk about writing." Karen held up a folder. "I brought along a couple of my poems—limericks really. I try to be funny. I do have a short story I'll leave with you. It won an award so someone thinks I know what I'm doing."

"Thank you. I need all the help I can get with my writing. I enjoy mysteries, but have trouble coming up with a good plot."

"I think I can help you with that."

As Hal returned and sat down beside Evelyn, Karen pulled a paper from file folder. "Shall I read one of my limericks now?"

"Please do."

"There once was a man who couldn't fly a kite, and he knew no difference between day and night. He spoke in self-defense, his words made no sense, so, all his friends told him he should write!"

"I think I fit that category," Evelyn said, grinning. "I've started three stories, and haven't finished any of them."

Karen nodded. "Writer's block. It's often a sign of not knowing your characters or the plot line well enough."

"That's what I need—instruction. But let's have dinner, and we we'll continue discussing writing."

Karen glanced at Hal. "I hope you won't be too bored."

Deep in thought, he paused before speaking. "Not a problem."

They made their way into the dining room. Evelyn directed Karen to a chair at the festive dining room table. As Evelyn turned to move toward the kitchen, Hal grabbed her arms in a quick movement. "Whoa, glad I caught you in time before you fell."

Scowling, Evelyn remarked, "I wasn't falling."

"You mean you won't admit it." He glanced at Karen with a cynical expression. "Recently, she nearly fell into our Jacuzzi."

"I did not."

"You don't remember?"

"When?"

"About a month ago. You slipped on the tile, and I caught you."

She shook her head, then glanced at Karen. "It's news to me if it really happened. I think it's another one of his fabrications."

Hal held up his arms in surrender. "Okay." He glanced at Karen with raised eyebrows. "I think she has vertigo. She won't see a doctor. I worry about her when she gets into the Jacuzzi alone."

Evelyn shook her head again and glanced at Karen. "I don't know what he's talking about."

He thought he planted sufficient seed to suggest his wife was accident prone. Hoping Karen heard his remarks about Evelyn's vertigo, he felt he needed additional anecdote of his wife's unstable condition even at the risk of overdoing it. He quickly thought of another fabrication to cement an indelible connection in his partner's mind.

"You don't remember what happened last year," he said, leaning forward in an aggressive manner.

Evelyn frowned her ignorance. "What?"

"When we took Rodney to the fair and went on the merry-go-round."

"I remember going to the fair and yes, we took Rodney with us on the carousel."

"It's what happened right after Rodney's ride. You complained of dizziness as we made our way to the next ride."

"I don't remember that."

"When we got home on your way to the front door you collapsed!"

"Good grief! You've got me confused with some- one else." She glanced at Karen shaking her head.

"You bruised your leg, don't you remember. I had to help you to the bedroom."

"No, I certainly would remember falling and get- ting hurt."

Hal looked at Karen with a tilt of his head. "I was there and saw her fall to her knees. Fortunately no skin was broken, but she took a couple of aspirin and went to bed."

"Did I see a doctor?" Evelyn quipped in a taunting manner.

"No, you didn't. Your exact words were, 'I'm not going to a doctor because of a stumble.'"

"I wouldn't have said something like that. Hal, you're confused."

Hal glanced back and forth between Evelyn and

Karen. He raised his hands, sucking in a deep breath. "Well, if she doesn't remember, she doesn't remember."

"It's time to change the subject," Evelyn said. "I'll get the casserole. Hal, pour Karen some wine."

They began eating and talked about writing.

"The story I'm stuck on now is a mystery, a who-done-it," Evelyn said. "I think I have something of a plot, but the main character doesn't seem real. He's the antagonist."

"That's the bad guy," she said to Hal.

Hal grinned. "Thanks for letting me know who the bad guy is. I could have used that info in our last case."

"Well the writing experts say you should know your main characters," Karen advised Evelyn, "like the back of your hand."

"How do *you* do it?"

"I make a profile, you know, listing the physical description and personality traits of all of the characters, especially the antagonist. I get to know the antagonist as if he were my family."

"Yes, that makes sense. I'll take your advice and write up a profile."

Karen sipped on her wine, then continued, "An author can usually instill more drama in a story showing the evil ways of the antagonist, rather than the good of the protagonist." She paused with a quick look to Hal. "The protagonist is the good guy."

He chuckled. "A rarity in our line of work."

"I don't want you to feel left out of our conversation."

He pretended to hold a book in his hands and added with a smug expression, "When I read my next novel I'll be sure to look for those two characters."

Evelyn leveled her eyes at Hal. "Don't be snotty."

"Without any conflict between the two, the story bogs down," Karen advised Evelyn.

After a sipping from her wine glass, Evelyn inquired, "Does your work at the department help you in your writing?"

"As a matter of fact it does." She glanced at Hal. "The homicide cases we work on often gives me insight on witnesses from the viewpoint of story characters. Especially suspects. I try to absorb every little detail of their personality hoping it will help solve the case. And it helps me in my writing. Even ludicrous limericks."

Hal nodded to his wife, grinning. "I believe that. If my partner was a suspect in a murder, I think she would get away with it because she scrutinizes every detail of the case with the eye of a fox bordering on obsession." After a pause he added, "But I commend her for a scrutinizing eye, searching for evidence. That's what it takes to stop a clever suspect from getting away with murder."

"Thank you, partner." Karen poked him in the arm. "You're more experienced at police work than I am. I think you'd be the one who could get away with murder." She laughed, then spoke to Evelyn. "We recently finished a murder case where the suspect almost got away with it."

"How was he caught?"

"His arrogance. He thought he could outsmart our lab technicians; his fatal mistake."

"Let's move into the living room," Evelyn suggested.

As Karen and Evelyn seated themselves on the sofa, Hal excused himself again, retreating into the hallway. He stood by the corner out of sight, tilting his ear listening."

"If I could have a copy of the who-done-it you're writing, I would be happy to critique it," Karen advised.

"I would like that." Evelyn gave a manila file to Karen. "It's not finished; but there's a summary of what's it's supposed to be about on the first page." She grimaced. "It's hard to concentrate on writing when I'm overwhelmed with Hal's behavior. I'm a nervous wreck lately. It's not worth it to me physically or emotionally to continue... I'm sorry, if I'm overstepping our friendship. I realize you work closely with Hal..."

"On homicide cases," Karen interrupted. "He has mentioned his confusion about not wanting to share his emotions with others. I don't know the reasons for your marital problems, and like I said before, I can't advise you what to do, sorry. I can only say, if it's affecting your health, appropriate action on your behalf is needed."

"Thank you for saying that." Evelyn nodded. "That's what I must do—protect myself."

"Do you really think he would harm you?"

"I don't know. Maybe not purposely, but anymore, I'm not sure what to expect."

"I should be going now," Karen said, getting up. "Thank you for the delicious dinner. I'll get back to you on your story, but it might be a few days."

"That's fine. I appreciate your help. And thank you for listening to my domestic problems."

As Evelyn rose out of her chair, Hal stepped into the room with an expression of surprise. "You're leaving already?"

"Yes. I have some shopping to do." She laughed. "Which takes up as much of my time I suspect as case work."

Having heard their conversation, he would try to convince Karen that Evelyn's concern for their marriage woes was overstated, that Evelyn tended to portray herself to others as a victim.

At the right time at work, he would tell his partner the marriage endured on a solid foundation.

It became clear to him that he had to be the credible one in their marital dispute. After the killing, Karen would be routinely interviewed, and her testimony might make the difference whether or not investigators viewed him as a suspect. He needed to soften Evelyn's portrayal of their marriage difficulties.

At the front door, Karen bid them good-bye and told Hal she would see him at the precinct in the morning.

After Karen left, while Evelyn cleared off the dining room table, she asked Hal, "What was all that nonsense about my falling?"

He paused, thinking. "Well, you looked like you were going to fall. Maybe I was mistaken."

"You know I don't have vertigo. Why did you say that?"

He shrugged. "I don't know. It just popped out."

"No." She shook her head. "Nothing you say ever pops out; you mull it over in your mind for a long time."

Forcing himself to appease her, he held up his hands in a show of resolve. "Okay, I spoke out of turn. My error. That's something we can discuss with the marriage counselor. Didn't we agree to work through our problems?"

"I'm beginning to think it's not worth the effort. Our personalities clash. Hal, you're too set in your ways." She stared at him. "The truth is—I don't think you love me anymore. And honestly, much of my love for you has gone by the wayside because of your attitude."

He didn't respond to her allegation.

"I believe I'd be better off on my own. I'm thinking more and more about ending the marriage."

Hal probed into her eyes. He could tell she had no respect for him. That fact bothered him the most. Without respect, soothing over their troubles seemed fruitless.

Unable to contain himself, he remarked, "I think I know what you're really saying."

"Oh really? Do tell me."

"You're after my money."

"What money? The small savings account that wouldn't buy a decent TV set? The meager mutual fund that grows about as fast as rhubarb? The only thing substantial is your retirement benefits. I'm not greedy, but I'm entitled to alimony and half of your pension."

"You won't get a penny of my pension," he said, folding his arms across his chest. He stared at her with teeth barred.

"We'll see about that," she said, getting up and defiantly stomped out of the room.

He walked out to the Jacuzzi disturbed by her last words. Believing that she would follow through with her threat of divorce, he needed to think about the options of killing his wife.

Falling on the Jacuzzi tile edging seemed to be the best scenario as he recalled the Buckingham case, and went over the facts of Sheila's *accident*.

He pulled on his earlobe, thinking, while studying

the layout of the Jacuzzi. Raised up above the patio floor, Evelyn would need to climb three steps and step over the raised edging to get into the water. The edging, an ideal point for a stumble, then falling forward and striking her head on the tile seemed plausible. He walked up the three steps brushing a foot against the lip, then moved his body forward assimilating a fall, but halted the process, regaining his balance.

He stepped down to the patio floor, strolled to the fence and looked at his neighbor's yard. The Jacuzzi, a good fifteen feet away from the fence, provided sufficient space to speak to his neighbor, Annette Greenville, without Evelyn hearing. All in all, his plan looked promising. He returned to the Jacuzzi enclosure staring at it for a moment. *Wait! What is the motivation to get Evelyn in her bathing suit and in the backyard at a precise time?*

He would invite Evelyn to join him in the Jacuzzi. Knowing that she enjoyed the soothing rest in the warm tub, he felt confident she would agree. But leaving nothing to chance, he would entice her by telling her he would agree to a divorce giving her half of his pension, a lie, of course, but he needed to make certain his plans were met without complications. Then inform his noisy wife he would be talking with Mrs. Greenville about replacing the slatted fence with a block wall for more privacy. The fake meeting would need to be previously arranged with Mrs. Greenville. Fortunately, his wife had an aversion to talking about construction projects. While speaking to Annette about changing the slat fence to a block wall, he would mention his wife in the tub reading a book. He knew Annette would greet Evelyn with a wave of hand, and Evelyn would reply. His neighbor would see Evelyn in the tub, alive and well.

Next, he would ask Mrs. Greenville to check on Evelyn before the end of the hour, Evelyn's normal time in the Jacuzzi, he would inform his neighbor. His reason for leaving—to attend an important meeting at the precinct. He would explain that when he wasn't there, it worried him that Evelyn might fall getting out of the tub because of her vertigo. After ending his talk with Annette, and seeing her go into her house, he would hit Evelyn with some hard object to her head, smear blood on the tub edging, then hold Evelyn's head under water until dead.

What then? Make sure the weapon is disposed of. Change out of the bathing trunks into street clothes. Jump in the car and drive to the precinct. He would wait for news of Evelyn's fatal accident. What's the reason for being at the precinct? A meeting with Karen previously arranged. It would add to his credibility with her there when notified of Evelyn's fatal *accident.*

Where would he hide the weapon of destruction? Remembering the poker case and Virgil Blydair's beer can in plain sight, he would have the object handy by the Jacuzzi control panel. If Evelyn asked, he would simply explain it to be a block used to support the panel which happened to be loose, another lie. The repairman had been informed, he would tell her, another lie, but credible. *A lie isn't a lie unless discovered,* he mused to himself.

He would need to get Evelyn out of the tub, and walk her back up the steps to make the *accident* as real as possible. *Wait! Why would she get out of the tub?* After a minute of scratching his head, he nodded. A fake emergency call from the house phone, and then as soon as she was out of the tub, making her way down the steps, he would tell her the call canceled. "No, I don't know who it was," he would say. "A woman's voice, wanting to give you some urgent message."

Taking the weapon from his waistband, he would follow her up the steps as she returned to the tub until she reached the lip. Next, grab her arm, turning her toward him, then striking her forehead with some hard object with a full swing of the arm.

Grab her before she collapsed into the water. He needed blood to smear on the tile at the point where her alleged fall would strike the tile edging. The only other uncertainty—how hard a blow would render her unconscious and what kind of hard object would do so?

Tomorrow he would buy a couple of cantaloupes to assimilate the human head. Practice smacking them with different force. Practice would give him the feel of it. He nodded and spoke aloud, "Good thinking, Hal."

But he must decide what hard object to use to knock out Evelyn, and break the skin so she would bleed? Remembering the Buckingham case, he quickly eliminated using a brick. Jack Buckingham had used a brick, he recalled, killing his sister; but the brick had broken in two pieces. Hal shook his head. Why Jack returned the brick pieces to his planter, he would never know. So now he needed something hard that wouldn't break, and that could be destroyed after its use. How about a piece of wood that would fit into the hand comfortably and was solid enough to knock someone unconscious?"

He went to the garage and sawed off a ten inch piece of two by four. Smoothing it out with sandpaper, he felt of it fondly, then pounded four nails toward one end leaving the heads sticking up a fraction of an inch. The nails gouging into Evelyn's forehead would assure bloodletting.

Then he did a strange thing, almost childlike, he thought, smelling the piece of wood, and licking the protruding nail heads. The metallic taste made him shiver slightly, and he smiled at the thought of his behavior, not so much odd, but that the action had become visceral. Although he knew his focus had to be based on intelligence, not instinct. Yes, his perfect murder would be faultless, as distinguished as an academy award.

Satisfied that he had thought of all contingencies, he decided to go to bed. Knowing Evelyn's habits, she had retired to the master bedroom, and closed the door to remind him of their sexual estrangement. He went inside and retired to the spare bedroom. Foolhardy, he felt, to expect his perfect murder to evolve without mishap, but ready emotionally and mentally to be successful in managing the perfect crime.

CHAPTER EIGHTEEN

TWO DAYS LATER, Hal adjusted the temperature to the lowest setting, then removed the control knob and put it in his pocket. He returned to the living room. "The temp control knob on the Jacuzzi is missing," he said to Evelyn who was sitting on the sofa reading a magazine.

She glared at him, dropping the magazine in her lap. "Well, I don't have it. See!" Shaking her head, she added, "How can it be missing?"

"All I know it's not there on the panel. So now we can't adjust the temperature. I'll call a serviceman."

"Is that necessary? It must be somewhere near the Jacuzzi. It wouldn't just disappear. I'll look for it."

"I've already searched. Never mind, I'll call a serviceman." Hal turned away from her and left the room, satisfied that he had adequately set up the scam.

At work, Hal make an appointment with a spa repairman. Returning home a few minutes before the scheduled appointment, Hal installed the knob on the temperature control panel just before the serviceman arrived. He told Evelyn her presence wasn't necessary, that he would talk to the servicemen. After a few minutes checking voltages on the heater unit, then adjusting the levers on the topside control box, the serviceman spoke to Hal. "I can't find anything wrong, except the temperature was set at the lowest scale."

Hal shrugged. "Really? I don't know. Maybe it

was turned down by mistake. I thought I turned the knob all the way up, but there was no temp increase."

"It takes a while. Did you give it enough time?"

"I thought I did, but maybe..." He grinned. "I admit sometimes I don't pay that much attention."

"No problem, sir. The heater temperature is now set between 80 and 102 degrees. You can adjust it to your liking with the knob on the control panel."

Hal shrugged. "Sorry if I got you out here for nothing."

"You should be okay now. Everything is working properly."

Hal paid the man and escorted him to the front door. After the serviceman left, Hal told Evelyn the serviceman put on a new knob and lied about adjusting the temperature control unit, but that the water temperature should be tested as soon as possible, and to give him a call if it wasn't working properly."

"Why didn't he test it when he was here?" she asked, frowning.

"He suggested we were a better judge of the temperature we wanted." Hal chuckled. "He said his finger wasn't a good referee of temperature."

"Well, don't procrastinate. Check it out, then. Meditating in the tub is one of my few pleasures."

"Well, you know I'm not good at detecting a change in the temperature. You use it all the time. Between the two of us, we can tell if the control settings are working."

She sighed. "When?"

"Tonight, after dinner." Smiling, he added, "I'll give you a back rub. I'll be talking to Mrs. Greenville about the fencing. Have you anything you want me to say to her about the fence?"

"No." She shook her head. "But it seems unnecessary since we'll be selling the house. Unless you want to give me the house in the divorce settlement."

He scoffed, ready to answer her comment with contempt, but realized he needed to be on her good side to simplify his plan of murder. Grinning, he said, 'We can talk about that in the tub."

Reluctantly, she agreed, but told him it would be after the dinner hour.

***

He returned to the precinct, sat down at his desk and looked at some papers absently. Finally the time had come to carry out his plan. He checked his watch. In about seven hours his pension would be safe. His perfect murder would soon be a reality. He glanced around the squad room. Karen wasn't at her desk, probably in the rest room. The familiar face of his nemesis, Gillan, appeared suddenly displaying an arrogant grin. How unfortunate that Gillan wouldn't know of his brilliance at achieving the perfect crime when the court ruled Evelyn's death accidental. The thought occurred to him that no one would know of the detailed planning, the thorough analysis of every eventuality he alone had thought of and accomplished. How sad.

"Did you get your hot tub fixed?" Karen inquired as she approached her desk.

He nodded. "I think so. The repairman made some adjustments. Evelyn and I will check it out tonight after dinner."

He excused himself to make a pit stop. He didn't want to be disturbed while planning Evelyn's demise. Fortunately, the current case required no urgency. He knew full well the importance of details in any murder. The poker table and the Buckingham cases were examples of the need for detailed planning. Evelyn's murder had to be performed with the precision of a tool maker. His first concern was how his wife's body would be discovered. He needed an alibi. Being at the precinct with Karen when notified of his wife's death would add credibility. A fail safe fabrication would justify their appearance at the precinct in the evening hours. Recalling the Kepler case, the wife's improper planning caused her death when she hired Utah as an accomplice.

Hal hurried to the restroom and occupied one of the stalls. Sitting on the stool with the door closed provided the seclusion he needed now while going over a thousand details nonstop. *Leave nothing to chance,* he told himself. He wiped his brow with a tissue. Another hefty problem—convincing Karen to meet him in the squad room later in the evening. A plausible reason for the get together a must. Above all, their meeting mustn't contain any suspicion of a co-conspiracy. Gillan had mention Karen and his relationship to be more than homicide detectives. Even though the rumor had little foundation, it provided too much of a motive for killing Evelyn. Hal knew it would take clear headed planning to come up with a solid reason for the meeting at the precinct in the off hours would require clear-headed thinking. To add to their credibility, two or three colleagues would also be working during the evening hours. Hopefully, Gillan wouldn't be there.

And a romantic rendezvous would more likely occur away from the station house according to Lt. Abrams' mind set. Hal made a mental note to inform the lieutenant of the meeting between him and Karen to alleviate any insinuation of a clandestine meeting. He went over the pros and cons of having his partner as an alibi, realizing when all was said and done, the advantage belonged to him with the knowledge and experience of a seasoned homicide officer.

With a confident smile he returned to his desk with one

last chore—convincing Karen to meet him later in the evening at work.

He got up from his desk hurriedly, tossing a sweater over his shoulder, and stopped at Karen's desk. "I have a big favor to ask of you."

"What?"

"We need to talk about the Lankershim case as soon as possible. New light has developed." He glanced at his watch. "But I need to head home for a few hours. Is there a chance we could get together later here at the precinct tonight?"

She grimaced. "I did have other plans. Is it important?"

"Yes. New evidence which needs to be gone over carefully. I haven't said anything to Abrams until I'm sure it's valid." He looked into her eyes eagerly. "I hate to impose on your free time, but I need your help."

Karen hesitated, sighed, then agreed. "Okay. I'll meet you here. What time?"

"Around eight. I'll give you a call on my cell. Thank you, partner."

Satisfied that he had covered all events that could jeopardize his scheme, Hal got in his car and headed home. More than ready, he felt eager to begin his mission of implementing the perfect murder, the epitome of a lifetime achievement.

***

At home, he tried to be pleasant, complimenting her as the occasion arose and even helped prepare dinner. Even though she may suspect his disingenuousness behavior, still, he wanted to be on the best side to encourage her cooperation. While Evelyn cleared off the dinner table and washed dishes, Hal took that opportunity to arrange a time to speak with his neighbor about the fencing, a ploy for the scene of the crime. On the phone he finally convinced Annette to meet him in the back yard at the fencing that separated their property at 7 p.m.

Time of the essence, he prided himself in arranging a meeting of the threesome for the purpose of discussing the construction of a block wall fence. Convincing Evelyn to join him in the Jacuzzi at that specified time required his best effort of diplomacy. Promising to discuss an equitable financial settlement had sealed the deal.

At fifteen minutes to seven, Hal paced back and forth in front of the bathroom waiting for his wife to put on her bathing suit. After a long moment of silence, Evelyn opened the door and walked out of the bathroom, frowning. "Do you have towels out there?"

"Yes. I even fixed you your favorite cocktail. He walked with her toward the patio door. She stopped suddenly. "I don't feel like getting into the water right now. My TV show is on. You go ahead and talk to Annette. I'll be out a little later."

From the tone of her voice he knew he couldn't change her mind. Now faced with an emergency, he anticipated her unwillingness to cooperate, but had to act quickly to accommodate the change.

Glancing at his watch, only minutes now when Annette would be coming out into her backyard, He went over plan B hurriedly. Call Annette. Change the meeting time to Seven-fifteen. Strike Evelyn with the wood block. Drag her to the Jacuzzi and hold her head under water until dead. Put her in the lounge chair. Don't forget to smear blood on the tile edging.

"Wait here just one minute, and I'll get your drink," he said to Evelyn.

He rushed to the Jacuzzi enclosure, called Annette on his cell phone, alerted her to the time change forward fifteen minutes, then he grabbed the wood block supporting the Jacuzzi control panel. He ran back to the patio door. Evelyn looked at him curiously, seeing an arm behind his back. "Are you hiding my margarita?"

He grabbed her arm with his left hand. With a full arm swing of his other arm, he struck her in the forehead with the wood block. She collapsed to the floor on her back. He saw blood on her forehead. He scraped blood with his finger, then rushed out to the Jacuzzi and spread the residue on the tile edging. He rushed back to the patio doorway, grabbed his wife by the arms and dragged her out to the Jacuzzi, then up the steps, over the edging into the tub. Panting, he paused trying to get his breath. Her arms jerked upward, and he could see her eyes flutter open, regaining consciousness.

He pushed her head under water holding her down. Feeling her struggle to get free, he continued the pressure. He felt her body go limp and checked her pulse. Grimacing, he glanced at his watch. More than six minutes had passed. Convinced of her death, he pulled her out of the tub, half-carried her down the steps to a nearby lounge chair. He sat her in the chair and swiveled it facing away from the Jacuzzi. Annette would be able to see his wife's legs from her angle at the fence. Taking another deep breath, he checked his watch. Seven-fourteen. Perfect timing. He stepped quickly to the fence, wiped his brow and tried to relax.

A minute later, Annette came out of her house and approached him, smiling. "Did you want me to come into your backyard for our discussion?"

"No, no. Actually, I have to cut this short. I need to go to the precinct now, sort of an emergency meeting. Sorry."

Annette stood on her tip toes, glanced past the Jacuzzi to the lounge chair and waved. "Hi Evelyn!'

"She's engrossed reading her book," Hal muttered. "But she'll be going into the tub in a few minutes. We'll talk later about changing our slat fence to a block wall. More privacy for both of us," he said hurriedly.

"Yes, that's true." Annette cupped her hand and called out to Evelyn, "With a high block wall, we won't be able to converse over the fence." Giggling, Annette waited for a reply.

"Evelyn heard you, but you didn't hear her reply," Hal muttered. "She said no problem."

"Well, tell her I'll talk to her later."

Hal nodded. "Yes, we'll all talk about the fencing later. I've got to go. Annette, would you do one thing for me?"

"Certainly."

"Check on Evelyn in about fifteen or twenty minutes just to see that's she's okay. She has vertigo. I worry when I'm not here that she'll slip and fall getting in or out of the Jacuzzi."

"I can come over now and watch her."

"No. She said she wants to be alone reading her book. In twenty minutes, just peek over the fence to see that's she's okay sitting in the tub. I've got to leave. Good-bye."

He waited until she disappeared inside her patio doors, then grabbed his wife, and drug her back into the tub. Rushing inside the house and changing into street clothes, he glanced at the wall clock. Seven-thirty. Just enough time to destroy the wood block and drive to the precinct. Remembering the Buckingham case, he vowed to leave no evidence of the murder weapon. In the garage, he tossed the wood block in a pail, added gasoline, then tossed in a lit match. Momentarily, flames reduced the piece of two by four to ashes. He put the pail in the trunk of his car and drove off, stopping only once at an apartment complex where he emptied the ashes in a dumpster. He phoned Karen and told her he was on his way.

He arrived at the precinct at seven-fifty-five, applauding himself for surmounting a possible disastrous situation. Entering the homicide department, he waved to a couple of detectives and a secretary, then walked calmly to his desk. He sat down, and waited for Karen to return to her desk. After a few minutes she walked briskly to her desk greeting him with a "Hi," but remained standing. "Did you want to use Lt. Abrams' office? It's a little more private."

"No. We're off by ourselves here in the corner. No one can hear us. This will be fine." He smiled at her, but his smile was self-serving now that he had accomplished killing his wife with a fitting alibi; the rest of his plan was frosting on the cake.

He wheeled his chair over to her desk sitting in a slouched posture. "You're not married," he began. That's both a plus and a minus. On the one hand you miss out having a lifelong souse, but are immune from marital arguments." He knew he'd need to be judicious with the conversation to make his meaning plausible. I love Evelyn, but lately she's become almost impossible to live with." He shrugged. "Maybe our personalities just don't mesh. I know we think differently. As you know, I'm laid back, not wanting to rock the boat. Evelyn, bless her soul, is an A-type personality."

With a confused look, Karen said, "Is this about the Lankershim case?"

"In a way, it is. From our investigation so far, Betty Lankershim has been missing for two weeks," he said quickly. "And evidence has suggested she's been murdered with blood splatter found in their bedroom."

"And the husband is our prime suspect," Karen added, "but there's no tie-in with him to a missing body. So, what's new?"

He handed her a sheet of computer paper. "This was on the secretary's desk when she came in this morning. Take a look."

> To whom it may concern.
>
> Betty Lankershim is a two-timing bitch! She's had numerous affairs, denying infidelity, even though friends have reported seeing her in compromising situations. I should know. She refuses to attend counseling with her husband. It's common practice for her to be gone for days at a time. If she's dead due to the hand of another, it's because of her wayward ways. Her husband is innocent, but I'm not."

Karen returned the paper to Hal. "Sounds like a confession by the husband. Can we trace it back to Lankershim?"

"Doubtful. But the gist of the accusation of her being hard to live with may be significant. I know about that. Except for the infidelity, Evelyn's way is the only way if you know what I mean."

"Why are you equating Betty Lankershim with Evelyn?"

"Well if the letter is from her husband, we have a motive—Betty's aggressive personality like Evelyn's.

"I don't know your wife that well. I thought things were okay with you two."

"I don't mean to be disrespectful of Evelyn, I'm just noting similarities."

"Really?" She looked into his eyes for clarification. I don't know what to say."

He nodded. "Right. I thought it was worth mentioning because of the computer printout. Actually, Evelyn and I are doing quite well in our marriage. Things are getting better. In the Jacuzzi tonight, we decided to see a marriage counselor. Talked about updating the house, adding a block wall to the property, maybe even taking a second honeymoon on a south seas cruise." He nodded with a smile. "Yeah. Vacation time is coming up. She suggested renewing our vows, and I agreed." Pausing, he inhaled a batch of air. "But I do worry about her. Despite her denial, her vertigo seems to be getting worse. I'm afraid she will fall. It could happen anytime, getting dizzy, unable to control her balance," he grimaced for effect, "God forbid, breaking a hip."

"Have you notice anything recently?"

"No, it's just a feeling I have, but as I told you, she's experienced dizzy spells before. I left her in the Jacuzzi. Insisting on staying in the tub longer, she promised to be careful getting out. I spoke to our neighbor to check on her."

"Maybe you should have canceled our meeting," she said, peering into his eyes to understand the connection to the Lankershim case.

"Well, I wanted you to know about this new evidence." He frowned for effect. "I needed to talk to someone. It's really bugging me that Evelyn's in denial about her dizzy spells."

"I'm sure there's medicine she can take for vertigo."

"Right. I'll get her into a doctor. Thanks. I love Evelyn." He chuckled. "She *is* opinionated, expresses her views openly. Much like you do." He grinned. "But I'm opinionated as well. I guess it's part of having a healthy ego. I need to accept it." He looked away for an instant. "I really hope I have the time to correct *my* behavior." He shrugged. "One never really knows what's going to happen in life from one minute to the next. We both know that all too well from the last three cases. Sometimes things don't go as planned. Sorry to trouble you with my personal problems, but you have a way of listening that makes a difference."

"Have you spoken to Michael about your concerns for Evelyn?"

"My brother?" Hal shook his head. "He wouldn't be any help or his wife. As you've probably guessed, we don't get together much. Even though we're twins, our personalities are like oil and water. After our father died, we sort of fell into the habit of seeing each other only on holidays and sometimes attending Rodney's activities. Michael is super busy with his work in corporate America."

Karen tapped the desk top with her fingers, then

looked up. "You seem unsure of yourself about Evelyn."

He grimaced. "I guess I'm more than a little confused. Too many ideas running through my brain. Well, maybe I'm thinking of the recent past too much. But after our talk in the Jacuzzi, my real concern is Evelyn's vertigo."

The only thing I can address is your feelings." She put on a positive face. "I'm happy to hear your relationship with Evelyn is improving. Always think positive. It can restore your emotional health." She pointed at the computer. "What shall we do about this new evidence?"

"See if we can tie it in to the husband."

"Is there anything else I should know?"

"No, I think that's it." Hal glanced around the room, noticing a few others busy at their desks. "Well, I won't keep you any longer. Thanks again for your caring ear, partner."

"Well, I'm glad to hear that's what partners are for—a good ear." She laughed. She was about to say something more when Hal's phone rang.

He picked up the phone. Anticipating news of his wife's *accident*, he put on a concerned expression. "Hello. Pause. "Speaking." Pause. "An accident? Oh no! "Is she okay?" Pause. "Yes. I'll come right away." He cradled the phone, staring at Karen with anxious eyes. "An accident at my house. Evelyn fell."

"How bad is it?"

"I don't know. The officer said to come home right away. Would you come with me?"

"Certainly."

They left the precinct. Karen went with him in his car. At a stop light, Hal turned to her and said, "I pray she's all right. Now I feel guilty leaving her."

"It's not your fault if she slipped and fell."

"When I left the house she was planning on going in the Jacuzzi. I had second thoughts about leaving knowing that she might have a dizzy spell. I should've called you and cancelled our meeting." As he continued the drive home, he went on to explain talking to his neighbor about a fencing change in the backyard, and that he asked his neighbor to check on Evelyn while he was away at the precinct."

Arriving in front of his house, Hal saw numerous patrol cars and an ambulance stood in the driveway. Hal rushed inside and was met by a uniformed officer he knew. "Where is she?"

"In the back yard. Hal, I'm sorry, she's expired. There's nothing you can do."

"I won't touch her, I just want to see her."

The officer escorted Hal out to the Jacuzzi. Hal stood watching, a palm pressed against his cheek watching, as the medical examiner bent over the body. Karen stood by, a hand on Hal's shoulder.

"We've called in CSI," the officer said.

Hal frowned. "CSI?"

"Your wife had a wound to the forehead, caused bleeding, but the coroner thinks it's from a fall against the tile on the Jacuzzi edging. We found blood on the edging. A detective will be out to speak with you. Just a formality. The M.E. is pretty sure the cause of death is an accidental fall, striking her head on the tile. An autopsy will confirm his ruling."

Hal nodded. The situation was progressing as he expected. There would be a formal inquiry, and he looked forward to it with enthusiasm. He saw his neighbor, Annette, talking with another officer. She appeared visibly upset. He thanked her under his breath for calling 9 1 1. Her testimony would give credence to his alibi.

Hal thanked Karen for coming with him. A patrol officer gave her a ride back to the precinct. After the CSI team took photographs and Evelyn's body was taken by the ambulance, Hal was finally alone. He sat down on the sofa drinking a cocktail. He had accomplished his task and the investigation proceeded as expected. He took a deep breath, proud of his achievement. As he gazed at the far wall, a new thought pressed against his mind with startling alarm—how would the inquiry go? Would he get away with murder? If so, who would know about his cleverness?

CHAPTER NINETEEN

After the autopsy, the medical examiner classified Evelyn Reiner's death accidental, but the D.A.'s office recommended further investigation by a grand jury. Dubious that the incision-type laceration was caused by a flat force against the forehead, the prosecutor speculated that a moving object had caused the wound. It became known that Mr. and Mrs. Reiner were having marital problems. The D.A. spoke to a circuit judge, and the judge agreed to a grand jury to determine if sufficient evidence existed to bring an indictment against Reiner.

At the homicide department, conversation among the detectives and civilian personnel centered on one of their own, Hal Reiner, a person of interest in the death of his wife.

At his desk, Hal could see into Abrams' office, and noticed Harold Gillan talking to the lieutenant. Certain they were talking about him, Gillian would be the one to accuse him of any wrongdoing. Hal leaned back in his chair somewhat pleased. Finally, his peers were giving him some attention even though the subject matter would be non-commendable from their point of view.

Abrams looked at Gillan with an expression of doubt. "What are you saying—Hal and Karen are involved in his wife's death?"

Gillan glanced through the window at Hal. "They're like two peas in pot off by themselves. More than once I've seen them laying hands on each other like young lovers."

"What did you see?"

"I saw Karen hug him; more than a friendly hug in my opinion; sort of a lover's embrace. She frequently rolls over to his desk in her chair speaking to him in close proximity which appears secretive. They don't act like partners." Abrams didn't reply, keeping his frown in place. Gillan strolled back to Abrams' desk and sat down in a chair. "We know Hal and his wife were having problems in their marriage. Karen could be the reason why. A tryst, you know what I mean?"

"Speculation at best."

"Yeah, but it might be true."

Abrams grunted. "Hal is only in love with himself, but one thing is certain. I'll need to separate them until this mess is all over. Karen will join you and Thompson. Avoid any of your speculation to her, understood?"

Gillan shrugged. "I was thinking I could check out..."

"End of conversation," Abrams said getting up. He called Karen and Hal into the office and spoke to Hal in a tone of apprehension. "Hal, until we hear the outcome of the grand jury, you'll be on desk duty. Work on the Williamson cold case."

Hal nodded anticipating the job change. The lieutenant turned to Karen. "And you'll be assigned with Gillan and Sikorsky as a temporary course of action."

Gillan ogled Karen to ascertain any unfavorable response.

Karen inquired of the lieutenant, "Do I have to join them at their desks?"

"No, we'll set you up nearby. No need cramping the hallway. Understand though, no discussion with Hal of on-going cases, understood?"

"Yes, sir." She glanced at Hal with an expression concern.

"I don't think you have anything to worry about," Abrams said to Hal. "Based on the evidence, the grand jury really can only render one conclusion—your wife's death an accident." The lieutenant made a motion with his hands toward the office door. "Okay, that's all for now. Everybody back to work."

Hal and Karen returned to their desks. Hal wasn't surprised. He half-expected to be expelled from the department during the time of the inquest. In a way he was happy even to be considered a person of interest. Maybe he could attend the hearing to enjoy the witnesses' account of uniqueness of Evelyn's *accidental* fall.

"I don't know what to say," Karen said to Hal.

"That's a first."

She smiled. "Yes. Don't worry about the inquest. I agree with the lieutenant. The jury has to agree to Evelyn's death as an accident. There's no evidence you were involved, and you were more than cooperative in the investigation.

"Well there's scuttlebutt going around," Hal said, glancing at Gillan, "that Evelyn and I are having marital problems."

Karen shook her head. "That's all in the past."

"Is that the official word?"

With a wry grin, she replied, "Well, it's *my* official word.

* * *

The hearing didn't come too soon for Hal. Even though the grand jury wasn't open to the public, the judge allowed Hal to sit in on the hearing where 20 jurors would hear testimony about Evelyn's death. The prosecutor began by summarizing the scene of the accident, and then presented a brief summary of the facts of the accident which he referred to numerous times. Hal watched the proceedings with eagerness. He hoped they would get into the details which would show the exactness of his planning.

Assistant D.A. Evans showed a video reenactment of various positions of falling into a raised Jacuzzi. "Ladies and gentlemen, there is only one way the victim could have fallen striking her head on the edging." He stopped the video and pointed a laser at the screen. "Tripping over the lip and falling forward striking the forehead on the far side of the tub. However, there are numerous positions the body *could have* fallen *not striking* her forehead on the edging."

Good, good, Hal thought to himself. *Keep going, Evans. See if you can outsmart me.*

The only expert witness testimony came from the medical examiner who spoke about Evelyn's wound. "The depth of the laceration is not usually conducive of a flat surface force."

One juror inquired, "But wasn't the victim's blood found on the edging? It seems to confirm the victim fell striking her head on the flat surface which caused the bleeding."

"Yes, assuming the blood was caused by a fall."

"What other reason could there be?" The juror inquired.

Good point, Hal mused. *There was one juror who was a thinker.*

"The injury to the head could have happened before falling, but of course that's pure speculation.

There's no evidence of that possibility." The M. E. summed up his testimony. In my opinion, based on the facts and the autopsy, there is no substantial evidence that suggests anything else but accidental drowning due to a fall on the Jacuzzi tiles.

Hal nodded, a skewed grin just noticeable. He was thoroughly enjoying hearing about his perfect murder, but to his surprise, the prosecutor summed up his case with a brief summary.

"Ladies and gentlemen of the jury, I must agree with the pathologist. There is no evidence of wrong doing; the speculation that the cause of the victim's death was not due to an accident is not supported by the facts of this inquiry. Thank you for your time and effort arbitrating this tragedy."

Disappointed of the shortness of the proceedings, Hal said to Karen, "Evans didn't say much about the possibility that Evelyn's death *wasn't* an accident. He hardly mentioned the laceration on Evelyn's forehead. I am surprised."

"What else could he say?" She glanced at him with an expression of curiosity." It's not like the Buckingham case where we found a bloody brick. Hal, you're exonerated as everyone expected. Aren't you happy?"

He paused before speaking. "Yeah. I just thought the prosecutor would be more aggressive." He shrugged. "So be it."

They waited while the jury deliberated for less than an hour. Returning to the courtroom, the foreman issued their finding. Emily Reiner's death was accidental. The final word--no suspicion of any wrong-doing on the part of the husband. Hal looked at Karen with a nod of acceptance, his smile only half genuine, as he tried to understand the reasoning of the jury. He should feel elated that he'd gotten away with murder. The thought occupied his mind for a moment, but he wanted to hear more from the proceedings. As he and Karen left the courtroom, he stopped several times. In the hallway he held his head as though burdened with a migraine.

"Are you okay?"

"I don't know. I'm feeling sick to my stomach." He paused then said in a moment of reflection, "Abandoned."

"Abandoned?" Karen repeated the word. She escorted him to a hallway bench.

A bailiff came over. "Is everything all right here?"

"He's feeling sick to his stomach," Karen told the officer. "It must be a reaction realizing the jury agreed not to indict him. Would you mind taking him into the men's room?"

"Come on, sir," The bailiff grabbed Hal around the shoulders, and escorted him into a nearby restroom. Hal went directly to a urinal and began vomiting. He stayed on his knees and continued to dry heave into the stool. The bailiff began to think Hal's problem was worse than an upset stomach. "Do you need medical help, sir?" When Hal didn't answer, the bailiff opened the bathroom and waved to Karen. "You better call emergency. Mr. Reiner's condition doesn't seem to be getting better."

"What do you mean?"

"He's on his knees bent over the toilet. Looks like he's frozen there. He's unresponsive."

Hal fell back onto his back, arms overlapping his chest, breathing deeply.

The bailiff hollered, "He may be having a heart attack!"

Karen got her cell from her purse. "I'll phone 9-1-1."

Hal raised an arm. "Officer! Don't call emergency. I'm all right now." He struggled to his feet. The bailiff held onto Hal and walked him to a bench in the hallway where Karen joined them.

"Will you be okay?" she asked Hal.

"The jury's decision not to indict me..." Hal paused. "It got to me."

The bailiff patted Hal on the back. "Well, sir, there was never any doubt; it had to be an accidental drowning. I must say, enjoy the decision. You should be feeling on top of the world."

Karen sat down beside him, and put her hand on his arm in a comforting way. "What are you thinking?"

Hal motioned for the officer to sit down. "The prosecutor didn't do a very good job," he began with a deep frown showing. "The jury got it all wrong. I've got to say what really happened."

Karen glanced at the bailiff with a questioning look. "Hal, what are you saying?"

"I killed her...deliberately. Yes, I'm proud of what I did, exhilarated really how I managed the impossible." He shook his head, scowling. "But what good is it if no one knows of my proficiency—of getting away with murder?"

Hal confessed in detail the planning and execution of his wife' murder, even the changes he had to make due to unforeseen events. He told Karen numerous times, "I did it. I committed the perfect murder. At least now someone knows."

As the bailiff handcuffed Hal, Karen said, "I hate

to bust your bubble, but you didn't commit the perfect murder."

"What do you mean?" Hal looked at her with dread showing. "Had I not confessed, no one would have known I planned it all."

"But you did confess. Which means it was your goof admitting the murder just as much as if forensic evidence proved you committed the crime."

Hal stood up at the bailiffs prodding. "Ironic isn't it? It was the last possible thing I could have imagined that would mess me up. Who would have thought I would sabotage my accomplishment, wanting someone, anyone, to know what I had done." He paused. "Here I thought I had planned for everything… but the one thing that failed me was my own ego—needing someone to know how I did it." Hal looked at Karen, an expression of hopelessness. As he was led away, he turned and said to Karen over his shoulder, "So much for the perfect murder. I guess I'll have to agree with you—it doesn't exist."

~*~*~*~

www.ingramcontent.com/pod-product-compliance
Lightning Source LLC
Chambersburg PA
CBHW051526260626
47170CB00003B/808